Straight Up

A TWISTED FOX NOVEL

CHARITY FERRELL

D1383999

PROLOGUE

Lincoln

THERE'S ROCK BOTTOM, and then there's the underbelly of rock bottom.

My underbelly?

Getting arrested and going to federal prison.

Today, I'm being released from the hellhole.

With my chin held high, I salute the guard and exit the place where I've been held hostage for two years.

There's no stronger high than freedom.

No drug.

No booze.

No sex.

Nothing.

Everything I took for granted in the past I'm grateful for.

Hello, fucking freedom.

It feels damn good, being released from prison for a crime I didn't commit.

I'VE BEEN HUMBLED like a motherfucker.

I went from owning a million-dollar penthouse to sleeping in a prison cell to crashing in my brother's guest bedroom.

From being the VP of a million-dollar empire to broke.

The feds took possession of nearly everything with my name on it.

Underbelly of rock bottom.

It's been a long-ass day. After leaving the prison, I was treated to a steak and lobster dinner, courtesy of my mother.

"I read that people like a nice, big meal after being released from incarceration," was what she declared.

I replied with a forced smile and enjoyed the meal.

Who turns down a steak and lobster dinner?

I didn't have the heart to tell her that all this guy wanted straight out of prison was solitude, peace and quiet. One more luxury I'd taken for granted.

After showering, I slide into the king-size bed—the silky sheets yet another relic of my old life—and snatch my phone. Just as I plug it into the charger, a text comes through.

Unknown number: It's Isla. Can we talk?

My blood boils, and my grip tightens around the phone.

How'd she get my number?

I had my brother, Archer, change it, so I could have a fresh start when I was released.

Cursing, I delete the text, toss my phone onto the floor, and sigh as I soak in the silence.

Had it not been for Isla, I might not have been incarcerated.

Had it not been for Isla, my father might not be in a prison cell, awaiting his own freedom.

CHAPTER ONE

Cassidy

"HAVE YOU LOST YOUR FUCKING MIND?"

Since I'm walking out of the county jail, my brother's question isn't a shocker. Barefoot with my heels in my hands, I hop down the concrete steps one at a time. Call me classy.

Don't judge.

Get Arrested wasn't on last night's bingo card.

Kyle leans against his Jeep with crossed arms and a deep scowl. I gulp back the dread of the interrogation he'll deliver on our drive back to my sorority house.

"Yes, you've definitely lost your mind," he adds when I fail to answer.

I squeeze my forehead to ease my pounding skull while facing him. "Can you not be so loud?"

My head throbs.

My body aches.

My heart is wounded.

Everything hurts.

A drove of emotions kicked through me while I sat in the jail cell, waiting to be bailed out.

Sadness. Anger. Abandonment.

Last night was supposed to be a parade of romance while celebrating six months with my boyfriend, Quinton.

Correction: *ex-boyfriend* after he deserted my ass.

What great taste I have.

Fall for a man who bails when the cuffs come out.

Instead, my night ended with me incarcerated and him walking free.

"What?" Kyle shouts.

I wince.

He raises his voice. "You don't want me to be loud?"

I roll my eyes, yank the door open, and hop into the passenger seat while Kyle slides into the driver's side.

"Thanks for bailing me out," I grumble. Frustrating or not, I have to respect the man who rescued me from jail.

He shakes his head and starts the Jeep. "You're not goddamn welcome."

"I should've called Rex." I jerk the seat belt across my body. "He wouldn't have freaked out like this." My younger brother would've arrived with an iced coffee and offered me a high five.

"Had I not been able to pull strings, I'm sure you would've."

Facts.

Kyle is a cop, and with his help, I hoped for a speedier release.

Which happened.

I chose less jail time over an iced caramel macchiato.

Proof I don't always make stupid decisions.

Kyle runs a hand through his dark hair. "You ready to face Mom and Dad?"

"Hell to the no." I pin my gaze on him. "Which is why, dear brother, you're keeping your mouth shut about this little adventure."

I'm twenty-one. My parents don't need to be filled in on every component of my life. There are things a lady should keep private and all.

"Too late. The university called to inform them of your

expulsion." A heavy sigh leaves him. "Hell of a wake-up call for Mom."

The fuck?

"They can do that?" I shriek. "Don't they have, like ... a HIPAA for criminal records?"

His lips twitch as he fights back a smile. "You lose confidentiality when you break the law."

"Remind me to write to the attorney general about that bullshit."

"I have more news." He offers me a pitying glance.

"This is all a prank, and I'm on some reality show?"

"You wish." He snorts. "Our next stop is your little sorority house to pick up your shit since they're evicting you."

My lips tremble. "How can they do that? What happened to innocent until proven guilty?"

When it rains, it apparently pours and kicks you out of college.

I'm throwing out humor. It's who I am.

On the inside? I'm choking back the urge to vomit.

The urge to break down in tears.

This arrest will ruin every life plan of mine: college, law school, becoming a successful attorney.

One mistake.

All aspirations shattered.

"This is ridiculous," I snap, tossing my bag on the floorboard.

"You broke the rules—broke *the law*."

I didn't break shit. I cried to the officers, claiming my innocence, but someone had to take the fall. That someone ended up being me. With tearful eyes, I begged Quinton to confess. He refused, and his lie resulted in my arrest. The asshole didn't even bother to bail me out either.

"Oh, like Becky didn't break the law, forcing us to take ecstasy during rush," I scoff. "Or when Sam drunkenly smashed a cop car's windows? Neither were booted."

Kyle shakes his head. "You should've taken tips from Becky and Sam on how not to get kicked out then."

I slump in my seat. "I'm fucked."

He nods. "You're fucked."

Expelled.

Kicked out.

Criminal.

All for a crime I didn't commit.

CHAPTER TWO

Cassidy

One Month Later

ONE BAD DATE destroyed my future.

Booted me from my sorority.

Granted me with a criminal record.

My present-day life, ladies and gentlemen.

Following my arrest, my world became a shitshow. My mom sobbed. My father threatened to ship me off to military school. I reminded him that wasn't possible since I was an adult.

What was possible?

Him cutting me off.

Which was what he did after my little *I'm an adult* remark.

"You're a college expellee and irresponsible," he said after breaking the news that he'd no longer support me.

They did at least foot the attorney bill that helped drag me out of the mess Quinton had thrown me into. My punishment ended in probation and community service.

Word of advice: don't listen to the sugary pop songs.

Bad boys are never good for you.

After collecting my belongings from the sorority house, I moved in with my older sister, Sierra, in our hometown of Blue

Beech, Iowa. News travels fast in small towns, so it didn't take long for my arrest to hit the gossip mill. Everywhere I went, I was asked about my jail stay.

"What did you do?"

"Are you a drug addict?"

"Were you, like, dealing with the Mafia?"

Like, no, Karen. I was put in a crappy situation and screwed myself.

No hot Mafia heroes here.

I decided it was time to leave my old life behind. The problem was, I was on probation, and I couldn't legally venture too far. Sierra stepped in and found me a job. I used my savings to rent a one-bedroom apartment in Anchor Ridge, two towns over from Blue Beech. Even with the short distance, there's a relief, walking into a coffee shop without being known as the troublesome daughter of Blue Beech's mayor.

Now, I'm just the customer who orders a deathly amount of espresso shots in her coffee. One employee actually wished me well in the next life, claiming no one could survive that much caffeine. Taking that as a challenge, I ordered an extra shot the next day.

All of that led me to my new job at the sports bar, Twisted Fox. Maliki's—Sierra's boyfriend—best friends own the place, and they agreed to hire me. My first shift is tonight, so I'm dealing with a ball of nerves in my stomach the best way I know how—by drinking two vanilla lattes and cramming four mini Snickers bars into my mouth on the drive there.

I walk into the crowded bar, and Finn, the bouncer, jerks his head in greeting. Casually dressed patrons with beers in their hands yell at the display of mounted TVs—a different sport on each screen. A long wooden bar is stretched along the back, a mirrored wall behind it, throwing back the reflections of the happenings in the building.

The sweet aroma of fried bar food trails with each step I take toward the employees-only door in the back, following the directions I was given. Venturing down a short hall, I knock on Cohen's office door.

The co-owner answers and waves me into the room. Since Cohen is Maliki's best friend, I've met him a few times. Last weekend, Sierra dragged me to his birthday party and introduced me to my new coworkers.

We briefly chat before he passes me a stack of forms to complete. Twenty minutes later, I return to the front of the bar in search of Georgia—my trainer for the night and Cohen's younger sister.

I do a sweep of the bar and spot Georgia waving me over in a similar fashion as her brother did.

"Hey, girl!" she shouts.

I wade through the crowd, dodging a group of guys arguing over a sports call while women yell at them to grow up, and join Georgia and her friends at the pub table.

"Hey." I pull out the stool and plop down next to her before exchanging hellos with her friends—Lola, Grace, and Silas—all people I met at the party.

While they make conversation around us, Georgia guides me through the employee handbook and training packet. I've never waitressed before, but the job seems simple enough. I'm a people person. I got this.

Georgia claps when we're finished. "You ready?"

"I think so." I twist my watch and do another scan of the room.

That's when my gaze lands on the man behind the bar, and all background commotion fades. A black shirt, sleeves rolled up and cuffed at the elbows, reveals his muscular frame. Biting into my lip, I drink him in as if he were the cocktail he's pouring into a glass, a bachelorette party cheering him on in the process. He's older—my guess, five to six years on me. Thick raven-black hair is trimmed short on the edge and longer on top. I play with my fingers, wishing I could run them over the scruffy stubble stretching along his cheeks and strong chin.

The woman's eyes light up with as much desire as mine as he slides the glass to her.

It's him.

The type of man I shouldn't want.

The type of man who is nothing but heartache and criminal records.

Dear heavenly father, please forgive me. I want to sin with this man.

"Who is he?" I point at my future boy toy. "I want him for breakfast, lunch, and dinner."

The table falls silent while all focus moves in the direction of the guy I'm nearly drooling after. The mood has shifted, and everyone's eyes avoid me.

"You might be eating those meals through a straw if you keep staring at Archer like that in front of Georgia," Silas says.

"Archer?" I shake my head and look away from my new man crush.

No wonder everyone is shooting me death glares. They think I'm referring to Georgia's boyfriend.

"Not him," I clarify before I'm fired or stabbed. "We met at the barbecue. I'm talking about the guy next to him." Mentally, I slap my forehead and inhale a sharp breath.

Dear heavenly father, it's me again. Please do not let that guy be one of the other girl's boyfriends.

That'd be just my luck.

"Lincoln?" Silas asks, cocking his head to the side while staring at me. "Archer's brother?"

My muscles relax, as a drink hasn't been thrown in my face. "If that's the man next to him, then yes. Is he single? Can I have him? What's his favorite breakfast, so I can make it for him on our morning after?"

Everyone laughs while I do the same.

"Be careful, newbie." Silas scratches his cheek. "We have a strict *no relationship between employees* rule around here. Too much drama."

I glance at Georgia, raising a brow. "Aren't you and Archer dating? They both work here."

"They're the exception," Lola states matter-of-factly.

I smile, perking up. "Maybe I can be the exception too."

Although I have no pull around here. Georgia has the advantage of dating the co-owner. Pretty sure they make the rules but don't have to follow them. Maybe I can have the benefit of nepotism on my side, and Archer will allow his brother and me to fraternize.

Instead of replying, Georgia checks her watch and stands. "All right. Time to get this training party started."

Georgia reminds me of myself. She's quirky and a ball of energy, and everyone loves her.

I slide off my stool and am on her heels as she gives me a tour of the bar and introduces me to the employees I haven't met.

Oh shit.

Here we go.

My heart freezes and then pounds when we stop at the bar. The new closeness provides me with a better look at Lincoln, a better look at every physical feature I find attractive.

I know; I know. Boys get me in trouble.

Literally.

Something about this man is different.

Maybe it's my being on a strict no-guys diet and my weakness is standing in front of me.

Maybe it's that the only *eye candy* I had for months was Blue Beech eye candy, and that shit hasn't changed since middle school.

A little flirting won't hurt, and it'll keep me entertained in this new, boring life of mine.

"You met Archer." Georgia's sugary-sweet voice snaps me back into reality. "And this is Lincoln. They're our bartenders for the night."

I display my flirtiest smile, hoping it's not overkill.

He returns the smile; it's friendly, easygoing, nowhere near as desperate as mine.

Dammit.

"Hi, I'm Cassidy." I step in closer. "Your future wife."

I was voted Most Outspoken in my senior class.

Talk to a crowded room? No problem.

Meet new people? Sign me up.

My lack of shyness and wit is why my parents said I'd make a great attorney.

Thanks for ruining that, asshole ex.

I went from studying the law to breaking it.

Georgia snorts behind me as I level my attention on Lincoln. He throws his head back and laughs. It's deep, rumbling, masculine—my new favorite sound.

"You working here?" He tilts his head forward and smiles. It's a smile that nearly buckles my knees. "Are you even old enough to legally buy a drink?"

Hot and a smart-ass.

One point for Lincoln.

This will be fun.

"Obviously," I fire back. "Or they wouldn't have hired me."

"I stand corrected." He winks. "I'm the fun bartender." He jerks his head toward Archer. "He's not."

Archer gives him a warning glare.

Lincoln shrugs with a smirk.

I grin harder.

Archer murders our flirting when he says, "You go train away, baby," to his girlfriend. He slaps her ass with a towel and kisses her.

I'd place my hand over my chest and moan *aww* had he not thrown off my flirting with his brother.

With a silent groan, I shuffle away from the bar on Georgia's heels, forcing myself not to check if Lincoln is watching me.

"So … why aren't you working at Maliki's bar?" Georgia asks.

I expected that question. Maliki owns the Down Home Pub in Blue Beech. It'd make sense if I needed a job, he'd give me one. He offered, but I declined.

"I got into some trouble." I mentally curse myself at the admission and backtrack to what I planned to say. "And we decided I needed to get out of town for a while."

I decided.

My mother claimed it was a terrible idea. My father swore I'd fall into more trouble, working at a bar.

Georgia perks up, fanning strands of thick brown hair out of her eyes. "What kind of trouble?"

"Just stupid stuff that got me kicked out of college." I wince, wishing I hadn't said that either.

"Oh, I'm going to get that story out of you some time." She laughs and swats my shoulder.

I'm grateful she doesn't push for more.

WAITRESSING ISN'T AS easy as it looks.

Twisted Fox's crowd has nearly doubled since the start of my training, and as the night grows later, the customers grow needier.

More handsy.

Ruder.

Drunker.

After shadowing Georgia for an hour, she gave me two tables of my own to serve. All of them are easy two-tops, but hey, I'll take it. She instructed me to tell Finn if anyone gave me trouble. As a girl who attended frat parties like they were her second major, my creep meter is legit. I can spot a dude who's contemplating catching a feel or slipping a roofie in seconds.

"You bitch!"

Whipping around at the comment, I spot Georgia across the room with a man standing in front of her.

He pulls his shirt out, his face wild and inebriation bleeding through him, and inspects a red stain. "You ruined my shirt!"

"You okay, Georgia?" I yell, a chill snaking up my spine.

Creep meter is losing its shit over here.

She nods, giving me a thumbs-up, and talks to the guy. When he grabs her ass, I dash in their direction. Her tray crashes to the floor, and he stumbles when she shoves him.

"What the fuck?" Archer screams, jumping over the bar like a damn hyena and storming toward them.

Oh shit.

My throat turns dry as I witness the fiasco along with everyone else in the bar. Not one TV is getting an ounce of attention at the moment. Not one drink is being sipped. This is now tonight's show, and it's better than any *Real Housewives* reunion.

"Archer, no!" Georgia yells at her boyfriend.

"Fuck that shit," Archer roars. "Move, Georgia." He levels his gaze on the asshole and tightens his fist.

The murderous glare on his masculine face has me convinced the drunk dude isn't leaving in one piece tonight.

"He's drunk," Georgia pleads. "Let Finn kick him out."

"Nah," Archer says, spit flying from his mouth. "I'll take the trash out myself."

I cover my mouth to conceal my chuckle.

Good comeback there, Archer.

Lincoln appears at his brother's side. "I got this." It's a failed attempt to ease his brother.

"Oh, look," the jerk mocks. "The assholes are coming to her rescue."

I throw my arms up.

Dude deserves at least one punch from Archer.

"Georgia," Archer yells, advancing toward the man, "goddamnit, move."

My attention flicks to Georgia when she calls out my name and asks me to round up Asshole's friends.

I nod and scramble toward their table. "Seriously, grab your friend and get out of here before he gets his ass handed to him." As much as I'd love to witness Archer teaching him a lesson, it can't happen here.

With a string of curses and glares, they down their drinks and stand. I snort when one mutters, "Chad is done being invited to guys' night. Dude is a fucking hothead."

We're too slow to save the day. Archer circles around Georgia to kick Chad's ass, and she attempts to block him. It all becomes a blur of movements and shit-talking, and in the end, Georgia falls and smacks her head on the ground.

CHAPTER THREE

Lincoln

IT HAPPENED FASTER than when I'd come the night I lost my virginity.

Two pumps, and I had been apologizing to my unsatisfied date.

Two seconds, and Archer attempted to kill the guy who had grabbed Georgia's ass.

The problem was, he hadn't planned on her jumping in to stop him.

I stand out of the way as the ambulance wheels an unconscious Georgia out on the stretcher. With flaring nostrils and not a word to anyone, Cohen rushes out of the bar behind them. Archer sprints out seconds later.

The instigator and his friends fled the scene at the mention of cops. When the cops and EMTs arrived, everyone turned silent, so there were no distractions as they took care of Georgia. An uncomfortable silence—something I'd never heard in Twisted Fox—hung in the air as people pleaded for Georgia to *just open her eyes*.

Terror took residence on my brother's face, regret flashing alongside it, and I cracked my knuckles. Everything would change after tonight.

How much? I'm not sure yet.

"You okay to keep the bar covered?" Silas asks, chewing on a toothpick while eyeing the bar—customers staring at each other in question, unsure if they should return to screaming at ref calls or go home.

Archer being gone leaves me slinging drinks solo. Not that I mind. Even if he'd tried to stay, I'd have forced him to go be with Georgia. Half the bar cleared out after the cops arrived, so it's manageable. Even if it wasn't, I'd lie.

"I got this," I answer with a nod.

"Appreciate it, man." He slaps me on the back. "Prepare to be there for your brother."

That's the understatement of the motherfucking year.

Whatever happens tonight, my brother will never be the same.

I nod again in uncertainty.

"You know my number if you need anything," Silas adds. "Finn will wait until close to leave, so someone will still be working the door."

I check my watch. "It's only an hour before close."

"You think she'll be okay?" He jerks his head toward Cassidy, who's headed in our direction.

The new girl was living in my head rent-free all night before the shitshow happened. She sprinkled flirtation with every drink order she called out to me, making it impossible not to laugh. In my short breaks, I eyed the men watching her strut through the bar, sleek and almost catlike. Her wavy blond hair feathered over her shoulders with each step she took, and it never took long for her petite frame to get lost in the sea of crammed tables.

"You good with working without help?" Silas asks her.

"Definitely." She shoots me an amused smile. "If I have any questions, I'll ask my man here." Her attention returns to Silas. "You going to the hospital?"

Silas plays with the toothpick in his mouth. "Yeah."

Cassidy snags the pencil behind her ear and shoves it into her apron. "Will you keep us updated on her condition?"

"I got you." He salutes us and leaves.

A flush creeps up Cassidy's cheeks as she rests her elbows on the bar and smirks. "Looks like it's just you and me."

I offer a polite smile. "Looks like it."

"We'll make a damn great team." She holds out her hand for a high five.

I high-five her with as much enthusiasm as a dude who just tested positive for the clap. It's out of character for me to be uptight, but tonight, concern pours through me. Hell, I'd take a curable STD over what happened to Georgia. Archer doesn't cope well with loss, people getting hurt, or when he seems responsible for something bad happening. If Georgia's condition is critical, it'll gut him. Turning the TVs back on, I hope the rest of the night flies by.

"Yo! Bartender!" a yellow-polo-sporting frat boy yells a few barstools down from us. "How about a drink on the house for that mood killer?"

"What an asshole," Cassidy says, not bothering to lower her voice. "Poison his drink ... or at least spit in it."

Frat Boy shoots her a glare.

She smirks in response.

Even though all I want to do is kick him out, I yank a glass from the stack and pour him a beer *on the house*.

The cheapest shit we carry.

The kind that delivers a hell of a hangover.

I hate fuckers who take advantage of vulnerable situations.

Asshole mutters a, "Thank you," and his friends blurt their *free drink* requests at me.

This will be one long hour.

In what seems like every five minutes, I check my phone for any updates on Georgia, and before I know it, it's closing time.

"Last call!" I shout.

Customers guzzle down their drinks and finish their games

of pool. The free-drink-loving frat boys are in the corner, throwing out desperate last shots at convincing a group of women to go to their place for round two. The man in front of me asks me to find his wife's name in his phone and calls for a ride home.

A typical closing night at Twisted Fox.

Different situations but always the same characters.

Finn waits to leave until the bar clears out, and while he's walking out the door, Cassidy reminds him to send her updates. I kill the TVs—what I always do first when closing—but the silence is needed more tonight than ever.

Dirty glasses and beer bottles clank together as Cassidy collects and tosses them into the garbage. Just like with Archer leaving me, Georgia's rush to the hospital left Cassidy alone for the night.

"If you want to go, I'll finish up," I say, dumping the contents of a red food basket into the trash before stacking it on top of the others.

She doesn't need to feel obligated to stay and close shop with a stranger.

"I'm good." She strolls to the next table. "It's my job."

My throat tightens.

Would she be okay if she knew who I was?

Where I've been?

My past?

My money is on no.

There's an automatic assumption when it comes to people like me.

An automatic notion that criminals are not to be trusted.

"Any updates on Georgia?"

Her question jerks me from my *woe is me* thoughts, and I cringe, remembering Cohen's latest text.

The good news? Georgia is doing well.

Bad news? Archer left the hospital, hasn't returned, and isn't answering his phone.

I clear my throat. "She's stable. They think it's a concussion." I scrub a hand over my face, adding a deep pressure with the tips of my fingers.

"Then why do you look so stressed?" She tilts her head to the side. A strand of blond hair tucked behind her ear falls free.

"Archer is MIA."

Whoa.

I retreat a step.

I'm a private person, never one to air out my family's business.

"What do you mean, MIA?" She stops cleaning and focuses on me. "Why isn't he there with her?"

"That's the question of the century." Holding in my aggravation over my brother's dumbass actions is a struggle.

"No offense, but that's messed up."

It is.

We've only known each other a few hours, but within that time, I've learned that Cassidy isn't a bullshitter. When shit with my brother blows over—which it'd better, or I'll kick his ass— she'll be a hoot to work with.

"He has issues," I say, snatching the disinfectant from underneath the bar and spraying the top down.

"They always do."

I set the bottle down and stare at her from across the bar. "What's that mean?"

"All hot guys have issues." She levels her deep hazel eyes on me, and I wish the lights were brighter so I had a better view of her. "So, what's yours, big guy?"

I quickly glance away in guilt. "Who says I have one?"

Shit, and who says I only have one?

I could write an entire damn novel on mine.

"Like I said, all hot guys have issues."

I point at her with the towel. "Don't let Georgia hear you call Archer hot."

She laughs. It's feminine, indulgent—a sound I wouldn't

mind having as my ringtone. "Considering Archer is MIA, I'm sure she'd rather me call him worse." She clicks her tongue along the roof of her mouth. "So … your issues?"

My stomach twists, and I hold up my hands. "No issues here."

"Mm-hmm." She strokes her chin, and her eyes meet mine. "I have an idea. When we're finished here, we'll embark on Operation Find Archer and Kick His Ass."

Relief settles through me at the subject change. I chuckle. "How about this? You'll go home, and *I'll* go hunt my brother down and kick his ass."

It'll be a hard enough job to get Archer to talk to me. If I have someone with me? No dice.

She shakes her head. "You'll need backup—like Batman and Robin."

"I show up with you, shit will get worse."

She sighs. "Geesh, you and your bro are serious buzzkills."

"My brother is." I shove my thumb into my chest. "Not me. I told you, I'm the fun one."

"Does the fun one have a girlfriend?"

I'm rendered speechless for a moment. I pause to study her, zooming in on the way she waits in anticipation—licking her lips, a smile twitching at them.

"I don't," I croak. Nor do I want or need one.

I got involved with a woman who fucked my entire world up.

"Perfect." The word slowly slips from her bubblegum-pink lips. "What's your breakfast of choice?"

I raise a brow.

"I need to know what to cook the morning after our first sleepover," she replies like *duh*.

I scratch my cheek. "You're pretty blunt for a girl."

"Girls can't be blunt?" Her eyes, brimming with mischief and challenge, meet mine. "If you don't like a blunt woman, this is where I retract my breakfast offer."

"Nah, I'm good with it." I share her grin, mine cockier. "I actually like it."

Resting her pink-manicured hand over her Twisted Fox tee, she pouts. "Are you going to ask if I have a boyfriend?"

I hesitate, my voice turning strained. "I think me asking that is dangerous."

If I don't know, I can convince myself she's taken and off-limits. Technically, she is off-limits. There's a *no fraternizing* policy here—which no one obviously takes seriously—and Cassidy is my brother's employee. Not only that, but she's also younger than my usual taste.

At least, I think that's what my problem was. Back then, as hard as I tried, there was no connecting with women my age. Maybe it was the chicks in my circle, in my world, but I never found anything in common with them. Cassidy, on the other hand, is proving every *she's too young for you* theory wrong.

There's this electricity between us that's zapping me to life.

"Why is that dangerous?" She makes a *hmm* noise in the back of her throat.

"You're trouble." It's a statement. A fact. A motherfucking warning to myself.

She rests her hands on her hips. "What's wrong with trouble?"

I gulp. "Trouble leads to more trouble."

I know that from too much experience.

CHAPTER FOUR

Cassidy

"TROUBLE LEADS TO MORE TROUBLE."

If that's not the understatement of my life.

Trouble finds me and then becomes a domino effect.

If I ever became a reality star on *The Real Housewives*, I'd make that my tagline.

After Lincoln calls me trouble, he hastily shifts our conversation a different route. While cleaning, we talk about customer reactions to tonight's disaster. Lincoln muffles out laughter at my jokes here and there, but my commentary isn't where his head is.

It's on his brother.

There's nothing sexier than a man who cares about others. That attraction is deeper now that I've had my fill of dating one of the most selfish men on earth.

Good-bye, self-absorbed men.

Hello, selfless ones.

Lincoln offers to walk me out when we're finished cleaning. "From now on, park in the employee lot in the back. You don't need to be walking through a parking lot where drunk people might linger. We always walk the female employees out after their night shifts."

I salute him, a sense of security hitting me. "Got it."

This man could tell me never to eat chocolate again, and I'd do it.

Okay, maybe I'd do it for a month.

A girl has to have her s'mores frapps in the fall.

The wind whines around us while we walk side by side, our strides coordinated. My skinny frame next to his muscular one. There's a sense of safety as I walk with this man. With another bite of the wind, I catch a whiff of his cologne—masculine, subtle, and expensive.

We stop at my car, the parking lot light shining over us.

I tug my keys from my purse. "What's your last name?"

He pauses and averts his gaze. "Why do you ask?"

"Just curious."

A flicker of anguish flashes across his face, and he forces a smile. "You plan to cyberstalk me when you get home?"

"Damn straight."

He shakes his head. "Nope, not letting you in on my secrets yet."

"Yet?" I raise a brow. "Does that mean there will be a time when you do?"

"Get in your car, trouble."

He chuckles and tips his chin toward my shiny red BMW coupe—another item my parents let me keep after the snip-snip of my financials. I unlock my car, and he opens the door, stepping to the side to allow me room to slide in. I start my car, rubbing my freezing hands together, and curse myself for not remote-starting it earlier.

"Good night, trouble." He peeks through the door. "Drive safe."

"Good night, Lincoln."

He offers me one last smile, gently shuts the door, and waits until I leave the parking lot before returning to the bar. I replay our conversations in my head on the ten-minute drive to my duplex. After parking, I grab my bag and scramble into my apartment.

Noise flows through my neighbor's walls. The closest we've been to a conversation is when he screams at his video games at three in the morning and I bang on the wall.

I check my phone for Georgia updates and then shower, savoring the steaming water pelting at my sore muscles. Tipping my head back, I groan as my real-life problems evade my thoughts. Work was a temporary reprieve from them.

A reprieve from Quinton.

Stepping out of the shower, I dry off. My skin crawls when my phone beeps with a text.

Quinton: Quit ignoring me. We need to talk.

I stopped blocking his number when he found other ways to contact me. He'd randomly show up where I was or call me from different numbers, and once, he even had some rando kid deliver a letter like we were in the Cold War and I was his wife, waiting at home for him. Answering his calls is easier than dealing with his weird alternatives.

I stab my fingers against the screen like I want to stab him.

Me: We've talked plenty.

Quinton: I don't trust you.

Me: I don't trust you. We're even.

Quinton: Don't make me fuck up your world.

You already have.

CHAPTER FIVE

Lincoln

A WEEK HAS PASSED since Georgia's fall.

A week that I've been covering for my pain-in-the-ass brother.

His absence has created a major disruption at the bar. I'm the only one who knows where he is, and I've refused to share that information, crowning me as the most hated coworker.

Out of guilt, I'm covering his shifts. It's not like I have shit else to do anyway. Working helps me pass the time, clears my mind from the bullshit, and it's better than sitting at home alone since Archer and I live together.

"Your brother pull his head out of his ass yet?"

I stop counting inventory at the sound of Cassidy's voice and sweep my gaze over the bar. Cassidy's marching in my direction, her hips swaying from side to side with each step. With me covering for Archer and her filling in for Georgia while she recovers from a concussion, we've been working together all week. Like with working, being around her keeps my mind off my problems.

"Hello. Good afternoon to you too," I say instead of answering her question—the same one she asks daily.

She wrinkles her nose. "I'm up for kidnapping his ass …
wherever he is …" She leaves the rest of her sentence hanging.

"Hmm …"

On the outside, I'm acting cool.

Inside, agitation speeds through me.

Archer's actions have been putting me through hell. I'm
trying to be understanding, but it's hard when everyone around
is pointing out what an idiot he is.

"If only someone—*say, you*—knew where we could find
him." Her oval-shaped eyes sharpen as she glares at me.

I ignore her comment, not even bothering to *hmm* this time.

Too bad Cassidy isn't one to steer clear of sensitive subjects.

"What's his deal?" She ties back her glossy blond hair in a
high ponytail. "Can't you force him to do the right thing or tell
Georgia where he is, so the girl can rip him a new one? She at
least deserves that."

"Archer is … complicated." Defending him makes my jaw
twitch. He doesn't deserve it.

"How about you *uncomplicate* the situation, force him to
pull up his big-boy panties, and face Georgia?"

I scrub a hand over my face. "You have siblings?"

"A sister. Two brothers." She pauses and holds up a finger.
"Shit, three brothers. I recently found out about a secret half
brother that my dad hid for fifteen years. And now, my brother
is marrying his sister."

I cock my head to the side, replaying her words. "Jesus. That
sounds messy."

"Yep." Her red nails make a *tap, tap* against the bar, and her
voice turns stern, almost parent-like. "I know complicated, and
if one of those siblings was acting as if they were still in Pampers,
I'd make them face the consequences of their actions."

"Your parents still together after the whole *secret baby* thing?"
I'm still processing what she told me *and* desperate to turn the
conversation away from Archer.

"Nope. They tried, but it was hopeless." She props an elbow

on the bar. "Not that I blame my mother for leaving him. If I found out my husband did what my father did, I'd file those divorce papers in a heartbeat." She smirks. "If I didn't kill him so he no longer had a heartbeat."

I can't help but chuckle.

Apparently, I find homicidal innuendos made by tiny blondes funny.

"What about you?" she asks. "Your parents still together? Any other siblings?"

My mouth turns dry, and I gulp in an attempt to fix it.

I shouldn't have asked her any family questions.

Should've known those questions always circle back.

"It's just Archer and me," I reply, a pain in the back of my throat. "And my father ... he's dead."

My chest tightens in surprise at my revelation. While I'm not as closed off as Archer, I don't openly talk about his death. It's a sore subject for me. I'm not sure when it won't be.

Her face falls in apology. "Lincoln, I'm so sorry. I shouldn't have asked."

He died in prison shortly after I was released. He died somewhere he shouldn't have. Sure, maybe he deserved his place of residence for his actions, but no one should die there.

That's why I fought so hard to prevent it.

And failed.

It nearly killed me when I got the call.

Slaughtered my mother.

Crushed Archer, even with their strained relationship.

Lucky for him, he had Georgia at his side.

Me? I had no one.

I clear my throat, shaking my head. "Nah, it's cool. I asked. You asked back. No biggie."

"You get to work with the cool bartender today, ladies and gents!"

Our attention shifts to Silas as he saunters across the bar. His leather jacket and shredded jeans break the dress code per our employee handbook, but from what I've discovered about Silas, he's the epitome of a man who gives no fucks.

I was him once.

Parties. Drugs. Booze. Sex.

I lived my life day to day and traveled to exotic locations on a whim, and rules were only for those who couldn't afford to break them. A slice of that changed after my grandfather's death. That was when I stepped up in our family business since Archer refused to. Within a year, I went from a highly educated trust-fund kid to the VP of a multimillion-dollar empire.

How did that *give no fucks* attitude evaporate from my body?

When my father started committing felonies and leaving me to cover up his crimes.

"I beg to differ," Cassidy argues, wagging a finger at him. "Linc is the coolest-slash-best-slash-hottest bartender here."

Her compliment wipes out the sorrowful thoughts of losing my father.

Not that they won't resurface later.

"That's my girl." I hold my arm across the bar.

She grins and high-fives me.

Silas jerks his jacket off his shoulders and peers at Cassidy. "I'll let you have that one because Maliki would kick my ass if I ever touched you."

She scrunches up her face. "You're not letting me have *anything*." She pats his chest. "No offense, pretty boy, but only one bartender has my heart." Blowing a kiss, she turns and strolls toward the employee entrance.

My gaze is trained on her, her curves, the pep in her step as she walks.

"Safe to say, she likes you, man," Silas comments, his lips curving into an amused smile.

I don't look away from Cassidy until she disappears through the door. "She's young."

"Twenty-one isn't that young," he scoffs. "What are you, twenty-six?"

I nod.

"Five years ain't shit. Which means you're using *age* as an excuse, and I have the best solution for that."

I raise a brow.

"Telling Cohen to schedule you and Blondie together."

"Girls are the last thing I need to worry about."

What do I need to worry about?

Getting my life in order, moving into my own place, and adjusting to this new world.

I'll never be the same man I once was.

SPORTS AND SHOUTING customers consume my environment as I sling drinks—a margarita here, a shot there, a beer here. I went from ordering drinks to serving them. Don't get me wrong. I'm thankful as fuck for the job. My only experience upon being hired was that I'd drunk a whole lot of liquor.

Bartending isn't my passion. Making small talk with people isn't my jam. Hearing people whine about their problems like I'm a damn therapist is hell. I came from the corporate world, and in the corporate world, we told people to shut the fuck up when they whined about their problems.

What was once my passion?

Business. Finance. A salary with six numbers.

That was the name of my game.

Until that game ended and I was the loser.

"Silas. Oh, Silas," Cassidy sings out at the end of the night. "I volunteer as tribute to take over your closing duties."

Silas stops collecting trash. "Seriously?"

All night, as I poured drinks and ignored people bitching, I thought about Cassidy. The girl, she's getting to me.

Whether it's platonic or sexual attraction, I want to spend all my time with her.

I want to learn everything about her, every single damn tidbit I can.

I want all of that … while also desperate she doesn't learn about the real me. As much as I don't want it to happen, it will eventually. My past hasn't been a secret, given everyone knows me as Archer's brother.

They all know my story.

Do they judge me for it?

I'd bet every damn dollar in my bank account that some did at the beginning.

Now, not so much. They invite me into their homes, they allow me in the bar's cash, and I've never given them a reason to worry.

Cassidy eagerly nods. "Seriously."

Silas peers over at me. "You cool with that?"

I shrug, striving to appear casual. "Sure. Whatever."

Cassidy helping means I'll leave later, and even though I'm as exhausted as people are after Thanksgiving dinner, I'd rather spend time with her than sleep.

"Cool." He snatches his jacket, and when Cassidy turns around, he elbows me playfully.

I shove him away.

"Catch you guys later!" Silas salutes us before leaving.

"Who volunteers for extra work?" I ask on my way to lock the door behind Silas.

"It's better than going home to an empty apartment," Cassidy replies with a shrug.

"I feel you on that. It's the same with Archer being gone."

"Another reason to drag his ass home." She clears a table of two drinks before spraying it down with cleaner and wiping it.

"Me doing that equals working less … which means less time you get to spend with me."

The towel falls from her hand. "He can come home *for Georgia*, and you can still work. Dude probably needs time to clear that stubborn head of his and grovel at Georgia's feet. I suggest he take classes on how to be a good boyfriend."

I bite back the urge to ask if she's ever been in a serious relationship. For someone who thinks she's Dr. Phil, has she even dealt with real-life problems yet?

"If you understood Archer and his past, you'd think differently," I reply.

She cocks her hip against the bar and levels her hazel beauties on me. "Tell me about it then."

Well, shit.

Not where I was going with that statement.

I thought it'd shut her up about my brother.

"Archer, he …" I clear my throat while searching for the right words. "He sees himself as the Grim Reaper. He thinks it's safer for Georgia to stay away from him. In his weird-ass head, he's punishing himself, not her, for what happened."

"He might think that, but Georgia is being punished in the process."

Returning to the bar, I snatch the universal remote and power off the TVs. "Trust me, I tried explaining that, but he's hardheaded."

So are all of us Callahans.

It's why my brother and father could hardly stand to be around each other.

"What about you? What would you do in that situation?"

I draw in a deep breath as her question sinks into my blood, pulling out honesty. "I wouldn't run." My response is a sellout to my brother—me agreeing with everyone but him.

A satisfied smile stretches along her lips. "Good. You weren't lying when you said you were the cool one."

I match her grin. "Told you so."

We make small talk while finishing up cleaning, and I learn:

She was voted Miss Teen Blue Beech, to which I replied, "That sounds like the honkiest shit I've ever heard." That resulted in a napkin being thrown in my direction.

The night she found out about her father's affair, she lit every birthday present he'd ever given her on fire.

She lost her virginity on prom night but lied about it because she didn't want to seem like a cliché.

What do I share with her?

I graduated with a finance degree from Stanford.

I used to lie about being allergic to shellfish, so I wouldn't have to eat nasty-ass caviar because my parents served it on the regular.

Before prison, I embarrassingly didn't know how to work a washer and dryer.

"Do you live around here?" I ask while we walk to our cars, leaves slashing along the concrete.

She nods, unlocking her car. "Like, ten minutes away. What about you?"

"About twenty." I fail to mention the reason I'm crashing with my brother. That the feds took nearly everything with my name on it, not caring if I had two nickels to rub together.

"I'll have to come see it sometime." Standing on her tiptoes, she smacks a kiss to my cheek and flashes me a playful grin. "You can give me a tour."

As she leaves, I glide my finger over my cheek, feeling the heat of where her lips were.

I grin like the damn Grinch.

"GEORGIA," I greet when she walks into the bar.

Georgia narrows her eyes in my direction. "Unless you're here to tell me where the hell your bastard of a brother is, I'm not speaking to you."

She's the CEO of my haters club—not that I blame her.

I'm also waiting for her to castrate me, per her threats.

As much as I want to defer the topic away from Archer, I can't. He called last night and asked for a favor. I drove to his hiding place—our grandparents' lake home—and prayed he decided to get his shit together. No such luck.

All the little prick did was hand me an envelope to give to Georgia. When I questioned what it was, he wouldn't tell me. I had an urge to open it on the way home, but I didn't. My brother might have thrown me smack dab in the middle of his mess, but I'm trying to distance myself from the situation.

And a mystery envelope isn't my damn business.

She stares at the envelope as if it's tainted when I pull it out and offer it to her. "What Archer needs to do is grow some balls, face me, and tell me why he left."

Facts.

I thrust the envelope closer. "Archer doesn't always do what he needs to do. You know this."

"What's his plan then?" Cassidy asks, leaning back in her stool and crossing her arms, always joining in conversations that have nothing to do with her. "He's just never coming back?"

"I think that's his plan," I reply even though I'm as clueless as she is.

Cassidy's eyes widen, and her voice rises a hitch. "What about you? Are you leaving too?"

I shrug, the thought forming a rock of dread in my stomach. "I have no idea." I thrust the envelope further toward Georgia. "Now, take the envelope."

"What's in it?" she asks with a glare.

"He didn't say. Only asked me to give it to you." I hold up my hands. "Don't shoot the messenger."

She snatches it from me and stares in my direction while ripping it open. All eyes are on her as she reads what's inside. I silently pray it's an apology letter.

"You've got to be kidding me," she hisses. "Tell me where he is."

I shake my head, my stomach churning at the anger in her eyes. It's more intense than it was before. "No can do, babe."

"Goddammit, Lincoln!" she shrieks, tossing the letter onto

the pub table. "Forget your stupid loyalty for one damn minute and tell me where he is." She flicks the letter away. "He's trying to sign over the bar to me."

"What?" I blurt.

She jerks her head toward the letter. "Read it."

With nearly shaking hands, I read the letter, my throat constricting as I take in every word in his handwriting. He's signed over his cut of the bar—fifty percent—to her. I shut my eyes in pain. Not because I'll lose my job, but because my brother is sacrificing his dream. After our grandfather's death, he turned his back on the millionaire lifestyle we'd grown up in. As soon as he had the perfect opportunity, he quit the company. Owning a bar is all he's ever wanted.

This bar, like Georgia, brought him happiness and peace he hadn't had in a while.

That's it.

This has to stop before he ruins his life.

I slam down the letter. "He's at our grandparents' lake house."

"Address, please," Georgia replies, her face unreadable.

I give her a *really* look.

"Directions," she demands.

"Fine, fine." My face falls slack. "But don't say I'm the one who gave it to you."

A hint of regret slivers through me before I brush it away. Archer can be pissed at me all he wants, but I'm not allowing him to fuck over his life.

Deal with your problems, Archer.

Cassidy chuckles, wearing a proud smile on her face. She's elated that I finally caved. "There's no way you're getting out of this one." She stands and slaps my arm. "Think of it as your good deed of the day."

I fight back a smile, her comment downsizing my tension. "Listen, youngster, don't you have some frat boy's heart to break or Barbies to play with?"

I'm unsure if our relationship is big brother, little sister or sexual tension we play off as humor. Most of the time, I'd put my money on it being the latter, but it's weird for me. I've never gone for chicks younger than me.

The problem is, we work together, and the timing sucks.

Cassidy flips me off. "Don't you need to go find your vitamins to keep your bones strong and pick up your Viagra from the pharmacy?"

I laugh, turning my attention to Georgia. "Georgia, since you might be the new co-owner, fire her ass."

Cassidy throws her head back. "Lincoln, dear, the chances of you being fired are much higher than mine since you're related to the devilish heartbreaker."

"He's going to kick my ass for this," I tell Georgia, rubbing my forehead in stress. "So, be happy that I like you."

"Just tell him I went through Lincoln's phone and gave it to you," Cassidy comments with a *give no shits, I'll piss off my boss* attitude.

Chick has balls of steel.

"I'll text you the address," I inform Georgia.

She replies with a pleased smile.

"You okay to drive?" Cassidy asks. "I can take you if you want?"

"She wants a front seat to the shitshow," I add.

"Rude." Cassidy shoots a glare in my direction. "I *also* want to make sure she's cool to drive."

"I'm fine," Georgia replies. "They told me to wait forty-eight hours before driving, and it's been a week. I haven't felt dizzy at all. All I need is for you to cover my shift tonight."

Cassidy points at her. "I got you. Good luck!"

Georgia dashes out of the bar, and I already feel bad for the wrath Archer will face if she goes to my grandparents'. I yank my phone from my pocket to give him a heads-up but then shove it back in place. I'll let this one be a surprise.

"Are you sure you're okay working a double?" I ask Cassidy.

She worked through lunch and the mid-dinner rush and was clocking out when Georgia arrived. I planned to pull a double to fill in for my jackass brother. Plus, I need the cash. The money is decent here, but it's nothing like what I made before.

It's not like I don't have *any* money. Call it foul, but my mother created a bank account to transfer my funds so I didn't lose everything.

"I have nothing better to do," Cassidy replies.

"That makes two of us."

Her phone chimes, and she rummages through her bag, searching for it. My eyes are on her when she reads whatever is on the screen. She stills, her face paling, and seconds later, as if someone snapped her out of a haze, she frantically shoves the rest of her shit into her bag. In the process, she drops her phone. When she ducks down to retrieve it, the bar conceals her.

"Everything okay?" I ask, standing on my tiptoes in an attempt to see her over the bar.

"Yep." She comes back into view, blowing strands of hair from her face. "Georgia's shift doesn't start for, what, another ten minutes? I need to run home really quick, and then I'll be right back."

"Cassidy." I circle the bar, my brow wrinkling.

"Gotta go." She rushes out the door.

My throat constricts as my intuition tells me something's wrong.

CHAPTER SIX

Cassidy

RULE NUMBER ONE IN RELATIONSHIPS: don't date the biggest drug dealer on campus.

In my defense, it's not like I knew Quinton was one when we started dating. We met at a frat party and immediately clicked. He became the perfect boyfriend—polite, never made me question his character, and decent in bed. His Mercedes, his wining and dining, and the gifts were never a red flag because he came from money. His family owns Landing Holdings, a large commercial real estate and investment firm.

Turned out, all that wining and dining wasn't on his parents' dime. It was funded from profits from selling drugs. When his car was in the shop, he borrowed mine while I was in class. Too bad I didn't know *borrow* was code for drug runs. We got pulled over on the drive to dinner—me in the driver's seat. The cop claimed there'd been a familiar make and model in a drug hot spot.

Knowing I had nothing to hide, I wasn't worried when they demanded to search my car.

Key word: *I*. I had nothing to hide.

Turned out, my boyfriend did.

And asshole had hidden it in my trunk.

I should've known something was wrong when Quinton told me not to pull over and make a run for it, like I'd graduated from sorority girl to Grand Theft Auto pro. I stupidly thought he was joking, and he cursed under his breath when I followed the law.

He muttered a quick, "Thank fuck," when the officer approached my window.

That followed with an, "Oh shit," when the other officer appeared.

As the cops searched my car, Rat Bastard stared at me straight in the face and said, "I don't know what kind of shit you're into, Cassidy, but not cool." His attention slid to the officer. "Those aren't my drugs. Can I call a friend to pick me up?"

The officer, who'd been cool with him the entire time while eyeing me skeptically, said, "Of course, man."

Then … they did the man hug.

Yes, my drug-dealing boyfriend did a bro hug with a cop.

A cop who then instructed me to turn around before slapping handcuffs on my wrists.

I cursed at Quinton.

Screamed.

Called him countless names.

But he didn't budge.

I sat in the back of the cop car, careful not to touch anything. The stench of rotten eggs and french fries along with the sound of AC/DC tortured me during the ride.

Quinton's betrayal shocked me.

My trust in people was a reality check.

Never to be repaired.

Not only did Quinton ruin my future, but he also ruined my insight on life.

On people.

Quinton called after Kyle bailed me out.

Over and over again.

Threatening me with a creative variety of things he'd do if I even muttered his name to authorities—slit my throat with barbed wire, cut my mother's uterus out, catch my house on fire.

You know, all normal things a man you dated should say.

I might've been ignorant enough to fall for the wrong guy— the *bad boy*—but I refuse to be stupid enough to cross him. I'll stay in line and keep my mouth shut until he leaves me the hell alone.

It's been a week since he graced me with a text. That changed ten minutes ago when he messaged me with a selfie of him sitting in *my living room*, blindsiding and scaring the shit out of me. Dude was even holding my favorite teddy bear. He's not supposed to know where I live, where to stalk me.

It's fall, but I'm sweating when I step out of my car. Dread accompanies each step I take toward my apartment. With shaking hands, I shove the key into the lock, only to realize it's unlocked.

Did he pick the lock?

Kill my landlord to get one himself?

I inhale a deep breath, terrified of what I'm about to walk into. Quinton is waiting for me on the couch. His arms are sprawled out along the back, and a Rolex dangles from one wrist as if he were a king awaiting his peasants.

Or prey, in my case.

I slam the door shut and toss my bag onto the floor. "Breaking and entering is against the law. Keep committing crimes, and I'll eventually turn your ass in."

You see, sometimes, I'm not the wisest with my mouth. I might be smart enough not to rat on Quinton, but that doesn't also apply to my sarcasm. He can't have both.

He drops an arm to rub the hard line of his jaw, and his lips curve into a sinister smile. "Say you'll turn my ass in again, and that sweet mouth of yours will be toothless."

Well then.

Not trying to have falsies before thirty.

I shut my mouth and curl my arms around myself. "What do you want, Quinton?"

Licking his lips, he eyes me up and down, his predatory expression stronger. "You look good, babe."

Ugh, vomit.

"And you look gross and criminal."

Again, this damn mouth.

When he rises to his feet, my back straightens, and the hair on the back of my neck stands, but I quickly fix myself. He advances toward me, needing to only take a few steps before he's inches away, tipping his head down to stare at me.

Don't let the psycho know he affects you.

I hold out my palm in warning. "Don't."

"Why?" He smirks. "I thought you liked compliments."

Yes, when I didn't know you were a damn monster.

Now, you make my skin crawl.

I retreat a step, my back hitting the wall. "What do you want?"

He doesn't move closer. "Just want to make sure we're still on the same page."

"Still on the same page." I gulp.

He eases closer, slow and wolfish, and caresses my cheek, causing me to flinch. His hand is smooth, yet there's a greasy coat over it. His breath, a deep cinnamon, hits my skin. "Good. Keep it that way."

I swat his hand away.

A hard chuckle releases from his chest before he turns and leaves.

As soon as the door clicks behind him, I snatch my teddy, which now feels corrupted, and throw it at the door.

How did he know where I lived?

I need to buy a baseball bat, just in case.

"EVERYTHING GOOD?"

I expected this, yet I hoped Lincoln wouldn't ask that when I returned to the bar. He had seen me when I read Quinton's text and witnessed the sheer panic on my face.

After Quinton left, I hurriedly locked the door and opened a meditation app my mother had been pestering me to try. Five minutes into forced reflection, my mind wasn't shutting off, so I quit.

Meditation isn't what'll work for me tonight.

I need vodka, or a Xanax, or a distraction.

Working will be good for me.

Nodding, I join Lincoln behind the bar and yank a bottle of vodka from the glass shelf. "Of course."

I snatch a shot glass, pour myself a double, and knock it back, relishing the burn as it seeps down my throat, hoping it'll bring a dose of forgetfulness later. His eyes are pinned on me as I set the glass down and wipe my mouth with the back of my hand like a lady.

"You sure?" He wrinkles his brows, his gaze shooting from the glass and back to me.

I give him a nervous smile while I consider pouring another shot. Too bad I'm on the job and I don't want to get fired. "Positive."

No one will find out about Quinton's visit.

It'll be my and my stupid tormentor's little secret.

Among many.

He reaches out, running his hand over my arm, as worry flashes along his features. "If you need anything, I'm here. You know that, right?"

If it were any other time, I would revel in his touch. Now, I can't keep my mind straight because all I'm thinking about is Quinton.

I tap his wrist. "You getting soft on me, Callahan?"

"Hell no." He snorts.

I do a sweep of the bar, noticing the growing crowd, and

know soon, there won't be much time for conversation. "Did Georgia find Archer?"

"Sure did." He smirks. "Archer texted me, bitching about not giving him a heads-up."

"Good girl." I smile, a real one this time, as I think about Georgia barging in on Archer. "Tell him it's time to rip off the Band-Aid."

"Trust me, I did. Who knows if he'll listen, though?"

"Make sure to keep me updated." I pat him on the back.

He groans. "Hard pass on keeping you updated with my brother's love life."

I mock his groan. "Fine, I'll be texting *you* for updates."

"Too bad you don't have my number."

"Too bad I do." I dance in place, Quinton temporarily dissipating from my thoughts. This is what I needed. "You're just lucky I haven't sent you nudes yet." I pause and press a finger to my mouth. "Or does that make you *unlucky?*"

He scrubs his hand over his face, peeking at me through the spaces between his fingers. "How'd you get my number, you little stalker?"

"There's a spreadsheet in the employee room in case we need someone to cover our shift."

"Remind me to have Archer change that."

"Pretty sure Archer has bigger concerns at the moment than me knowing your number."

"Nope." He presses his hand to his chest, feigning defensiveness. "That's a serious violation of privacy."

This is how it is with Lincoln.

I spend time with him, and all my frustrations fade.

I shove him at the same time I say, "Shut it. Who else will I call when I'm lonely at night?"

"Fine. *Only* if I'm the last resort … *and* you tell me what's going on in that pretty head of yours."

"YOU WANT to talk about what's been on your mind tonight?" Lincoln studies me as we walk out of the bar.

I blow out a ragged breath when we reach my car. As hard as I tried to act normal while working tonight, a sudden chill would rush down my spine at times. I'd anticipate Quinton standing behind me. My throat thickened when I checked my phone, in fear I'd find another text from him.

If he knows where I live, surely, he knows where I work.

I shift from one foot to the other. "Have you ever loved someone you shouldn't?"

I'm disgusted with myself at times.

Disgusted that I thought Quinton was a nice person.

That I allowed someone so shitty to take a piece of my heart.

Lincoln's mood changes at my mood-changing question. "I don't know if I've ever *loved* someone I shouldn't, but I've been involved with someone I shouldn't have been."

"Sounds scandalous." I perk up in curiosity. "Details, please."

He cups my chin in his hand, sending ripples of goose bumps over my skin. "I'll give you details when you tell me what made you run out of the bar as if it were on fire."

Our eyes meet under the streetlight.

His full of questions.

Mine filled with answers he won't get.

I place my hand over his. "Looks like I'll get those details another time."

CHAPTER SEVEN

Lincoln

"THANK FUCK you got your head out of your ass," I tell Archer over the Bluetooth in my car.

The news of him and Georgia making up is the best I've heard all day.

Hell, all month.

I brake at a stoplight and tap my fingers along the smooth leather of the steering wheel. The feds might've seized the bulk of my assets, but I'm also not a complete dumbass. I got smart before they put their grimy hands on everything. Archer packed up my belongings and stored them at his place, and my grandparents purchased my Porsche, which they gifted back when I was released.

"How'd it happen?"

Jesus, I sound like Cassidy, wanting all the relationship gossip.

This is my life now—questioning my brother about his love life since mine is in the tank.

"None of your business," he grumbles with a huff.

I chuckle. "Happy for you, bro."

"As bad as I want to kick your ass, thanks for telling Georgia where I was; it really cemented reality into me that I needed to stop acting stupid. I'm a grown-ass man who shouldn't run away from his problems."

"Damn straight. I'm on my way to Mom's. You coming home?"

"Nah, I think Georgia and I are crashing here again tonight."

"You kids have fun."

The light turns green, and I whip into the local coffee shop's parking lot. I order an iced coffee for myself and some fancy shit for my mother. Just as I'm about to turn onto the intersection, a flash of blond hair catches my attention. Slowing down, I peruse the group of people picking up litter off the side of the road and pull over.

Rolling down the window, I stick my head out for a better view.

No fucking way.

It's her.

I'd know that body and hair anywhere.

It belongs to the woman I can't stop thinking about.

I cup my hand over my mouth and yell, "Yo! Did you get a new job?"

Cassidy veers to face me, stunned, and mutters, "You've got to be kidding me."

Not that I hear her. I'm just decent at reading lips.

She shuffles toward me as if I were a dreaded stepparent she had to spend the weekend with, wearing plastic gloves and carrying a trash bag along with a picker.

When she reaches me, she stabs at loose strands of hair falling from her hair tie.

I lean farther out the window, sticking my head out like a turtle from his shell. "If you need more hours at the bar, I can ask Archer." There's no stopping my lips from twitching into a smirk.

"Shove it," she grumbles, chewing on her plump lower lip. "This is my community service."

"Community service?" I shift my car into park. "What do you have community service for?"

This woman grows more interesting by the hour.

Her gaze drops to the ground, and she kicks at the tiny rocks in the gravel. "I don't want to talk about it."

"I do." I want to know every damn detail.

She moves from one foot to the other. "Too bad it isn't happening."

I frown. "How many hours did you get?"

"I have one more day. Saturday morning. Then, thank the Lord, I'm finished."

"Hey! Excuse me!"

At the gravelly, smoke-cured voice, our attention swings to the middle-aged woman stomping in our direction. A neon-orange vest is draped across her shoulders, and a clipboard is gripped in her hands.

"No talking to men in cars like some hooker!" she yells, snapping her fingers. "Get over here before I report you for breaking guidelines!" She releases a final huff while glaring at Cassidy.

"Ugh," Cassidy groans, rolling her eyes before shooting me an apologetic smile. "Thanks for stopping and talking shit. It's always a pleasure."

"Anytime, Cass." I wink.

"Looks like I'm not the only stalker in this relationship of ours." She winks back more dramatically, holds up her trash picker, and walks away.

"TACO TUESDAY, BABY!" Silas calls out, slamming his palm on the bar and pointing at Cassidy. "You coming?"

"Sounds tempting," Cassidy replies, biting into her lower lip before locking eyes with me. "Lincoln, are *you* attending Taco Tuesday?"

"Of course he is," Georgia answers for me. "No one misses Taco Tuesday. It's one of the rare nights the entire crew has off."

Cassidy takes a sip of her vodka cranberry. She sometimes has a drink before going home after an early shift. "I'll be there."

"Awesome!" Silas whistles. "See you there. Bring your appetite for some guac."

"You mean, for queso," Georgia corrects.

"Jesus. I need to talk to Cohen about how he raised you," Silas disputes. "Guac is where it's at."

The two then start arguing about which is better, their passion as strong as those who argue over politics.

"It's guac," I state to Cassidy, out of their conversation. "Definitely guac, but it has to be good guac."

"Nope." Cassidy shakes her head while scrunching up her nose. "Queso is delish. Smooth white cheese you dip a tortilla chip in. *Mmm.* Queso has never let me down. Guac, on the other hand? I've had people completely destroy guac."

"You taste my guac, and I guarantee, you'll never think about queso again."

A woman I dated pushed me to take a cooking class with her in Spain, where I learned all the inside tips on making the perfect guacamole.

She raises a brow. "Does that mean you're making guac tonight?"

"Considering we're going to a restaurant, it might be rude to crack mine out at the table."

"Hmm …" She taps her chin. "Looks like you'll need to make me dinner one night, so I can taste your guac."

"I'll think about it."

"Eh, I'll let you *think* you'll think about it, but you're doing it. Until then, don't you dare bail on me tonight, or I'm kicking your ass."

"Hmm …" I tap my chin the same way she did. "I'll think about it."

"Like with the guac, there's no *thinking* about it. We're the newbies of the group, so we must stick together." She pouts. "I like having you around so I don't feel left out."

The feeling is mutual.

The group—Archer, Cohen, Finn, Silas, Georgia, Grace, and Lola—has been tight for years. It's not that they exclude new people; it's just hard not to feel like the odd one out. You don't have the history, know the inside jokes or shit that happened years ago, like they do.

"I'll be there," I reply.

She claps her hands and squeals. "It's a date."

I shake my head. "It's not a date."

"Oh, it's a date, babe."

TACO TUESDAY IS BEING HELD at La Mesa.

It's the only taco joint in Anchor Ridge. From a guy who's wined and dined all over the world, I have to say, La Mesa has some damn good tacos.

Are they the best I've tasted? Nah.

Are they better than tacos I've paid double for? Hell yeah.

Our table is nearly full when Archer, Georgia, and I arrive. I sweep my gaze over the faces, in search of the one I've been looking forward to seeing.

The one with cute freckles that dust over her nose and cheekbones when she doesn't wear makeup.

The one whose smile can light up a damn bar.

The one who's given me a reason to smile nearly every damn day—something that was once forced.

That face isn't present.

Georgia and Archer take their seats while I nudge myself into a chair near the end of the table. The only one with an empty seat next to it. An empty seat that had better be occupied with Cassidy's ass soon, or she'll be hearing from me in the form of endless texts. She can't break our newbie pact.

Just as I'm easing my phone from my pocket to text her, I hear Lola say, "Damn, Cassidy! You look hot."

My gaze shoots to Cassidy as she struts toward us.

Lola isn't lying.

Cassidy is breathtaking.

A black sweater revealing a hint of cleavage and tight black jeans.

Tousled blond curls.

Ruby-red lips.

There's something about red lipstick.

Something about a girl you know who's trouble, rocking red lipstick.

I'm so fucked.

She greets everyone, a slight shyness in her tone, and doesn't hesitate to plop down next to me.

As soon as her ass hits the seat, I lean into her, inhaling her sweet floral perfume. "Nice of you to finally show … *late*."

She swats at my shoulder. "Oh, shush, Callahan. No one has ordered, and I couldn't get my mother off the phone. She thinks I'm going to some huge party even though I insisted countless times that it was just dinner."

I cock my head to the side. "Why's she so worried?"

"She doesn't want me hanging around the wrong crowd."

"Did you used to hang out with the wrong crowd?" The community service and sudden move are enough that I shouldn't need to ask that question.

"A little, yes."

"Good thing you found me because I'm the best crowd." I theatrically push my chest out.

She laughs, rolling her eyes. "So damn cocky."

We're interrupted when the server stops to take our order. Everyone makes small talk as we wait for our food, and my stomach grumbles at the mouthwatering smell of fresh tortillas. My mouth waters each time a waiter passes us with a sizzling plate of fajitas, going straight to another table.

Everyone is here, including Cohen's very pregnant girlfriend Jamie, and his son, Noah. Jamie, a doctor, isn't around as much as the other girls, but I have great respect for her. She's stepped up as a mother figure for Noah—even in the tough situation of Cohen being her sister's ex.

"How's it at the love-rekindled shack?" Cassidy asks when our food arrives, and we dig in.

Archer crashes with Georgia most nights, but they make appearances at our penthouse. It's funny at times—my brooding brother dating the spunkiest, loudest, and most outgoing person I've met in my life.

"As much as I'm glad they're back together and that my brother is happy, love can be gross." I bite into my carnitas and groan at how much more delicious it gets with each chomp.

"If you ever want a break, you can stay at my place." Her lips tilt into a smirk. "My bed is *always* open."

I chuckle, shaking my head, and decide to change the subject before taking her up on that offer. "You have community service tomorrow, right?"

"Ugh." She throws her head back and groans. "Yes. The last day of hell awaits me."

"Is it an all-day thing?"

"Nope, just until noon."

"Picking up trash again?"

"Unfortunately."

I bite back the urge to ask what she did to earn community service. This isn't the time or the place to ask. I know from experience, from when I've had someone blurt out questions regarding my past in front of people, it's not a good time. It's humiliating—something I'd never want Cassidy to experience around me.

The woman eating a quesadilla while dancing in her seat is becoming one of my closest friends. And if I dig deep into my soul for answers I've shoved away, just like I'm biting back that urge to ask questions … I know there's the urge to have more with her.

CHAPTER EIGHT

Cassidy

MY COMMUNITY SERVICE OPTIONS SUCKED.

It's not like in the movies, where you get a simple task of painting a wall or washing a car, and then when you arrive, a hot guy is working. You bond, fall in love, and live happily ever after. No, my type of community service isn't Hallmark movie–worthy.

Mine is picking up litter.

The guy I'm working with? Said I was cute for a girl with a small ass.

I check my watch for the thousandth time and sigh in relief.

My work here is done, ladies and gentlemen.

I'm ripping the latex gloves off my hands when a car similar to Lincoln's parks on the curb next to me. The window rolls down, and sure enough, Lincoln is perched up in the driver's side, staring at me with interest.

How can he afford such an expensive car?

A Porsche this nice isn't something a regular paycheck can purchase, especially one on a bartender's salary. Hell, even with my parents' money, they don't roll around in vehicles that cost six figures. He and Archer have high-end rides, never seem to be in need of cash, and even though they don't walk around in expensive clothes, theirs aren't cheap.

I know quality clothing, and they wear quality clothing.

Maybe they come from money.

And that's how he can afford such luxury.

It's hard for me not to be curious about these things anymore. Quinton came from money, so I never questioned how he afforded his Mercedes, the five-hundred-dollar meals, and Tiffany jewelry. It turns out, most of it was probably purchased with money he'd earned selling drugs to my fellow coeds.

Lincoln's voice snaps me out of my questioning haze. "You finished yet, my little criminal?" The midnight-blue baseball hat he's wearing covers his ebony-black hair and shields half his face.

As I step closer, a gust of wind whips around, pushing the masculine scent of him mingled with the tropical air freshener in his car toward me.

"All done." I toss the gloves into my trash bag. "What are you doing?"

Not going to lie, him being here is mortifying. It was the same the last time. There is nothing worse—okay, other than being arrested because you dated a criminal—than the guy you're crushing on seeing you picking up trash, looking like the so-called convict you hate. And it's not like I dressed up for the occasion in my old jeans and ill-fitting sweatshirt.

He shifts the car into park and relaxes in the leather seat. "I was in the neighborhood and figured you needed lunch after a hard day's work."

I need lunch, a shower, and then a shot of vodka.

With the sun shining in my eyes, I lower my hand over my brows to get a better view of him. "Your treat?"

"My treat, you little hellion."

I half-shrug. "Sounds good to me."

Whistling, he jerks his thumb toward his passenger seat, and I hear the click of the doors unlocking. I make a pit stop to check out with Helga, the monster in charge of community service.

On my first day, she asked if I was ready to get whipped into shape and said, "Helga doesn't like slackers. Helga sends slackers back to jail. Don't piss off Helga."

I'm pretty sure I pissed her off as I snorted to hold in my laughter.

After tossing the bag into the trash, I stop at my car to grab my purse and pour sanitizer into my hands on my walk to Lincoln's car.

"Okay, it smells like my first piña colada in here," I say, scrunching up my nose as I slide into the passenger seat and inspect the car. "I took you for more of a woodsy-scent kinda man."

He playfully glares at me. "My mom gives my car fresheners to me, and what the hell is wrong with piña colada? You get in my car, and it's like a mini vacation to the Caribbean."

"Nothing is wrong with piña coladas … if you're a fifteen-year-old girl getting her first drink." There's no holding back my smile.

This.

This is why I love hanging out with Lincoln.

As soon as I saw him, my thoughts weren't stuck on hating community service, or losing my future, or my crazy-ass ex. His presence eases my mind and soul.

There's no better company than this man.

"Keep insulting my air freshener taste, and *my treat* for lunch will be a cup of water and three french fries."

"Fine," I groan. "For the sake of my stomach, I shall stay quiet … *for now*. Once I'm fed, I can't make any promises." Shifting to grab the seat belt, I buckle up. "Where to?"

"Anything you're in the mood for?"

I spent my morning picking up trash, cigarette butts, and a few used condoms—*who the fuck tosses condoms on the side of the road?*—so I'm in need of a reward, like a nice steak and lobster.

But as great as that sounds, I'm not a brat who expects people to buy her expensive meals, so I say, "Surprise me."

Anchor Ridge is a small town, known for its local restaurants, shops, and bars. With the exception of Burger King, McDonald's, and Starbucks, there aren't many chains. My choices are limited, and since I haven't ventured out much, I don't have an answer that doesn't involve an Egg McMuffin.

Lincoln nods. "I got you."

I'm updated on Georgia and Archer's love situation while he drives out of Anchor Ridge and along the outskirts of town, closer to the city. He flicks his turn signal and cuts the wheel into the parking lot of a quaint yellow home that's been converted into a restaurant. A bright pink-and-yellow sign reads, *Yellow Peep*.

"Have you been here before?"

I shake my head. "Nope." I've heard of it, and it's definitely no McDonald's. In alarm, I glance down, inspecting myself, and tug at the hem of my sweatshirt. "I don't think I'm okay to go into a place like this."

He scratches his cheek. "I'm not catching your drift."

I throw my hand down, gesturing to my homely appearance. "Uh, I look like someone who was picking up trash on the side of the road. *Literally*."

"Babe"—his voice is stern, but his eyes are soft—"picking up trash or not, you're fucking gorgeous. I wouldn't think twice about walking in there with you."

I blush—like seriously blush—in a way I've never blushed before. "Stop lying."

"Not lying. You look damn good." He kills the ignition. "Now, let's get you fed. You deserve a good meal after today's contribution to society."

He steps out of the car, opens my door, and extends his hand. I grab it, the warmth of his large hand burying mine underneath it, and we walk into the restaurant.

Hand in hand, like we're a couple.

A relaxed ambiance collides with us the moment we enter through the doors. A man in the corner is playing piano as people sit at white-clothed tables—some with mimosa flutes in their hands, some with waters, and some with coffees. No one is dressed like me—no freaking one. Sure, there are some casual diners, but no one underdressed, who was picking up condoms ten minutes ago.

As much as I want to haul ass out of here, Lincoln's words ring through my thoughts, crashing through my insecurities.

Fuck it. I'm starving.

Who cares?

It's not like I'm interested in anyone but the man who already told me he gave no fucks about what I was wearing.

We stop at the hostess stand, where menus are stacked up with a basket of rolled silverware placed beside them. The girl behind the counter, complete in a white button-up shirt and black slacks, greets us before leading the way to our table in the corner of the room.

"I'm going to wash my hands," I tell Lincoln before scurrying to the restroom and returning minutes later. Lowering myself onto the chair, I set my eyes on him. "You so planned this, didn't you?"

He unrolls the cloth napkin and drapes it over his lap while I do the same. "What do you mean?"

"You planned to find me finishing community service, so you could take me to lunch *because* you love hanging out with me."

He shoots me an amused smile. "What can I say? You're cool ... like a little sister."

I cringe at those words.

Little sister.

That's the furthest from what I want him to see me as.

"Oh God, never call me your little sister again." I rub my forehead with the heel of my hand. "That'd mean you're like my big brother … and no way in hell can I say I'm sexually attracted to my brother."

As if with perfect timing, the waitress approaches our table at the same time those words leave my mouth. The way her eyes widen, her jaw drops open, and her gaze pings back and forth between me and Lincoln confirms she heard my little comment. My head spins, and swear to God, I'm tempted to dash out of this place. I might be able to handle looking like a hot mess, but our waitress thinking I want to bang my brother, that's where I draw the line.

I cast a quick glance at Lincoln, who doesn't look fazed by my comment. In fact, he only appears entertained at my awkwardness.

"Hello," the waitress chirps, gaining control of her thoughts. She's my age, and fingers crossed, she realizes it was a sarcastic statement. "I'm Taylor. Can I start you off with something to drink?"

I quickly peruse the drink menu and order a mimosa while Lincoln asks for an ice water. Taylor scurries off to grab our drinks, and Lincoln's eyes level on me, humor shining in them.

"Should we make it clear that I'm not your brother?" he asks with a raised brow.

"I'm sure that would be *more* awkward." My cheeks redden.

He smirks.

"All right, here ya go," Taylor says, dropping off our drinks.

"Thank you," I say. At the same time, Lincoln replies with, "My girl here wants to make it clear that I'm not her brother."

I freeze, mid–mimosa grab, and want to drown myself with the liquid.

No, he didn't.

Taylor stares at Lincoln. I'm unsure if it's in captivation or if she's speechless at what he said. I'm leaning a bit toward captivation, though. When she took our drink orders, she was so flustered that she barely looked him in the eye. Now that she is, she's realizing she likes what she sees.

I set my drink down.

He wants to have some fun? Let's have some fun.

I shift my attention to Taylor, and mischief barrels through my belly. "You see, I *don't* want him to see me as a little sister, though."

Taylor nods, catching my drift, and sweeps her long black hair off her shoulder as her gaze leaves the guy I wish hadn't just said I was like a sister to him.

"Ah, I get it now," Taylor says, her voice no longer timid, her tone now confident. "He's dumb if he doesn't see you as more because you're gorgeous."

Yes.

A girl's girl.

I like her.

Taylor's gaze nervously slides back to Lincoln. "And if you're paying the bill, don't use that against me with my tip, please."

Lincoln holds both hands up. "I'll be tipping you more for your honesty."

A rush of relief leaves her. No doubt, she didn't plan on that little outburst. "Thank you. Now, what can I get you?"

Our conversation turns more professional as she rattles off the lunch specials. We order, and she shoots me a smile before scurrying away.

"I can't believe you did that," I comment, wrapping my fingers around the stem of my glass.

"And I can't believe you did that," he replies.

"Touché." I smile. "You wanted to make things awkward, and I needed to up the ante."

"You sure did." He takes a long gulp of his water. "You working tonight?"

"Nope." I moan at the first sip of the sugary mimosa. It's been a while since I've had one. I tend to save them for days I'm nursing massive hangovers or for weddings. "We both have the night off."

"How'd you know I have the night off?" He tilts his head to the side and chews on his lower lip.

"The schedule."

He waggles his finger at me. "My little stalker, you."

"You love it."

"Any big plans tonight?"

I ignore the chatter around us and focus on Lincoln. "Possibly."

"Like what?"

"Sex." I lick the rim of my glass in a failed attempt to appear seductive. *Yeah, I most likely look like a baby licking a toy.* "Lots and lots of sex."

Unfortunately, my response doesn't choke him up as I hoped. Lincoln is hard to rile up, to my surprise, and my humor never shocks him.

He scoffs, "Bullshit. My money is on you staying home, watching cartoons, and cuddling with a stuffed animal you've had since you were two."

"It sounds like you're speaking from experience." I crack a smile and tap his hand. "Is that what you were doing at twenty-one, Grandpa Bartender? When did you finally break up with your baby blanket?"

He chuckles. "Nah, you got it all wrong, babe."

"I bet it was Ninja Turtles ... am I right?"

He stays quiet, fighting back a grin.

"Oh my God!" I cover my mouth to hold in a shriek of laughter. "I'm so right."

"Wrong." He plucks an ice cube from his water and flicks it at me. "My baby blanket—which I haven't used in years, *thank you*—was Mickey Mouse."

I thrum my fingers along the edge of the table, engrossed in this conversation like it's a revelation as deep as how the world will end. "Do you still have it?"

He swipes his palm over his chin. "My mom probably does."

"Ask her because I'd love to give it to our kiddos when the time comes."

He throws his head back and laughs. "What am I going to do with you?"

"Marry me. Knock me up. Whatever you'd like." I chug my mimosa and motion toward him with it. "But not anal. I don't do anal, prewarning."

Call Taylor the CEO of poor timing because it's at *anal* when she returns with our plates.

"Uh …" she mutters, searching for the right words before quickly placing our plates in front of us.

This time, Lincoln is the one covering his mouth to contain his laughter.

CHAPTER NINE

Lincoln

DAMN, does it feel good, having the night off.

As much as I love the mental interruption the bar provides, a break is nice. A grip of disappointment squeezes at my core, though. I'm home alone with no plans and no one to make plans with. Archer is working, and my bet is, he'll go to Georgia's when he gets off.

Before my life fell apart, I had friends.

By the dozens.

Friends I partied with, traveled with, acted like spoiled rich kids with.

Fake-ass friends—most of them dropping me like flies when news broke.

A few were at my side during litigation, but after I was locked up, they were ghosts. No letters. No visits. No calls.

After my release, my mother threw me a *welcome home* party. Some of those *friends* came. I said my hellos, but just as they'd done to me, I wanted nothing to do with them. Hell, I hardly want anything to do with the old life I once had.

Loyalty—it's a big damn deal to me.

If you're not loyal, if I can't trust you, then there's the fucking door.

I've kept my mouth shut to remain loyal.

Got time for staying loyal.

If I say I have your back, I have your back.

I'm channel-surfing when my phone rings.

Cassidy.

"Hello?" I answer.

"Hi, handsome," she says, her voice casual as if this were a daily occurrence for us. "Whatcha doing?"

I scratch my neck, savoring the sound of her voice. It flows like an expensive ink, and I could soak up every drop. Cassidy's voice doesn't match her appearance, doesn't match your typical sorority girl.

"Not much," I reply. "Just chilling."

"By yourself?"

"Why?"

She's so nosy, and for some damn reason, I love it.

"Answer the question, Mr. Complicated."

"Yes"—I chuckle—"I'm alone."

"That's my good future husband."

The call ends.

The fuck?

Pulling the phone away, I stare at it in confusion. Just as I'm about to call her back to see if we lost connection, a FaceTime call comes through.

Cassidy.

I accept the call, and a zoomed-in Cassidy pops up on my screen—her face makeup-free, her blond hair swept back into a messy bun with stray pieces hanging loose around her eyes, and a knotted tie-dye headband pushed at the top.

"What movie do you want to watch?" When she shifts to make herself comfortable, her upholstered headboard comes into view.

I raise a brow. "Huh?"

"What's tonight's movie of choice?" She adjusts the collar on her silk pink-and-white striped pajama top. "Do you have Netflix?"

"Yes." I stare at her, blinking.

"Coolio." She leans forward, positions the phone so she's hands-free but still in view, and grabs her remote. "What are you in the mood for? Action? Comedy?" She glances away from the TV and shoots me an amused smile. "Me personally? Romance is the name of my game."

"Babe," I breathe out, "you need to clue me in here."

She plays with the remote in her hand. "Both of us are home, solo. Might as well watch a movie ... hang out."

"Hmm ... from what I remember, you said you'd be having *lots and lots* of sex tonight."

Nausea permeates in my stomach at her sleeping with a random guy who doesn't deserve her. That nausea morphs into satisfaction that she's not with a guy tonight.

No, she's with me.

Virtually.

But I'll take it.

I'll take any extra time I can have with her.

She scoffs, "You're dumber than I thought if you believed that."

I knew she was fucking with me.

The thing is, I love fucking with her right back.

"You have six seconds to decide before I take matters into my own hands," she says, breaking me out of my thoughts. "And trust me, it'll either be a serial killer doc, a cheesy romance, or some tiger people's drama."

I kick my bare feet up on the concrete coffee table. "You plan to come over?"

She shakes her head. "We're watching a movie via FaceTime."

There's no, *Do you want to?*

Cassidy—my new bossy best-friend-slash-coworker—has no problem telling me what *my* plans are for the night.

"Ah, is this what the cool kids do these days?" Observing my surroundings, I search for the perfect phone stand and decide on a leather pillow. Snagging the pillow, I settle it on the coffee table and balance the phone against it—a setup similar to Cassidy's.

"Nope. We typically Netflix and chill. Netflix and chill is when—"

Not wanting to hear about her Netflix-and-chilling with anyone, I talk over her, "I know what Netflix and chill is. I'm not *that* old. You pick the movie. I'm down for whatever."

"Let me grab my movie snacks."

Movie snacks?

"I wish you had given your boy a warning, so I could've grabbed some movie snacks."

"Joke's on you. Everyone should have movie snacks on hand at all times. Next time you go to the store, I'm tagging along to make sure you're loaded with the good stuff." Blowing me a kiss, she jumps off the bed, providing a short glimpse of her in her short pajama shorts, and disappears from the camera's view.

I train my eyes on the screen, not wanting to miss a second of our conversation. Minutes later, she returns with a bowl of popcorn, movie-theater snack boxes, and a Coke. My mouth waters, practically tasting the buttery popcorn.

She darts a quick glance in my direction, as if double-checking I'm still with her, and settles her snacks onto the bed. Sliding back onto the bed, she fluffs out a pillow and makes herself comfortable.

"Want a virtual kernel?" She holds the bowl toward the phone.

"Funny." My stomach grumbles like a chain saw. "You're making me hungry."

"Be better prepared in the future." She pops a kernel in her mouth and shoots me a sly grin.

I frown in disapproval. "Give me a heads-up next time."

"I love that you're agreeing this will happen again." She

winks before tearing open a box of Junior Mints and tossing one into her mouth.

"Pause and let me see what I can wrangle from the kitchen." I drop my feet and groan as I stand.

"Wrangle? What are you, a cowboy going to hunt for his next meal?"

I flip her off before heading into the kitchen in search of snacks. Since Archer and I prefer takeout to cooking, I don't get my hopes up on matching Cassidy's snack game. Rummaging through the cabinet and fridge, I return to the living room with a bag of pretzels, a beer, and a box of Thin Mints.

How the living hell my brother managed to have Girl Scout cookies is beyond me.

I plop down on the couch at the same time I rip open the pretzels. "Choose our movie."

She nods, chewing the popcorn in her mouth, and rattles off some romance movie title.

Suppressing a groan, I type it into the search bar. "Got it."

"All right," she says, simulating a game show host's voice, "one, two, three, hit start."

We hit the button on our remotes at the same time, and the movie starts. Instead of watching the movie, I stare at Cassidy— all creeper-style but also justifying it as this is what she wanted. I soak up her surroundings, of the small area I can see of her bedroom.

"It sucks you're over there," Cassidy says, sliding the popcorn bowl onto her nightstand before tugging a white blanket up her chest. "We could snuggle." She *snuggles* into the blanket, into the bed, the same way I'd want to with her.

It does suck that we can't.

It's also good for us that we can't.

My heart quickens at the thought of her in my arms, but instead of agreeing, I say, "Eh, I don't know. I'm putting my money on you not only being a bed hog but also a snorer."

I joke.

It's in my nature.

My defense mechanism without sounding defensive.

Humor is what steers me away from conversations, from honesty I'm too scared to admit.

She wiggles her finger in a *come-hither* motion. "Come and see for yourself then."

I repeatedly shake my head. "Trouble, trouble, trouble."

Our attention returns to the movie, and every so often, one of us will comment about it. Mostly Cassidy, who has no problem telling movie characters they're being stupid. Even though romance movies aren't typically my jam, it's not terrible.

After a long spread of no Cassidy comments, I glance over to find her sleeping. Her mouth somewhat open, her chest dropping in and out slowly, and the box of Junior Mints is gripped in her hand. I hesitate, unsure of what to do, but decide to keep watching the movie.

If she wakes up, she'll know I didn't bail on her.

She's still crashed out when the movie ends.

Whispering, "Good night," and hoping the mints don't spill all over her bed, I hang up.

And just like that, I had my first virtual … date … hangout … with Cassidy.

"I'M THROWING Archer a surprise birthday party," Georgia announces while walking into the bar.

Georgia and I have gotten along since day one. She and Archer … well, *Archer* was in the midst of denying his feelings for Georgia then. She flirted with me, resulting in my brother wanting to kill me. I knew he liked her, so I told her to keep doing it until he got his head out of his ass. When our father died, I called Georgia to be there with Archer. She was who he needed.

Even in the small amount of time we've known each other, I can depend on Georgia.

I respect Georgia.

I hope to God my brother never fucks up the good thing he has.

I snort. "Yeah, he won't be happy about that."

"Yes, he will," she answers with certainty as if there'd never been a truer fact.

Archer and surprise parties go together like the Pope and a strip club. My brother would probably choose to have his balls tugged off than attend a party solely for himself. Although, now that Georgia is in the picture, he's changing. The dude is becoming more of a social man. And given the hell he put Georgia through when he was working through his issues, he's nearly bowing down to her.

He won't love the surprise party, but he'll enjoy it for the sake of his relationship.

He'll enjoy it because his girlfriend threw it for him.

I chuckle, shaking my head. "You and my brother being total opposites yet also obsessed with each other would confuse the smartest dude on the planet."

"Opposites attract." She taps her finger against the side of her mouth. "Sometimes."

I cock my head to the side. "What's that supposed to mean?"

"Sometimes, cut from the same cloth attracts each other too." She offers me a bemused smile. "Like you and Cassidy."

It's a struggle, hiding my bullshit. "There's no *me and Cassidy* unless you're referring to our friendship."

"Yeah, okay." Sarcasm covers her tone. "Anyway, I'll give you time to come to terms with your liking her. Your grandparents offered the lake house for our little soiree. So, it'll be an overnight thing. Be there, or I'm shaving your head next time I sleep over."

A sinking feeling sets in my stomach. "You sure that's a good idea?"

Concern etches along her face. "Do you not think so?"

Archer doesn't mind the lake house.

He goes there all the time to clear his head.

Me? That's who I'm worried about.

There are too many memories there.

Regret rushes into me like a scorned ex as I remember what took place there.

But like I tell my brother, you have to face your shit, not run away from it.

"Nah, it's cool." I gulp. "He'd rather have it there than at some club."

The worry on her face dissolves, and she claps her hands before releasing a squeal. "I invited the crew, and hopefully, everyone can come."

I nod. "Let me know if you need me to do anything."

"You're the best." She blows me a kiss before scurrying away at the same time Cassidy comes into view.

"Gotta say, babe"—I shake my head in exaggerated disappointment—"you suck as a movie-watching partner."

My thoughts retrace to last night and how she made it seem less lonely, made me feel as if I had someone, a friend other than my brother. Someone I can call anytime, who I can ask to hang out, and who enjoys my company as much as I enjoy theirs. I'm damn grateful for this woman squeezing her way into my life.

She twists her ponytail around three fingers and laughs. "Look, a girl can be tired after picking up trash all morning. You didn't catch me at my movie-watching peak."

"And you say I'm old. You didn't even make it past midnight."

"Had you been there with me, I would've stayed awake *all* night."

I confine a laugh into a snort.

"Will you be in attendance at your brother's birthday party, old man?"

I nod. "Yep. You?"

"Georgia invited me, so I'm considering it." She grins. "It'll be a good time to show you how great my night-owl movie-watching skills are."

"My sidekick had better show up." I click my tongue against the roof of my mouth. "Can't leave me hanging as the odd one out."

"I'll be there. I'm Batman. You're Robin. Sidekicks forever."

"Whoa, whoa. I'm Batman. You're Robin."

I shake my head and snort. "I'm Batman."

She throws her arm out, signaling to her body. "Green isn't my color. It washes me out. Therefore, I can't be Robin."

"Too bad. You're *my* sidekick."

She rolls her eyes. "First, you're *my* sidekick. Second, here soon, I'll be moving my way up to the love of your life."

I cover my face to conceal a snort. "Swear to God, you and your craziness will be the death of me."

"Craziness? You haven't seen anything yet. Just wait until you get me in the bedroom."

The glass in my hand slips through my fingers and shatters on the floor. The thought of having Cassidy, of kissing Cassidy, of sliding into her warmth, into a pussy that'd probably be the best I've ever had, sends my heart into overdrive.

I am so screwed with this woman.

NO MATTER how much time has passed, a grim cloud will always be over my head when I visit the lake. What was once an enjoyable hangout for me is now nothing but a pitiful reminder of who I lost.

"Don't worry about hiding," Lola says, walking into the cabin with Silas trailing her. "The surprise is ruined. There will be no shocking gasps from Archer when he walks in."

Grace sighs, her hand covering her mouth. "What?"

"We parked down the street for this," Finn adds. "And it's fucking chilly outside."

Silas scoffs, "Dumbass. Did you honestly think Archer would hang out in the car, *blindfolded*, for hours? A hundo he *maybe* lasted ten minutes before he tore the damn thing off."

Lola shakes her head in disapproval. "What a pain in the ass."

Silas drapes his tattooed arm over her shoulders. "Don't act like you wouldn't do the same."

"Wrong. I enjoy being blindfolded." Tilting her head back, she peers up at Silas with a teasing smile. "I'd keep it on *all* night."

"What am I going to do with you?" He drags her against his chest and wrinkles his hand through her midnight-black strands before she smacks his hand away and smooths down her hair.

Silas and Lola are best friends.

Or so they say.

Something I've observed about my brother's circle is, people are in love with each other.

Archer and Georgia are obviously now dating.

Silas and Lola act like an old couple.

Finn acts as if he's Grace's bodyguard, her protector, and keeps a constant eye on her. While she stares at him with stars in her eyes.

Way more than friendship between them.

Briefly, I consider their viewpoint of Cassidy and me. They've made comments about us dating and being into each other.

Speaking of Cassidy, she declined my offer for a ride here and rode with Lola and Silas instead. She mentioned something along the lines of finding new friends. Which I get. Working so much, she doesn't get out much. Neither Grace nor Lola work at the bar, but they hang out at Twisted Fox like it's their second job, and she spends time with them during her breaks.

Everyone's attention shifts to the front door when it flies open.

Forgetting what Lola said, we yell, "Surprise!"

False alarm.

Instead of the birthday boy coming into view, it's my mother and grandparents. I smile, appreciative that Georgia included them. My mom has gone through hell the past few years, and with my father gone, she's lonely. When Archer and I were younger, we hardly spent time with our parents. Now, I check on my mother a few times a week, have dinner with her, watch movies—anything to get her mind off her loss.

"Wrong person." My mother's brown eyes widen with concern about ruining the surprise. "Although I'm sure Archer won't be upset about missing the surprise part." She struts into the house, and her heels clack against the wood floor. A Prada bag hangs off her shoulder, and she's wearing a white pantsuit.

To a lake house.

Josephine Callahan doesn't do casual.

Hell, I'm not sure she even owns a pair of jeans.

Designer pantsuits and dresses are her fashion choice.

Behind her are my grandparents, walking hand in hand.

"Although I did enjoy a greeting like that." My grandmother —barely wrinkled with the help of Botox—scrunches her face as she grins.

The room erupts in laughter.

Cassidy lifts on her tiptoes next to me and whispers, "Is that your mom?"

I nod at the same time my mother reaches us. Cassidy retreats a step, allowing my mom room to wrap her arms around me in a hug and smack a kiss to my cheek.

Before the *incident*, my mother wasn't a hugger.

Kissing cheeks was more of a formality than maternal.

My father's death changed her.

Changed her outlook on life and she tapped into her inner self.

Same shit with me.

"Okay, you're absolutely gorgeous," Cassidy blurts out.

My mother beams at the compliment, her pearly veneers showing.

I hold in a chuckle and gesture to Cassidy. "Mom, this is Cassidy. Cassidy, this is my mother, Josephine."

"Oh, I like her. Are you two …?" She signals back and forth between us.

"Not yet," Cassidy answers before I can. "Your son is quite stubborn."

My mother offers me a nod of encouragement as Lola calls Cassidy over.

Cassidy holds out her hand toward my mother. "It's really nice meeting you. I can't wait for us to shop for my wedding dress when the day comes."

My mother squeezes her hand once and then twice while grinning at her.

Just like how those maternal instincts kicked in, my mother has started asking when I'll settle down, when I'll find a nice girl like Georgia, when I'll stop wanting the *bachelor* lifestyle. I don't live the bachelor lifestyle. I'm living the survival lifestyle— working my ass off, fighting my demons, and not wanting to punch the world in its face every time I think about how it's fucked me.

That isn't me being a whiny bitch either. I'll accept responsibility for what I've done and the choices I've made, but there are people in high places who hate me. And they brought me down.

"Why haven't you asked her out?" my mother rushes out as if she's been holding on to it like a breath underwater. "She's better suited for you than … others you've dated."

A fucking Kit Kat bar would be better suited for me than the women I've dated … well, was involved with because *dating* is a heavy term. A term I've never used with a woman—nor have I had to with the type of women who found their way, sneaking into my bed.

I scratch my cheek, averting my gaze to the opposite end of the room—to where Cassidy is talking to Lola and pouring herself a drink. Talking about the women I've *dated* is the last talkfest I want to have with my mother. The situation, the women I was involved with, is awkward enough.

I clear my throat, hoping to dispose of the uneasiness. "We're just friends. She's young and—"

"Honey, honey," she interrupts. "She isn't that young. And so what if she's a few years behind you? She's full of life, and she obviously likes you … and from the way you've been staring since she walked away, I'd say the feeling is mutual. She reminds me of Georgia. Look how good she is for Archer."

"Georgia and Archer are different." I slip my hands into my jean pockets. "Archer has his life together, and his past isn't as fucked up as mine."

My mother's fair-tinted face falls while she captures my hand in hers. "I'm sorry for what happened, but in order to be happy, you have to move on from the past. We're suffering the same pain—in different ways but still similar. I want you to rise above it more than I want it for myself. All it takes for you is a reason, an incentive, a realization that not everyone will judge you for your past."

"I know; I know." The thought still sends nausea through my stomach.

Thankfully, Archer and Georgia walk in, interrupting our conversation. The surprise is delayed this time, happening a good minute after they come into view, and everyone cracks up in laughter. Archer, not appearing one bit surprised, thanks everyone for coming.

Georgia ordered a taco bar that I picked up on my way to the lake, and Lola brought enough drinks to last us a week. We eat, drink, and celebrate my brother's birthday.

As the sunset transitions into darkness, I say good-bye to my mother and grandparents and walk outside. I accept the bite of the wind as I stroll down the wooden dock and settle myself on the edge. Shutting my eyes, I soak up the silence and absorb the semblance of my surroundings. There's something about the lake, the rhythmic echo of the water, that lends a hand to your psyche and relaxes you.

Yet at the same time, the solitude of the water forces you to remember.

The two-story home, complete with a wraparound porch and wall-to-wall windows, has been in the Callahan family since my grandfather bought it in his thirties. It's been renovated a few dozen times by my mother, whose interior style is a revolving door of changes.

After my grandfather's death, the home was passed down to my father. It was supposed to keep that same course—the home being passed down from generation to generation. Too bad that didn't last. The feds wanted it, and before they managed to get their grimy hands on one of my favorite childhood destinations, my mother's parents stepped in and purchased it from my father. That way, it could stay in the family, and we wouldn't lose yet another thing. The lake house is modest compared to our other family homes, but it was my grandfather's pride and joy. We'd already annihilated the business he'd built from the ground up; we couldn't lose the lake house too.

"Hey, party of one out here."

I glance back to find Cassidy stopping behind me.

"Can I join you?"

I pat the space next to me. "Sure."

If it were anyone else, even Archer, who'd asked that question, I'd have told them I needed alone time. But not with Cassidy. I'll never decline a second with her. Like the serenity of the lake, she's practically a sedative for me. And this isn't about me being codependent with a girl; it's about being around someone who shines so fucking bright that I can't help but be zapped with her energy.

About a woman I can sit here with, not say a word, and she'd understand.

Or I could ramble off about the most random shit, and she'd understand.

Or I could ask her to leave, and she'd also understand.

Cassidy is understanding, and in the world of the rich and felons, that isn't a common trait.

She plops down next to me, our shoulders brushing as she settles herself. "This is gorgeous." With a sigh, she leans back on her elbows and lifts her head, studying the open sky. "I could stay out here all night and take in the stillness of this place."

"This is where my father's ashes were spread." The words, unrelenting, spill from my lips like a waterfall.

Fuck!

Regret seeps up my throat.

I should've kept that to myself.

Way to morbid the night up, Linc.

"Oh." Dead air passes before her voice softens, and she stretches out her arm to rest her hand over mine. "That has to be hard."

That's an understatement.

It ripped me apart.

I was close with my father.

After graduating college, I took over the VP position at Callahan Holdings since Archer refused to. My father and I worked together every day and got along great, and then he hired Phil, his longtime friend. His shady friend who had too many ideas but not enough sense.

That friend convinced my father he could avoid repercussions from breaking the law because he was rich and had a company to stand behind. I warned him, threatened the friend, begged my father day after day to stop. It generated a wire of tension between us that was never uncut. He was breaking the law, and all I could do was sit back and watch the fire spread, praying to the good man above that my father would come to his senses. Archer, not giving a shit about family loyalty, resigned the moment he found out.

Me? I stayed. Callahan Holdings had been ingrained in our blood, and I'd never turn my back on blood.

Then I also went to prison with my father and Phil.

"He died while serving time in prison." Another unstoppable confession.

"What?" There's no stammer in her tone.

"He was in prison, had a heart attack, and died."

She shifts to face me, and under the brilliance of the light seeping from the front porch, I spot the curiosity swimming in her eyes. I wait for the endless questions, but they don't come. Cassidy, my mind-reading confidant, understands I'm here to reflect upon my past, my father, and not confess the wrongdoings of a man who's no longer with us.

"It's nice he can rest somewhere so peaceful ... so pretty."

I nod. "It is."

I never perceived it that way, but Cassidy has a point. My father loved the lake; it was his resting place, so it only makes sense it's where he was finally laid to rest. Criminal or not, he deserved a proper good-bye, a proper place for his soul to reside.

Cassidy, the girl who never stops talking and bullshitting, sits silently next to me. Eventually, she rests her head on the crook of my shoulder, and I wrap my arm around her back, tugging her closer to me, nearly on my lap.

"You cold?" I ask, peering down as she rubs her hand over her goose bump–covered arm.

"A little," she whispers.

I tighten my grip on her, hoping to transfer a sliver of my body heat, and run my hand up and down her arm—similar to what she was doing. Her skin is soft, smooth like the organic apples my mom overpays for. When the goose bumps don't disappear, and she shivers, I slowly pull away, already missing her warmth, and stand.

I hold out my hand, and there's no hesitation before she

takes it, allowing me to pull her to her feet. Only inches separate us. Our breaths meet, and my heart thrashes against my chest in uncertainty of what's to come.

She licks her lips.

I do the same.

The desire of this woman cuts through my veins, as if it's begging to be let free.

I inhale a deep breath.

No, I can't ruin our friendship.

I lower my voice, swiping flyaway strands of hair from her eyes. "My sidekick."

"Your sidekick," she whispers.

Without thinking, without considering the repercussions of such a reckless move, I bow my head and rest my forehead against hers.

"Lincoln." She says my name in a shaky breath.

Her voice. That tone. It ruins me.

It's the push that leads me to drop my lips to hers.

She kisses me back, her lips plump and soft.

As we kiss, it's as if she's breathing life back into me.

Yet also casting a calmness alongside it.

When she opens her mouth, sliding her tongue along the seam of my lips, reality shatters through me.

My head spins when I break our connection, retreat a step, and catch my breath. "Shit, Cass. I'm so sorry."

This time, she's caressing my arm while appearing unfazed by my pulling away. "No, it's fine." A hint of a smile crosses her face. "In fact, I'm down to do it again."

I hesitate.

That urge that caused me to kiss her moments ago resurfaces.

My mouth already misses the taste of hers.

"Yo! Party ditchers!" Finn calls out into the night from the back porch. "Get your asses in here!"

And just like that, Finn saves us from ruining our friendship.

"I'm going to punch him," Cassidy grumbles. "In the balls. Then the kneecaps. Then the balls again for good measure."

I chuckle, and my hand is sweaty when I grab hers. I wait for her reaction—whether she'll tug away, try to kiss me again, or ask about the kiss. With a sigh, she squeezes my hand, and I lead her back into the house, where everyone, except Georgia and Archer, are in the living room. Drinks are in their hands, and some trivia show is playing on the TV, all of them screaming answers at the contestant.

"We thought you guys had gotten lost out there," Finn says, falling down on the couch next to Grace.

"Prepare to have mosquito bites out the ass," Lola comments, shuddering as she peers back at us from the front of the couch. "Those things are brutal around here."

Finn slides his hands together. "I don't know about y'all, but I'm exhausted. The birthday boy has retired to his bedroom, and that means we can crash at any time." He does a once-over of the room.

I peer over at Cassidy and drop her hand. "You staying the night?"

A sleepover was Georgia's plan. It's a four-bedroom, providing plenty of room for everyone. Archer and I are crashing in our bedrooms, which leaves the master and guest bedroom.

Cassidy nods. "Sure am."

"What are the sleeping arrangements?" I ask everyone.

Lola yawns, stretching out her arms. "Grace and I are crashing in the master." She shoots a glance at Cassidy. "We can squeeze your tiny butt in there if you want?"

Cassidy laughs. "That might be a little too uncomfortable. I'll take the couch. No biggie."

"Eh, I'm taking the couch," Finn says. "Silas and I flipped for the guest room, and I lost."

"You can have my bed, Cassidy," Silas offers. "I'll crash on the floor." He winks at her, sending a streak of jealousy through my blood.

"Nah, take my bed," I interrupt. "It's more comfortable than the guest bed, and I'll crash on the floor."

"You don't have to do that," Cassidy replies, biting into her lower lip—a lip that I now know the taste of.

For someone who's talked plenty of shit about being in my bed, she sure seems shy about it now.

"The floor is comfortable," I add. "I like sleeping on it."

She rolls her eyes. "You are such a liar."

"Punish me for my lying by taking my bed then." I smile. "You know I'm the perfect gentleman."

"Okay," she dramatically groans. "But don't say it's my fault when you're sore from sleeping on the floor."

CHAPTER TEN

Cassidy

"OH MY GOD, you're such a bullshitter," I say, laughing when Lincoln drops down to pull out a bed from the couch in his bedroom.

He smirks. "What?"

"You were acting like such a gentleman, offering to give me your bed and sleep on the floor, when in actuality, you have a damn pullout bed."

"Hey, I'm giving you my bed, aren't I?" He places his hand over his heart. "I'd say that's a damn good gentleman. I could be making *you* sleep on the pullout, which isn't nearly as comfortable as my Tempur-Pedic."

"I can take the pullout." I hate inconveniencing people.

"No, you'll take my bed." He shakes his head. "There's no changing my mind."

Dropping my overnight bag onto the carpet, I size up his bedroom. "This is cute."

It screams *I played lacrosse, come from money, and haven't been here since my high school years* with its plaid wallpaper, black furniture, and blue bedding.

He raises a brow. "Cute?"

"Definitely an adolescent teen's bedroom."

He advances the few steps to the closet and gathers sheets and a blanket. "No judging. I didn't stay here much growing up." He stops, a flash of regret on his features, and scratches his scruffy cheek. "I didn't spend much time with my family back then, so my mother didn't bother renovating rooms that weren't being used."

"Why didn't you hang out with your family?"

Even though my family could have a two-part special on *Dr. Phil*, we're close. My mother held mandatory dinners, and I regularly came home from college on the weekends. My parents' marriage might've been messy, but my mother made sure to build a strong support system within my siblings.

I stroll around the bedroom, as if I were in a museum, and inspect everything. Grabbing a framed photo, I hold it up. "Is this your dad?"

His face is unreadable as he nods and stares at the photo. "Yeah."

I eye the man's features. "He and Archer are spitting images of each other."

"Yeah, they were nearly twins."

Unlike Lincoln, Archer has broad shoulders, thick hair that reaches his neck, and a wide face. Lincoln is slimmer with short hair, and while they both sport facial hair, Lincoln's is cleaner cut. The similarities between his father and him are limited. While Archer took after their father, Lincoln resembles more of his mother.

I gulp, setting the photo down, and snag another of him in a tuxedo. His arm is wrapped around a girl, who is sporting a frilly, gaudy-as-hell pink dress.

"Girlfriend?" I jerk my head toward the photo.

"Prom date."

"Did you bang her?"

He cracks a smile. "None of your business."

"Secrets don't make friends, Callahan, and if I recall

correctly, that's what you keep saying we are. *Friends*. So … let a friend know."

He shakes his head. "It was prom. I was a stupid teenager. So, yes."

I love that he's honest with me. After what happened with Quinton, honesty and trust are my biggest turn-ons. Quinton did a lot of fucked-up things to me, and the biggest takeaway from it was, trust is an important component of a relationship.

Well, behind not dating a criminal.

The next photo I pick up is of Lincoln in a lacrosse uniform. *Shocker.*

"You were hot." I smile. "I so would've dated you in high school."

He stops in the middle of making up his bed and wrinkles his nose. "Only in high school?"

"Shut up." I return the photo to the dresser. "You know I'd date you so hard *right now*. And don't bother saying the same because I know if I were old, *like you*, you'd date me so hard."

"But unfortunately, you're too young for me."

"And you're too dumb for me for saying that."

He winces. "Ouch."

My chest tightens, but I'm strong enough to maintain a straight face. We're joking, being good ole buddies, ole pals, but it pains me every time he mentions our age difference, when he calls me too young. It's not like he's Hugh Hefner and I just graduated from high school. Yes, there's a *slight* age difference but nothing too out of the ordinary. Hell, Georgia is years behind Archer.

That heartache of the topic hits harder now that we've kissed. I had known kissing him would be exciting, but it was more than I'd expected. It was perfection. Never before had just a kiss dragged out emotions so strong, a need so heavy, a compulsion to want to have everything with a man. Him kissing me verifies he feels the same way, but in true Callahan boy fashion, he's hiding.

Now, he's acting as if it never happened. Since we're in a house full of people and I'm not sure where the conversation would lead, I decide to save it for later. If he says the wrong thing, it's not like I can storm out of here and leave. Walking home or asking Grace to leave in the middle of the night aren't options.

There's a time and a place to talk with the guy I'm falling for. A time and a place to bring up the kiss. My stomach sinks at the realization that he might think said kiss was a mistake.

Kneeling, I unzip my overnight bag and yank my pajamas from it before snagging my toothbrush. "I'm going to change and get ready for bed."

He salutes me as I stroll into the adjoined bathroom. With a large glass shower and a blue rug, it doesn't provide as much character as his bedroom does. Walking out in a silky camisole and plaid pants—I packed casually but still kept a hint of sexiness—I find Lincoln changed into a white tee and gray sweats. I blush, taking him in, before noticing the candy pile on the bed.

"What's this?"

Lincoln glances up at me. "Movies and snacks until we crash out ... until *you* crash out."

And just like that, the tension over our kiss unbinds.

Temporarily washes itself out of my thoughts at him remembering our movie night.

"Sounds like a plan to me." It's hard to contain my happiness as I plop down on the bed, stomach first, and allow my feet to dangle off the end as I inspect the candy selection. "AirHeads, Starbursts, Nerds, Junior Mints. Jesus, you hooked a girl up." Rolling over, I bring myself up and rest my back against the headboard. "You planned for this, didn't you?"

"I might've made a pit stop on the way here." He snatches the pillow on the pullout and fluffs it out. "You're my sidekick, remember? We gotta look out for each other."

I cock my head to the side. "How'd you know I'd be in your bedroom?"

"That I had no idea. I figured we'd hang out in the living room, but this is better."

"Oh, really? Why's that?"

"No one can jack our snacks."

"Good point." I snatch the Nerds, open the box, and pour the mini candies into my mouth. "I've had alcohol, and now, I'm about to sugar binge. I'm either going to be up all night like a crackhead or crash out in twenty minutes. There's no in-between."

"Hmm …" He taps the side of his mouth. "What was it you said before? If I were with you, you'd stay up all night?"

Ugh, I hate when my words come back to bite me in the ass.

"Who said that?" I look from one side of the room to the other. "I don't know who said that. You got the wrong girl, buddy."

Marching toward me, he plucks the AirHeads box off the bed, opens it, and grabs a blue one. "I say, you put your candy where your mouth is."

"What does that even mean?" I stare at him with raised brows.

"I have no idea actually. It sounded much better in my head." He chomps off the end of the AirHeads.

"I sure hope so."

He collapses next to me on the bed and stretches out his legs. "What are we watching tonight?"

"I chose last time." I chew on my lower lip. "It's your turn, *but* I have a few rules."

"Rules suck, but throw them at me."

"No unrealistic action movies. Otherwise, prepare to hear me bitch about how it's not physically possible for a forty-year-old with a dad bod to beat up three ninjas and sixteen gun-bearing men and then get away with the millions in cash from jumping building to building in a Corvette."

"Babe," he groans. "Nearly all action movies are unrealistic."

"I guess that means all action movies are vetoed."

He chuckles and points at me with his wrapper. "I see what you did there."

"What?" I shrug innocently.

He shakes his head and lounges next to me. My breathing stalls at us being so close *in a bed* while the touch of his lips still lingers on mine. He allows me to choose the movie, and this go-around, I choose a romantic comedy. We make ourselves comfortable, selecting our movie snacks, and watch the movie.

As I do, thoughts of our kiss return.

Thoughts of how broken his face was when he confessed what he'd been thinking about while sitting on the lake dock, his feet dangling where his father's ashes had been spread. As we stood, as he warmed me up in his arms, there was a spark—a spark that had been heating me from the moment our eyes met —and I saw desire flicker through like a flame.

There was a connection unlike anything I'd shared with someone before.

Not much time passes before my eyes are heavy and I'm fighting to keep them open. We haven't even hit midway through the movie before I cave in to sleep.

I talk a lot of shit for a girl who can't stay awake for an entire movie.

I WAKE up in an unfamiliar bed with a familiar scent.

A scent I wish I could bottle up and keep forever.

Moaning as my body slides along the expensive, chilly sheets, I rise to find the room Lincoln-free.

No Lincoln, but plenty of memories of our kiss last night. My spine tingles at the recollection. I cast a glance at the pullout bed, wondering if he slept there or in bed with me. We could've slept together. Granted, there was no intimacy happening, but it was *kind of* a date, right?

Lincoln could have pulled a move on me last night. He could've kept kissing me, laid me down on the dock, and I would've been down for whatever he wanted. He could've brought me into his bedroom and put the moves on me. I would've gone down on him, ridden his cock, done anything he wanted. Coming from a sorority girl whose men consisted of frat guys, it's what I'd expect from a sleepover with a guy.

But Lincoln isn't just any guy.

He isn't a stupid kid or a guy who only wants one thing from me.

He's so much more.

And I'm terrified he'll never want those things ... because I do.

And it's not just sex I want from him. I want his friendship ... his heart ... so that way, I can give him mine in return. I can trust Lincoln with my heart, just as he can trust me with his.

I slide out of bed, brush my teeth, wash my face, and am bunching my hair into a ponytail as I walk downstairs to where I hear commotion. Everyone is in the kitchen, the smell of bacon wafting in the air, and Silas is at the stove with multiple pans in front of him.

My stomach growls, pleading to balance the sugar I binged last night with a supplemental meal.

"Morning, sunshine!" Lincoln greets, and a trail of hellos and mornings follows from the group. "How'd you sleep?"

His smile is bright as he stands in the kitchen, his fingers wrapped around a coffee mug, wearing the same sweats he wore last night. Gray sweats are where it's at, ladies. Don't think I wasn't looking in that waist area for a sneak peek of what Lincoln has to offer.

"Good," I reply around a yawn.

"My bed is pretty damn comfortable, eh?" He winks.

I roll my eyes. "Joke's on you though because I'll be demanding to sleep there every time I'm here."

"You two will be dating soon," Lola states with a tone of certainty. "I doubt there will be an issue with you being in his bed."

Lincoln swiftly looks away at her statement and stops our playful conversation.

If only I could read what's dancing through his mind.

We eat breakfast—this is the moment I realize Silas is amazing in the kitchen—and drink the mimosas Georgia whipped up.

After hanging out for a few hours, the lake house starts clearing out. Those few hours, I got a different Lincoln from last night, from the one who had greeted me this morning. Lola's comment had changed his attitude toward me, and even though he sat at my side as we ate, he didn't mention the kiss. Nor does he as we say good-bye.

And so, I wait for the perfect time to bring it up … along with other questions.

CHAPTER ELEVEN

Lincoln

"YOU TWO ARE ADORABLE," Grace singsongs, answering the door in an *Alice in Wonderland* costume.

It's two nights after Halloween, and she's throwing a costume party with Georgia. Since Halloween is one of the busiest nights at Twisted Fox, we all had to work, so we're celebrating now. What I'm learning from Archer and his friends is, they like to celebrate shit and party. They're different *parties* than what I'm used to.

They have kid-friendly pool parties at Maliki's, Cohen's best friend.

Birthday dinners for each of them.

Barbecues at Cohen's.

They're tight-knit, *who's bringing what food* parties.

"Look at you two, all matchy-matchy," Georgia shouts, coming into view with a mixed drink in her hand. "I am obsessed with it."

Georgia has to be the most supportive person I've ever met, everyone's biggest cheerleader. I've never known a friendlier soul. A sarcastic-as-fuck but kind soul.

Had I not overheard her and Archer bickering earlier, her Bride of Chucky costume would've been a surprise. I nearly spat out my water when Archer appeared in the living room in his Chucky costume—complete with the spiky orange wig, striped shirt, and overalls that were a good three inches above his ankles. He put his foot down when it came to makeup, only allowing Georgia to make one face scar.

"It had to have been planned," Grace says. "It's adorable."

"We didn't plan it," I argue.

"Um, we *so* planned it," Cassidy corrects, bumping her hip into mine. "In fact, Georgia, it was all your future brother-in-law's idea."

Georgia's face lights up at Cassidy's comment. Archer hasn't popped the question yet, but everyone knows it's coming. The other day, when I caught a ride with him, a jeweler's card was in the cupholder. No doubt, he'll have something custom-made and hit it out of the ballpark. He loves spoiling Georgia.

"Batman and Robin! Hell yes!" Finn calls out. "Or should I say, Batwoman and Robin?" He stomps our way in his Mad Hatter costume—one that matches Grace's Alice costume.

The couple of costumes are a trend, I see.

One Cassidy and I also followed with our Batwoman and Robin getups. Last night, Cassidy instructed me to pick her up for the party and informed me she had my costume. I scoffed and stated I wasn't wearing a costume, let alone allowing her to dress me up as some Ken doll.

When I arrived at her house tonight, she greeted me, wearing a black faux leather dress that landed inches above her knees and showcased her tanned legs. My mouth nearly dropped to the floor, and my dick hardened as I took in her thigh-high black boots that brought her closer to my height.

While I urged my dick to calm itself at the view of her, she shoved the Robin costume into my chest and directed me to the bathroom. Compared to her, I don't look nearly as hot in my costume … in my goddamn tights.

Yep. She dressed me in fucking tights.

A green-and-red jumpsuit, complete with a foam utility belt

and cape. The polyester is scratchy, and my nuts screamed at me when I shoved them into the jumpsuit. To top it off, my black mask won't stop falling off the side of my face.

I look like a damn joke.

But Cassidy told me to do it, so I did.

Call it friendship-whipped.

"Hey!" Noah, Cohen's son, shouts when we walk into the living room. He's on the couch with a caramel apple on a plate sitting on his lap.

Next to him is a very pregnant, looking close to bursting, Jamie, dressed as Jessie the Yodeling Cowgirl—I know who this is because my cellie's daughter was obsessed with *Toy Story*—and Cohen, dressed as Woody.

"I was Batman last year. This year, I'm Buzz Lightyear!" With carefulness, Noah settles his plate on the coffee table and jumps off the couch to show off his Buzz space suit—lifting one foot, then the other, and then spinning around fashion show–style.

Cassidy laughs and drops to one knee, so she's at his level. "That's awesome! I bet your Batman costume was way cooler than mine."

Noah's face lights up as he eats up her attention.

Tugging on my mask, I stare at them, devouring the scene. She's talking to Noah, giving him her full attention, and my breathing catches in my throat. Never have I been turned on by seeing a woman with a child, but watching Cassidy and the way she throws her head back laughing while talking to him is hot.

"What's up, big man?" Silas asks, slapping me on the back—knocking me out of my Cassidy trance.

I burst into laughter as I turn to him. "Dude, what the hell are you wearing?"

And I thought my costume was bad.

"What?" Silas grunts, his lips parting into a grin. "Don't be jealous of my ensemble." He performs a move similar to what Noah did.

"I'm far from jealous." I shake my head, feeling embarrassed for him.

"Lola," Silas shouts, wrapping his hands around his mouth. "Lincoln is talking crap about my costume!"

Silas's leaf-covered romper makes sense when I see Lola wearing a matching dress. At least Cassidy didn't decide for us to be Adam and Eve. A jumpsuit was pushing it. My ass will never be in a romper. I don't care how much Cassidy begs me.

Lola smooths her hands down her long black hair before playfully flipping me off. "Don't be jealous that Silas can show off his legs."

I snort. "Silas can definitely be the romper-wearer of our group."

"I'm going to miss this," Grace whines, peering over at Georgia and plopping down cross-legged on the floor. "Miss us hanging out here, drinking wine, gossiping, and watching reruns of *Schitt's Creek*."

Georgia, who's sitting on Archer's lap in a chair, peers at Grace with sad eyes. "You can come over anytime you want for wine time *or* just move in with us."

"Whoa," Archer grunts behind her. "Where's she going to sleep? The couch?"

"No, we'll add a bedroom to the penthouse," Georgia replies.

"Yeah, that'll be easy to do on the top floor of a building," I comment.

Grace's shoulders droop. "It's fine. I'll just move in with my parents or something."

"Why?" Cassidy asks, shooting a glance to Jamie. "Did you sell the place?"

Jamie rented out the townhouse to the girls after moving in with Cohen.

"Nope," Jamie answers. "It's all *love's* fault."

Cassidy's head tilts to the side in question.

"Here soon, Georgia is going to move in with Archer," Grace

explains before narrowing her eyes at Lola. "And *my other* best friend won't fill in the roomie role."

"Uh, I can't just break my lease." Lola stares at her with apology. "If I had an open room, I'd so give it to you."

"I told you, I won't move out until we find you another roommate," Georgia says.

"I can move in," Cassidy says. Her cheeks redden as all attention turns to her. "I mean, if that's okay with you? I live alone but am down for having a roommate."

Grace's face lights up. "Really?"

Cassidy nods repeatedly. "Really."

Grace squeals before jumping to her feet and hugging Cassidy. "Yay! Georgia moves out next week, and then the room is all yours. Tell me what you can afford rent-wise, and we'll work something out."

"Shit, Grace would let you move in for free," Finn inputs.

"See! There you go!" Georgia throws out her arms. "Everything worked out, and you don't have to move back in with your parents."

"This calls for a toast," Finn announces. "Everyone, to the kitchen!"

Cohen stands, holding his hand out to Jamie, and pulls her up while she groans. Cassidy loops her arm around mine, and we follow everyone to the kitchen. Finn and Lola start passing out drinks.

"All right," Finn calls out, "grab your beers, your wine"—he stops to glance at Noah and Jamie—"your Capri Sun and seltzer water and hold them in the air."

Noah's grin takes over his entire face at being included and raises his arm as high as he can.

Finn lifts his beer. "To friendships, to roommates, to Halloween. May we always celebrate our holidays together— even if it's days later—and always have each other's backs."

"Hell yeah," Silas says.

At the same time, everyone else shouts, "Cheers!"

"Georgia is moving in, huh?" Cassidy asks as everyone starts conversing. "Looks like you'll be third-wheeling all the time."

I shrug. "I don't mind. Archer is happier when Georgia is around. A plus for me. Georgia also doesn't mind making coffee runs. Another plus."

Georgia brings life into my brother, is a blast, and even helps when I'm feeling down. I'm happy my brother has found a great partner.

"Just wait until we start dating and I move in with you." Cassidy winks, gently elbowing me. "We can go on all the coffee runs together."

I chuckle. After the kiss, our jokes hit differently. I can see it in her face when I make an innuendo, and I'm sure she sees it in mine. There's now an underlying realization that it's not just *joking*. It's more.

"If you agree to coffee runs, tell Grace she's losing her roommate now, and you can sleep on the couch."

She rolls her eyes. "Your bed or no new roommate."

"Charades time!" Grace yells. "Let's get teams together."

Grabbing our drinks, we return to the living room, where we play charades until everyone is yawning. A few years ago, I'd have called something like this lame—it's something I'd have laughed at—but not anymore. I actually enjoy this shit.

In the past, my idea of good times with friends was expensive clubs, traveling abroad, or snorting lines.

"You need a ride home?" I ask Cassidy as the townhome starts clearing out.

"Obviously." She smacks my arm. "You picked me up. You're responsible for getting me home."

"Like your babysitter."

"I was thinking more along the lines of *like your date*."

Her words smack into me like a train. If you looked up the definition of *date* in the dictionary, it'd be what I've done tonight —drove to her house, picked her up, and attended a party together. Sure, during the drive, I told myself I was picking up a friend, but it's growing harder and harder to keep up with that lie.

Neither of us has mentioned our three-second kiss at Archer's party—shocking, considering Cassidy loves talking about everything, especially conversations I'd kill to avoid. You don't kiss people unless you're attracted to them or have feelings for them. If she asks me why I kissed her, I'd have to admit to both of those reasons.

I say my good-byes while Cassidy gives out hugs and tells Jamie that she can't wait to meet her little girl.

By the time we're walking to my car, our masks are off, and her cape is balled up in her hands. As soon as she slides into the passenger seat, she starts a series of yawns.

"Ugh," she moans around another yawn. "I could sleep for nine straight days and still be exhausted."

I crank up the heat and our seat warmers. "You been partying too hard?"

She works all the time, but she could be fitting in clubs and parties in her spare time. If she does, she never talks about it.

She shakes her head, rubbing at her eyes. "Just haven't been sleeping well."

"Why not?"

"Maybe it's the apartment … living alone …" She tips her head down and studies her red nails. "At first, it was nice. Now, it's just … weird sometimes."

She's not telling me everything. I know when Cassidy is holding back.

"Why? Your neighbor giving you a bad vibe?"

"No, not at all," she rushes out. "All my life, I've been surrounded by people, and now, I'm not. It's different, is all." Perking up in her seat, she releases a ragged breath. "We made a pretty good Batwoman and Robin tonight, huh?"

I chuckle. "Gotta say, with the exception of Buzz Lightyear, we had the best costumes tonight."

"Team Batwoman and Robin for the win." She holds out her

fist, and I bump mine against it before she pulls the seat belt across her body. "Now, this superhero needs her beauty sleep."

"Aye aye, boss."

I shift the car into drive, and it's a short ride to her duplex. Without a word, I unbuckle my seat belt, step out of the car, and open Cassidy's door—all date-style even though this isn't a date, right? My hand finds the base of her back when she steps out, and as we stroll side by side to her unit.

During the drive home, worry followed me with every mile over her comment about not sleeping well. I could be reading too much into it, but there has to be a reason. At times, I've slept terribly, but it's always been because of underlying issues. I'm almost tempted to invite her to my place and give her my bed while I take the couch.

My hand doesn't leave her back until we walk into her apartment, and she starts flipping on the lights. Her apartment is small and doesn't display much of her character. A deep red sectional rests against the living room wall with furry white pillows scattered along it. There's miscellaneous pink and feminine wall art. Across the room is the kitchen and an area where a pub table sits.

Cassidy shoves away a few pillows, collapses onto the couch, and eyeballs me, her gaze sharp and searching. "All right, Callahan, are we ever going to talk about our kiss, or shall we act like it never happened?" Her tone is clear—no bullshit, no beating around the bush.

My chest seizes with pain, and I force a laugh while attempting to calm my mind. "I was hoping we'd act like it never happened."

She sucks in a breath, disappointment clouding her features. "That sure makes a girl feel good."

I tug at the neck of my costume, wishing I could kick my own ass for kissing her. Not that there was no attraction or that I didn't want to do more. No, I wanted to drag her to my bedroom and do more than watch TV and eat snacks. I wanted *her* to be my snack, wanted the movie to be the background noise while I fucked her in every position possible, and then I wanted to feed her breakfast in bed the next morning.

Unfortunately, my dumbass has only managed to complicate our friendship.

"My answer has nothing to do with you and everything to do with me," I grind out, more disgusted with myself with each word of bullshit I deliver. With the time I've had, you'd think I'd have come up with a better reason for shutting us down.

She cringes as if she'd been slapped in the face. "That's a pretty crappy reason, by the way. I'll take *bullshit* for three hundred dollars."

I throw up my arms before allowing them to fall to my sides. "Cass, right now, you're pretty much my best friend." I swallow hard at my confession, at me putting all my honesty out there. "I don't want to fuck that up because we kissed. I don't ... I don't want to *lose you*." My voice breaks with the last two words the same way my soul would if our friendship turned sour.

Even before my life changed, I never had fun with someone like I do with her. I never bantered, had witty conversations, found someone I could vocally spar with like I have with her. I never thought about someone so damn much. And I don't want to lose her.

She blinks at me. "Why would that mess things up?"

"Kissing leads to feelings." I rest my back against the door and pinch the bridge of my nose. "Feelings lead to problems, fallouts, *hate*."

Every relationship—scratch that—every hookup I've had has ended in messiness.

She's quiet for a moment, as if digesting my words. "Kissing can also lead to better." She raises a brow and licks that plump bottom lip of hers. "*Hotter* things."

Fuck.

I need to abort mission before this friendship of ours takes a leap into something not platonic ... into something we both crave but shouldn't. Continuing this conversation can only result in two outcomes: us kissing again—most likely *hotter*, as she said —or me pushing her away, resulting in her hating me. The weight of guilt presses against my chest, making it difficult for me to breathe as I mentally rifle through my options.

Fixing my gaze on the woman I'm falling for, I take long strides across the room and stop abruptly in front of her. My neck strains as I stare down at her. Her gaze meets mine, her eyelids fluttering.

I clear my throat, wanting to be as straightforward as possible. "Those *hotter things* come with risks."

She nods. "I'm aware."

"They can ruin us."

"They won't."

"They will ruin you with any other man."

"I won't ever need another man when I have you."

Her response is my undoing.

Her confession deviates my train of thought, turning them from alarmed to desire. We hardly drank at the party tonight, so we can't blame this on liquor tomorrow. This won't be a night of fun we can pretend to forget in the morning. What happens in the next five minutes will solidify our relationship.

I gulp before asking, "When you talk about us getting married, about us being together, you're joking, right?"

At first, it was fun and games for me.

Flirting here and there.

But somewhere along the way, it shifted into more than that.

She chews on her bottom lip. "Yes and no."

Not the response I was searching for.

My voice turns weak yet rugged simultaneously. "That's not a clear answer."

Before I make any move, we need to be on the same page. I need to know where her head is. Maybe she's looking for casual. I'm unsure if that'd be a relief or torment for me. If she says she's joking, it would kill the thoughts in my head about her that shouldn't be taking residence.

"I mean …" She hums softly, as if searching for the appropriate words. "Yes, I joke about it—have since day one at Twisted Fox. In the beginning, it was innocent flirting, but the more time we spend together, the harder my heart races, and the more I like you, Lincoln." She sighs, averting her gaze to the other side of the room and away from me. "Like really, really like you."

Tension and lust carry through the air.

Heat spreads through my chest. I look at the ground before letting my gaze return to her face.

To the flushed face that's done nothing but consume my mind.

"Tell me you feel it too, Linc," she whispers.

My head spins. "I do."

"Then do something about it."

She stands, as if in mutual understanding that this is happening. I catch her chin between my thumb and forefinger, caressing it as our gazes meet. Hers eager. Mine gentle.

"I've wanted this for so long," I say.

She squeezes her eyes shut. "Me too."

That's when I claim her lips.

My claim is demanding and impulsive—a drink we've slowly sipped that we're ready to fully consume. Her tongue darts into my mouth, colliding with mine, and we devour each other. Our lips meshed as one.

I'm catching up on breaths as she breaks away. "My bedroom. Right now."

Yeah, I have no argument against that.

Interlacing our hands, she leads me down the short hallway, through a doorway, and flicks on the light. Before I'm given the chance to look around, her lips are back on mine.

While keeping our connection, I guide her to the bed before

slowly pulling away, already missing the feel of her lips on mine. "I want to see you. *All* of you."

I retreat a step as she stands before me, intense emotion filling my lungs, and she slips me a sinful smirk before gesturing to her outfit.

"Unzip me."

That's when I realize we're still in our costumes. I was so consumed by her that I forgot I was trying to seduce a woman while wearing a damn Robin outfit.

Yeah, this shit definitely needs to come off before it becomes a mood killer.

As bad as I'm aching to unzip her dress and touch every inch of her, I need this damn thing off first. The room is quiet with the exception of our breathing—heavy and layered with need— and she watches in interest as I hastily kick off my shoes and undress. Flinging the costume across the room, I stand in front of her, wearing only boxer briefs. There's no missing my rock-hard cock, standing at attention, confirming that all it wants is her.

Since we started developing a connection, Cassidy has been the only woman on my mind as I jerked off, stroking myself as I imagined it was her hand instead of mine.

I haven't touched another woman.

Kissed another woman.

Thought about another damn woman.

Cassidy has overtaken me.

And I wouldn't want it any other way.

Her lips are swollen from our earlier kiss, and she swipes her tongue along the bottom one as her eyes level on my erection.

That's for you.

All for you.

"My turn," she croaks. "But I need a little help." Turning around, she slides her hair off her shoulder and stares over it at me.

I gladly accept the invitation, advancing toward her, and I

stop so close that my cock brushes along her leg, causing her to shiver. I shove the zipper down, listening to the loud *zip*, and the dress pools at her feet, giving me the best damn view ever. Cassidy wearing only a black lace thong and matching bra. Her ass cheeks perky.

She gasps when I deliver a quick smack to each globe before cupping both, loving how they fill my hands to perfection.

"Your ass is amazing," I whisper into her ear, slowly licking along the lobe.

Pressing my lips to her shoulder, I inch her bra strap down. A light hiss releases through her lips when I suck hard on her skin. It'll most likely leave a hickey, and my dick stirs at the thought of marking her. Of making her mine.

"Climb on the bed," I say, releasing her and taking a step back.

She nods and doesn't glance back as she does, that plump ass sticking in the air. She slowly arches her back, causing her ass to jiggle, and swear to God, I'm about to come all over her white rug. Unable to stop myself, I wrap my hand around my cock and slowly stroke it as she flips onto her back and rises. Pushing her elbows out, she leans back on them to stare at me, raising a brow in question.

I take in the sight of her, my gaze traveling up and down her body, soaking up her smooth skin, her curves, and the way her breasts bounce with every sharp breath she inhales.

No more.

There's no more holding back.

Desire permeates through me like a drug.

"I could watch you do that all night," she says, drawing my attention back to her face.

I smirk. "Or we could do better things." Dropping my hand from my cock, I join her on the bed, slightly crawling over top of her, putting all my weight on my forearms to hold myself up.

I tilt my head down, and she offers a gentle smile before reaching around, gripping the back of my neck, and dragging my mouth to meet hers. This kiss is slower than the others as we soak up what the other enjoys, as our tongues tangle in a web of our attraction to one another.

She gasps when I pull away and then shudders as I rain kisses down her chest, along the cup of her bra, before directing her to rise so I can unsnap the band. As she stretches out her arms, I gently slide off the fabric, revealing more of her beauty.

To reveal the body of a woman I'm falling into a deep pit of lust with.

To reveal every inch of the woman I want to keep forever.

My mouth waters as I lick a circle around her nipple before sucking hard, feeling it harden between my lips.

Raising my arm, I push my weight onto the other while sliding down her body. She rubs her toned legs together in anticipation while I toy with the slim string of her panties with my pointer finger. Without warning, I jerk them down her legs, causing her to lift them, before I fling the thin material across the room.

I press my erection against her thigh as I slip a finger through her soaked folds.

Up and down.

Up and down.

Torturously, as she writhes underneath my touch, waiting for me to push my finger inside, to relieve her, to play with her pussy until she's crying out my name.

"Please," she breathes out. "Give me more."

Her pleas.

Jesus.

She could ask me to do anything in that voice of hers, and I'd do it in a heartbeat. Using my elbow, I lever it between her thigh to open her wider before shoving three thick fingers inside her. She's tight, her warmth wrapping around my fingers like a harness, and I swiftly pull out, not wanting to hurt her.

With how tight she is, I'm not sure she can handle my cock, but I want to take things slow. I want to play with her longer, for days, which means I don't want her to be too sore for me. This time, I slip two fingers into her, the pad of my thumb traveling to her clit, slowly moving it in circles.

"Oh, wow," she moans, rotating her hips, swiveling them to meet my strokes.

I've spent hours sitting around and wishing for this moment, longing to have Cassidy moaning as I touched her begging pussy, and it's better than what I imagined.

Wetter.

Hotter.

Louder.

Needing more, I plant a kiss on her belly button, shifting so I'm kneeling between her legs, open her folds and lower my head.

Only to have her grab my hair, nearly ripping it from my scalp, and stop me.

Having my hair gripped? Normal.

But it's usually as the girl is about to get off on my tongue.

Not before. Never before.

"Whoa," she rushes out.

I lift my face, resting my chin above her clit while pushing my palms up the inside of her thighs, and stare up at her in question.

"I don't …" She hesitates, her cheeks turning pink. "I don't do that."

"Do what?"

She gestures to where I am. "Faces down there."

There's no containing my snort to her explanation. "You've never been eaten out before?"

"I tried it once for maybe two seconds but stopped …" She shakes her head. "It's weird. I feel too … on display."

"That's the point. You put your pretty pussy on display for me, and I fucking worship it."

A wave of satisfaction charges through me that no other man has gotten her off with his face between her thighs.

Her face is unreadable as she stares down and studies me. As badly as I want to taste her, if she doesn't want it, I'll pull back and go another route to please her. No matter what, Cassidy needs to feel comfortable with me.

Her pleasure is what I'm thriving for.

I couldn't give two fucks about mine—even though eating her out would make my damn year.

I squeeze her thighs. "Do you trust me?"

She nods. "I trust you."

"If you don't like it, tell me to stop."

"I guess I have to try everything once."

"That's my girl."

I slide my body down, lower my head, and suck on her clit.

I'll prove to her there's nothing she'll enjoy more than my tongue in her pussy.

Well, other than when I fill her with my cock.

CHAPTER TWELVE

Cassidy

MY BACK BUCKS off the bed when Lincoln's lips suction around my clit.

Jesus Christ.

My heart thunders in my chest, a jolt of electricity passing through like a storm, as I peek down at the man having a snack between my legs. I'm consumed with not only my need for him but also slight premature embarrassment.

I stress about my OB/GYN—*who's a woman*—inspecting my lady parts.

How am I supposed to be chill when it's the man I've wanted for months down there, seeing me so up close and personal?

Are vaginas even pretty?

I've never been one of those women who sits in front of a mirror and examines her kitty. It's always been a strange concept to me. It's not like I'm a virgin and I've never been touched there. It's just typically sex that unfolds in the same trail of events—making out, five seconds of finger foreplay, and then sex. Never have I been with a man wanting as much foreplay as Lincoln.

Also, never have I wanted foreplay as much as I want with Lincoln.

My muscles are quivering, my body tingling with need for this man. At this point, I'll allow him to do anything, stick his face anywhere, to get relief from the pleasure streaming through me, begging to be released.

Those other guys?

They never kissed me like that.

Never touched me like this.

Never made my body burn hot.

Never made me want to push away all my boundaries.

My ribs tighten as I spread my thighs more, providing plenty of room for him to have his way with me.

Chills cover my naked body when his mouth leaves my clit, and his skilled tongue slides through my folds, sending a rush of shivers through my body. I inhale a deep breath, unsure what to expect. This is the moment when I made the last guy stop.

It felt too personal.

Too intimate.

Which is funny because I was getting intimate with the guy.

As I brace myself, Lincoln shoves the tip of his tongue inside me. My back shoots off the bed as a desire I've never experienced courses through my blood.

Lincoln licks.

He sucks.

I'm on fire.

This is what the hell I've been missing?

How was I so stupid not to want this?

I arch my back and release a moan.

Who am I kidding?

No way would it have felt like *this* with any other man.

Bursts of pleasure ride through me as I gasp. "This feels amazing."

He doesn't lift his head, but he does raise his voice as he says, "Do you like that?" against my core.

The room grows hot when he shoves a thick finger inside me and then another in addition to his tongue.

My breaths knock from my lungs in harsh pants, nearly fracturing my ribs, as I try not to come yet. As badly as I want to drag this out for as long as possible, I'm dying for a release. Delving my hand into his thick hair, I grip it tight. Not to stop him this time, but to hold his mouth there as I ride his face.

My hips buck against his mouth as he gives me everything I need and more.

When he plays with my clit, a wave of pleasure rockets through me.

It's over.

I'm coming on his mouth with no regrets of allowing this to happen.

As I whisper his name, I already know I want this to happen again.

And again and again.

I'm catching my breath when he pulls away, his lips and chin wet from my juices. He uses his tongue to scoop up the excess on his bottom lip. His grin is cocky, and his face is patterned with the same lust that's overtaking me.

I throw my arm across the bed and point at my nightstand. "Condom in there. Get inside of me before I die, please and thank you." I can't wait for him to fill me to my core and thrust inside me.

He shakes his head. "We're not having sex yet."

I wince. "What?"

"We're not having sex yet."

With the exception of his panting and his erection brushing against my leg, you'd think he wasn't fazed by my nakedness or what we did.

"I heard you loud and clear." My tone grows aggravated because, dammit, I want that large cock inside me. "*Why?* I'm not a virgin, nor will I get crazy emotionally attached, if that's what you're worried about." Okay, the second statement is somewhat of a lie. I'm already pretty emotionally attached to this man.

"Not what I'm worried about at all." He rests his palms on the sides of my face, and his chest rubs against mine as he pulls himself forward, up my body. "I'm more worried about myself getting emotionally attached." He says the last statement so softly underneath his breath that I'm questioning if those words left his mouth.

Stroking my cheek, he peers down at me with an expression I've never seen from him before—an expression I've never witnessed from anyone—a mixture of arousal, concentration, yet also contentment. A smirk is on his face as he dips his head down and places a quick kiss on my lips, where I briefly taste myself.

He just pleasured me in endless ways, hasn't received any for himself, but appears content. Lincoln looks as if he's on top of the world after eating me out, not even concerned about me returning the favor.

I rise up onto my elbows, our faces only inches apart. "Come on. You seriously just gave me an incredible orgasm. It's not fair for the favor not to be returned."

His lips brush against my nose before he pulls back. "First, my mouth on your pussy wasn't only a favor to you. Babe, it was a favor *to me*. You know how many times I've watched you, wondering how sweet your pussy tastes? How many times I've watched you lick the rim of your glass, wishing I could do the same to your clit?" He shakes his head. "Jesus, fuck, Cassidy. You handed me everything that's been on my mind for months." He smirks. "And I love that I proved it wasn't weird. I love that you trusted me enough to give me the honor."

"So give me the honor of getting you off," I argue with a pout.

He moans when I reach for his cock and run the tips of my fingers along the massive length. I eye it, my mouth watering, and wonder how well it'd fit inside me. It's the largest I've ever seen, and that's coming from a girl who watches porn on the regular to get herself off.

He draws back, away from my reach, causing me to frown. "How about you lie there, looking hot as fuck and all orgasmed out by yours truly?" He wraps his hand around his cock and starts jerking himself off. "That's all I need from you."

I groan, throwing my head back like a toddler close to a tantrum. "How's that fun? I let you go down on me, so it's only fair I get to do the same."

"Small steps, baby." His breathing turns ragged as his gaze moves down my body in appreciation.

"Small steps is licking and sucking on my vagina?"

"Damn straight."

He loses himself in his strokes, his pace growing, and I'm invigorated at the view of him jacking off in front of me. He inches closer, and I wait for my perfect opportunity. He grunts when I reach out and wrap my hand around his, joining him in pleasuring himself. He throws his head back, savoring the moment, and I take that weakness as an advantage for me.

Dropping my hand, I grip both his shoulders and push him onto my bed, back down. I climb over him in seconds, slide my hair over my shoulder, and say, "Trust me," before sucking the head of his cock.

"Jesus, fuck," Lincoln hisses, rotating his hips.

I work him with my mouth and fingers, tasting the saltiness of his cock as pre-cum leaks from the tip. His fingers find their way to my hair, and he runs them through the strands.

"Shit, I'm close," he hisses.

I peer up at him to find his eyes shut at the same time I swallow his cum.

"Fuck," he groans, coming down from his orgasm high. "That was … holy shit."

Licking up and down his erection, I clean him up, worshipping his cock. "I'm glad you enjoyed it."

ORAL SEX WITH LINCOLN ...

There's nothing like it.

Nothing hotter.

I can't even imagine how actual sex will be with him.

We're in my bathroom, naked and cleaning ourselves up—along with taking off the Halloween makeup. When I saw myself in the mirror, I was horrified. Runny mascara, smeared lipstick, and patches of glitter described my face.

A silence hangs in the air, but it's comfortable. I'm riding off the high of being with Lincoln, and exhaustion is starting to sink in from my orgasm and giving my all while sucking Lincoln's cock. My goal was to get him off faster than any other woman who'd had her mouth on his dick.

Walking back into the bedroom, I open my dresser to snag my pajamas as Lincoln stands in the doorway, still naked. He retrieves his boxers from the floor and pulls them up his legs.

There's a question riding on the tip of my tongue that I'm nervous to ask. I say it while pulling the shirt over my head, so he can't see the hesitation on my face. "Are you staying over?" I sound somewhat muffled when the cotton rubs against my lips.

"Cass, I just had my mouth between your legs," he replies with a hint of amusement in his voice. "You think I'm going to walk out of here ten minutes later? Abso-fucking-lutely not."

My body relaxes as I yank the shorts up my legs and tighten the string around my waist. Not only is it amazing that he's staying but I also know I'll sleep better with him at my side. There will be no Quinton fears when I'm in Lincoln's arms.

When Lincoln slides into bed with me, it's comfortable. Without hesitation, he wraps his strong arm around me and drags me into him, my back pressing against his chest.

Lying in his arms, I've never felt safer. At the point when I thought I was done with relationships, done with men, when my trust was the lowest it'd ever been, he stepped into my life and changed that.

For the first time in what seems like forever, I fall to sleep without fear.

Without wondering if someone will be sneaking in my house.

I fall asleep in the arms of a man I know is perfect for me.

And a man I'm afraid of losing.

CHAPTER THIRTEEN

Lincoln

MY FIRST MORNING waking up with Cassidy.

We're lying in her bed, side by side, having our own form of pillow talk. It's been endless conversation since we woke up, our limbs tangled together like lost ropes and the heat of the other's body a comfort. I fell asleep with Cassidy in my arms and woke up the same way—fucking heaven. As she slept, I stared down at her, not muttering a sound, and admired the woman who'd been stealing my heart little by little, day by day.

If someone had told me before the party that this was where I'd end up this morning, I would've told them to shut the fuck up. No way did I think I'd finish the night with my tongue between Cassidy's legs, tasting her sweet pussy, and then wrapping her in my arms.

What led us here?

Hours upon hours of conversation.

Random phone calls and movie nights.

A bond stronger than a diamond, shaped from friendship to intimacy.

Sense of humors blended together like an expensive painting.

Never has a woman understood, gotten me, or matched my personality better.

I inhale a series of deep breaths as Cassidy curls up closer, her chest nearly pressing into mine, and I drape my arm over her waist.

She sighs, resting her chin on my forearm to stare at me. "Remember when I asked what your favorite breakfast was all the time?"

I chuckle at the memory. "Oh, I remember."

I always laughed and blew off the question, claiming she was crazy. Her interest wasn't only on breakfast either. Over the course of us knowing each other, we revealed our front-runners of everything—breakfast, lunch, TV shows, movies, sexual positions.

If Cassidy was curious about something, she asked.

The same went for me.

She smirks before dropping a kiss to my arm. "I have maple, strawberry, apple butter, and raspberry."

I raise a brow in question.

"Pancakes are your favorite breakfast, *but* you never revealed your favorite syrup, so I bought a variety pack for when this morning came."

My gaze lingers on her, as I'm mesmerized that she took the time to do such a thing. "All this time, I assumed you were fucking with me."

"In the beginning, it was more of a flirt-buddy situation. I had recently been screwed over, so I wasn't looking for a relationship. Guys were the last thing I was worried about ... what I planned not to be worried about until you bulldozed your way into my life."

"Until I did? Babe, we know you came barreling into Twisted Fox, ready to set my world on fire." I squeeze her waist. "And who screwed you over?"

My mind wanders back to the day she asked if I'd ever loved someone I shouldn't. A gloominess shadowed her that week, an anguish when she walked into work, and whenever I asked if everything was okay, she blew me off.

Her face falls, a twinge of sorrow tilting into her mood, and her lips press together in a tight grimace. "Just a guy I dated."

"What did he do to screw you over?"

If this were anyone else, if past relationship problems were introduced, I'd throw my clothes on and duck out. The thing is, this isn't anyone else. It's Cassidy, and we talk about everything. The difference between her and anyone else is that I want to know every detail of her life.

Our conversations have been endless, but they've never deviated out of small talk. We've never ventured into our pasts, old relationships, or why we were both in trouble with the law. Hell, she doesn't even know I've been in trouble with the law. But after last night, we need to drag our demons to the light and fight them together.

She bends her knees and then straightens them before releasing a harsh sigh. "He was a lying jerk who really messed with my head … with everything I thought was real." She shuts her eyes, a pained expression crossing her features. "Before him, I was softer. I trusted people, and I was happier. I saw life differently. The old me, she was friends with everyone and never questioned allowing anyone in. Now, I have major trust problems." She levels her gaze on me. "Prewarning."

I gulp, a heaviness pinning my body to the bed. "Looks like I'd better prove myself then."

Drawing her arm out from underneath the blanket, she reaches up and traces the line of my jaw with her finger, running it along my facial hair. "Just never lie to me, okay?" Her tone softens. "And if I ever confide in you, then that needs to stay between us."

"You can always trust me." I curl my fingers around her wrist and pull her hand to my lips, kissing it. "I'll never betray you."

"I was arrested." That soft tone diverts into coolness with her confession.

It's not much of a confession to me—no new insight into Cassidy. Since she was serving community service, I figured she'd been in trouble. Most likely nothing too serious, given she was sentenced to pick up trash on the side of the street and not time served.

I stay quiet while waiting to see if she'll provide more.

I won't push.

Won't throw out question after question.

This is her truth to tell me on her time and in her own way.

Her gaze darts from one side of the room to the other, and when she speaks, my breathing grows a little easier.

She trusts me.

She wouldn't be opening up like this if she didn't.

"I dated a guy in college and let him borrow my car while his was in the shop. What I didn't know was he sold drugs as a hobby and was using my car to do said drug dealing in. We got pulled over, he said the drugs in the car weren't his, and I had to take the fall for it." She holds up her hand. "They weren't, FYI. I experimented with some uppers in my sorority house, yes, but they were never my thing. I like to be in control too much. Anyway, he walked free. I was arrested and charged with a misdemeanor."

I grind my teeth, hoping she doesn't feel my body tensing. "The guy, where is he now? That fucking bastard shouldn't get away with what he did."

She bites into her lip. "I'm not sure. I just want to move on from him. It happened, I did my time, and now, I'm only looking forward."

"If you ever want to speak out, to turn him in, I'll be by your side, you hear me?"

"Thank you." She shivers in my arms. "And please don't say anything to your brother, Cohen, anyone. You're the first person I've shared the full story with. My brother is a cop, and he, along with others, have been up my ass to give them more information."

"You can always trust me to keep your secrets."

As much as I hate that she won't turn the asshole in, I have to respect her decision. She knows what's best for her, more than anyone.

"I know. That's why I'm opening up to you." She shuts her eyes, inhaling a ragged breath before loosening her muscles. Her tone turns playful as she asks, "How about those pancakes, huh? I know I said I'd make your favorite breakfast and all, but don't judge if they're burned. I'm not the best in the kitchen."

"I'll be your right-hand man. We'll make them together."

Sliding out of bed, I hold my hand out. Taking it, I drape her over my shoulder, hearing her laughter as I walk us to the kitchen. Somehow, before the pancake mix even leaves the box, she ends up spread out on the pub table with my mouth between her legs.

Playing with Cassidy will be fun.

The heartbreak that might come after? Not so much.

CHAPTER FOURTEEN

Cassidy

"WHAT ARE you up to after this?" Lincoln asks, coming up behind me and wrapping his strong arms around my waist as I clock out in the employee room. "We can head to your place and have some fun."

I squirm in his hold as he rains kisses along my neck. "We are in our place of employment, young man." Laughing, I pull away from him.

He groans, "I know; I know."

Two days have passed since the Halloween party. The next morning, after pancakes, we agreed to keep quiet about us hooking up. Witnessing everyone, myself included, in Georgia and Archer's love life was a warning to keep private until we're ready to talk about it. I don't want to start my *whatever this is* with Lincoln alongside everyone asking questions and invading our privacy before we even have the opportunity to form a healthy relationship.

Another reason is fear.

What if things don't work out with Lincoln?

What if we try something more serious than being friends and end up hating each other?

What if he isn't as much into me as he said?

Quinton really messed with my head.

I'm scared to put everything out there, only for Lincoln to break things off later and make me look like an idiot.

I shove my wallet into my purse. "Jamie gave birth to baby Fox, so I'm stopping by the hospital to give her the adorable onesie I bought and to meet her. Want to tag along?"

He rubs his chin as if in deep thought. "Sure."

"Don't act too enthused now."

Placing his hands together, he holds them to his heart and mocks my voice. "Oh my God, yes! I want to bring all the baby gifts with you."

I click my tongue against the roof of my mouth and point at him. "That's more like it, Callahan."

"Your car or mine?"

"Mine."

"Your place or mine later?"

"Mine, considering neither your brother nor Georgia can know about us yet."

A flicker of disappointment flashes over his features when he says, "Okay."

Lincoln remote-starts his car to warm it up, and before we get in, I grab the baby gift from my back seat. On our way to the hospital, we make a Starbucks pit stop, where he gives me a quick peck on the lips before handing over my iced caramel mocha.

I gotta give it to the man. He knows how to turn on the romance in and out of the bedroom. Well ... the *foreplay* in the bedroom since we've yet to have sex. Every time I try, he says we're not ready yet.

When we walk into the hospital waiting room, we find Georgia and Archer sitting next to each other. "Hey, guys!" I flick my wrist in a wave.

Georgia smiles, returns the wave, and then whispers into Archer's ear. Archer nods in greeting, nearly all his attention on his girlfriend, while Lincoln and I take the chairs across from them.

With my insecurities creeping in, I wrinkle my nose while fighting back a frown. When someone whispers, I automatically assume it's about me. Blame it on growing up, competing in stupid beauty pageants, and living in a sorority house full of competition and toxicity. You only whisper if you're gossiping about someone.

"I hate when people whisper around me," I tell Lincoln, my throat tightening.

"Get used to it around those two." Lincoln dips his head down, his mouth moving to my ear, and talks softly, so only I can hear him, "Plus, my hearing is impeccable. Georgia is betting him orgasms that something will happen between us."

I lean into him, my insecurities morphing into eagerness. "Really?"

He grins. "Really."

"Looks like Archer will owe her some orgasms."

"Yeah ... when you decide you want to tell them."

Before I can ask how he truly feels about us waiting to share with our coworkers and friends that we're oral buddies, Silas and Lola walk into the waiting room.

Silas gestures from Georgia to Archer. "When you two have a baby, you'd better hope it has your personality, Georgia."

Georgia grabs Archer's chin and playfully moves it from side to side. "Why? You know he has a shining personality."

"Only for you, babe," Archer says, winking at Georgia.

I look over at Lincoln with a smirk and smack his thigh. "I think our baby will have a combination of our personalities."

"Your baby?" Silas asks. "What did I miss?"

Lincoln shakes his head and stretches out his legs.

"Hypothetical baby," I say.

"There will be no babies," Lincoln corrects, still shaking his head while fighting back a smile.

"I mean, first comes marriage," I say before peering over to Georgia. "You'll be such a good sister-in-law, Georgia."

Georgia laughs, and we stop when Cohen walks into the waiting room. I've never seen a happier man.

"You ready to meet my daughter?"

Before standing, I look over at Lincoln and whisper, "In order for us to have babies, you have to have sex with me first."

"We'll have to work on that then, won't we?" He winks.

ISABELLA FOX HAS to be the cutest baby I've ever seen with her peach fuzz and wrinkled forehead.

"Do you want kids?" I ask Lincoln as I run a finger over her soft cheek.

I gulp back the regret of asking him that question.

It's something I've never thought twice about, but after finding out Kyle's girlfriend can't have babies, I've learned to be more sensitive. It's a conversation I now tread lightly on. Sometimes, the answer is more complicated than yes or no. But this is Lincoln, and with Lincoln, I've tried to be as transparent as I can be. Plus, I'm super curious about his answer.

"I do," Lincoln replies, leveling his strong gaze on me. "There was a time when I thought it wasn't an option, but someday—*in the future*—I do. What about you?"

"I do … *in the future*." I sigh and lower my gaze to Isabella. "For a while, I questioned myself. As a little girl, I dreamed about being a mother, but after everything fell apart with my parents, I told myself I'd been fed a lie. Marriage, love, kids, family—it all seemed like something that wouldn't work, you know?"

His eyes don't leave mine. "What made you change your mind?"

"I realized my parents shouldn't be my only influence on my

outlook on love. I witnessed my brothers and sister find love. Kyle with a woman who hated him. Maliki and Sierra, who did nothing but fight for years. And Rex with his best friend. There's hope out there for me." I stare at him, unblinking. "Like I told everyone, I think our baby will have a combination of our personalities. Hopefully, he or she will have my sense of humor."

He chuckles, shaking his head.

I hold out my hand and fake inspect it. "I can't wait to see the ring you propose with."

"One from a candy machine, of course."

I bump his shoulder with mine. "Where are we getting dinner after this?"

"Wherever you want."

I perk up. "And then can I be your midnight snack?"

"I've created a monster out of you, haven't I?"

"Sure have."

I'm falling in love with this man, and the fear he isn't falling as hard feels like a brick to my chest every time I think about it.

I OFFICIALLY HAVE A ROOMMATE.

The townhouse is larger and nicer than the apartment I moved out of, and the rent is the same price since I'm only paying half with Grace. My brothers and Maliki helped me move all day today. Lincoln had offered, but I didn't want him to call off work at the bar.

Grace struts into the living room with a sparkly gift bag in her hand. "To my new roommate." Her strawberry-blond curls are in braids down each side of her head, and her pajamas are floral print.

I smile, grabbing it from her while sitting on the couch, and she plops down on the other side. "Aw, you didn't have to get me anything."

"You saved me from moving back in with my parents." She gestures to the bag. "I owe you, like, fifty of those."

I laugh, tugging at the tissue paper. "You couldn't swing rent by yourself?"

They say it's rude to ask about finances, but I'm genuinely curious. Grace teaches in an upscale private school, her father is a judge, and she never seems pressed for money. The few hundred I'm paying in rent doesn't seem like it'd be enough to push her out of the townhome.

"It's not about the money." Grace rests her hands in her lap, all proper and ladylike. "I don't like to live alone."

"I get that." I tried it, and it wasn't all sunshine and rainbows.

But then again, I also have a crazy ex who keeps popping up, adamant on scaring the shit out of me.

I tear the rest of the tissue paper out of the bag to find a box inside. Opening it, I find a mug with my name scrawled across it in pink glitter and a cartoon figure of my face.

"It was an inside thing with Georgia and me," Grace explains. "Nearly all of our mugs had our names on them."

I smile, holding up the mug. "Thank you. I really appreciate it."

When I was expelled from college, I lost contact with most of my friends. Some of them because they looked down on me for being arrested. Others were too busy, which I understood. I've been invited to parties on campus by some of my former sorority sisters, but it seems too weird to go back there. I also don't want to risk running into Quinton.

Grace stands. "You have the mug. Now, we make the roomie hot chocolate."

"The roomie hot chocolate?"

"Yep." She jerks her head toward the kitchen. "Come on. You're going to love it."

I follow her into the kitchen, and she opens a cabinet and pulls out a matching mug with her face and name. She sets it on the counter before gathering the ingredients, consisting of milk, hot chocolate, whipped cream vodka, and marshmallow vodka.

"Do you need any help?"

"I got it," she replies, warming the milk.

We make small talk while she prepares the hot chocolate, pours it into our mugs, and hands one to me.

"Will this get me drunk?" I ask, moving the mug in circles, watching the chocolate swish in the cup.

I'm not a lightweight drinker, but the amount of vodka Grace poured in might have me hugging the porcelain throne if I get too crazy. It was so strange, seeing someone who appears so put together and proper pouring an exuberant amount of vodka in hot chocolate.

"Possibly." She grins before holding her mug up in a *cheers* gesture. "To being roommates."

I smile and bump my mug against hers. "To being roommates." Taking a sip, I moan. "This is officially my favorite hot chocolate. I'm going to insist they start selling it at the bar."

"Georgia tried, but Archer and Cohen vetoed the idea, calling it too complicated to make. They also didn't think it'd be too popular in a sports bar, so we just drink it when we're here."

We walk to the living room and plop down on the couch.

"Roommate task number two," Grace says. "We find a new show to binge."

We go through the options, finding one neither of us has seen, and promise not to watch an episode without the other. Grace—the shy and conservative Grace—is beaming with a personality I've never witnessed from her before.

As we're in episode three, my phone beeps with a text.

Lincoln: You all moved in?

I grin while replying.

Me: All moved in.

"Uh-oh, who's the guy?" Grace singsongs.

I drop my phone into my lap to look at her. "Huh?"

She gestures toward the phone. "The one you're grinning at while texting."

"Oh, it's just Lincoln, asking if I got moved in okay."

"You and he …?"

"We're, uh …" I hesitate, running my fingers through the fur of the throw pillow next to me.

"Don't worry." Grace taps my hand playing with the pillow. "Anything we talk about stays between us. I promise."

"We're just"—I shrug—"hanging out … seeing where things go."

She nods, playing with her braid. "Lincoln is a nice guy. You two are good for each other."

The corners of my mouth turn up at her response, and a sense of relief hits me. "I think so too."

"And just like when Archer was dating Georgia while she lived here, he's welcome to hang out here whenever."

My smile grows.

I peer at my phone still in my lap when another text comes through.

Lincoln: Want some company when I get off? You can give me a tour of your bedroom.

I grab the phone to answer.

Me: You won't be exhausted?

Lincoln: Nah. I'll leave a little early and let Archer clean up. He owes me that.

Me: I'll be here.

Lincoln: See you in a bit.

Had Grace not said anything about him being welcome here, I would've questioned asking him to come over so late. I know Archer used to stay over with Georgia all the time because Grace would sometimes call him her second roommate. I think the more people there are around, the more Grace is happy. She seems to be a people person who doesn't like being alone.

I relax into the couch, sipping spiked hot chocolate while

bonding with my new roommate, and wait for my man to get off work.

LINCOLN: **You awake?**

My grin takes over nearly my entire face.

Call me desperate, but I've stayed up to see if he forgot about me.

Me: Awake and waiting for you to get here.

Lincoln: I'll be on my way in 10.

Me: See you soon.

Jumping out of bed, I dart to the bathroom and inspect myself in the mirror. Pulling my hair into a ponytail, I check my teeth before strolling into the living room. Grace went to bed a few hours ago, and I don't want to wake her.

Lincoln texts when he's outside, and I scurry to the door, unlocking it, then stepping to the side to allow him room to come in. A dark beanie covers his head, and a black coat is tight over his muscles.

He wastes no time before ducking his head down to press his lips against mine. "Hey, babe."

"Hi." I peek up at him, blinking, as an abrupt wave of shyness hits me.

"Let's see this bedroom of yours."

He tosses his overnight bag over his shoulder and interlaces our fingers, and I lead him to my new bedroom. The room is a decent size—larger than my old apartment and bedroom at the sorority house, but not as big as the one I had growing up. As the daughter of the town's mayor, I lived somewhat of a privileged life.

After pushing my queen-size bed in, there wasn't much room for more furniture. A simple white nightstand sits next to one side of the bed, and I have a standing mirror against a wall along with my desk.

Breaking away, I jerk my thumb toward his bag. "A little overeager there with the overnight bag, huh?"

He chuckles, slightly holding up the bag. "Eh, I figured you'd need assistance with testing out your new bedroom."

"Fine." I dramatically groan while fighting back a smile. "For testing purposes, I'll allow it."

To be honest, I'd have been disappointed had he not planned to spend the night since that's what he's done the past few nights.

I wonder where Georgia and Archer think he's staying.

Do they even keep tabs on him like that?

Lincoln drops his bag onto the floor and does a once-over of the room. "This is cute, babe."

"Thank you." I shut the door behind us. "Hopefully, I can see yours soon."

"You can come over anytime you want." Wandering into the room, he takes a seat on the edge of my bed, over the white duvet cover. He leans forward, resting his elbows on his knees, and focuses on me. "Cass, you know I always want to be honest with you."

I freeze, my pulse thrumming in uneasiness. "Good." I clear my throat and lower my voice. "I want you to always be honest with me."

Surely, he wouldn't have packed an overnight bag if he planned to bail on me tonight?

Unless he just changed his mind at the last minute.

There's a brief stillness, a lapse of time where he gathers his words. "There's something I need to tell you."

I clasp my hands together, hold them to the front of my body, and for some reason, prepare for the worst. "Okay …"

"I'm a felon."

The three words are a fist crushing my soul.

The memories of what happened with Quinton crawl through my thoughts.

No.

Just when I thought Lincoln was different, he tells me that.

"What did you do to … become a felon?" My last word is practically squeaked out.

"Aiding and abetting."

"Aiding and abetting for what?"

"Money laundering."

I'm quiet, digesting his words.

It all reminds me too much of Quinton.

Law breaking.

Secrets.

"You're mad," he says, his voice soft. "I get it. That's why I tried to keep my distance."

I inhale a steeling breath before answering, "Why didn't you tell me?"

"Being a felon isn't something I go around bragging about."

"We've spent enough time together for you to tell me."

A blend of irritation yet also understanding seeps through me. I get him keeping it from me when we were friends, but I opened up to him, so he should've done the same with me. I told him about my arrest and Quinton. That was a big step for me.

"That's why I wanted to start tonight by talking to you about this. I don't want any secrets between us, and from your reaction, I can see it's a big deal for you. I'm a felon. I was in prison. And if you're not comfortable with that, I understand."

"Wow." I slump down on the bed next to him and blow out a downward breath. "Prison."

"Prison," he repeats, mirroring my breath. "If it makes you feel any better, I *technically* didn't commit the crime."

I imagine most people would snort and roll their eyes at his declaration, his plea of innocence, but knowing the situation I was in, it's believable. I once wanted to be heard, said the words that I didn't commit the crime, and was mocked and ignored. I'd never do that before hearing someone out.

I swallow before speaking, "Okay."

He turns to face me, our eyes locking, and his face is pained. "I know it's stereotypical for criminals to say that, but hear me out." He shakes out his hands. "My crime was not turning my father in for corruption. I was the VP of the company he was laundering money through, and I kept my mouth shut, so I was brought down with him." He drapes his hand over mine. "You're the first person I've really talked about this with."

I battle with my internal emotions.

Back and forth.

Right and wrong.

Good guy or bad guy.

I'm not sure how much silence passes before he says, "Do you want me to go?"

Pulling away, he levels his palm on the bed to pull himself up, but I stop him.

"No, please don't," I whisper.

Prison was Lincoln's past, not his future.

He's done nothing to convince me otherwise. If he were doing shady shit, there'd be too many inconsistencies, people would be talking at the bar, and no way would Maliki and Sierra let me be around him.

Unlike Quinton, Lincoln is admitting to his wrongdoings.

Unlike Quinton, Lincoln took the fall, even when he hadn't committed the crime.

He's nothing like Quinton.

He's the man I wanted Quinton to be.

"Stay." I grab his hand and place it back over mine. "Always stay."

The initial shock has dissipated, reality bleeding through in its place. No way will I lose him over something like this.

His tense shoulders slump, releasing pressure, and he kisses my forehead. "I'll always stay ... for as long as you'll have me."

And just like that, I know this is a man I can trust.

This is a loyal man who I can tell my secrets to and who will keep my secrets.

But what happens if I'm not ready to tell him all of mine yet?

What happens if he wants me to be as open with him as he was with me tonight?

I'm not sure that's possible if I want to protect us.

Knowing how Lincoln is, if he finds out Quinton is messing with me, he'll intervene. If he's a felon, it'll send him right back to prison. Lincoln isn't getting in trouble over Quinton's dumbass. I'll handle his stalking on my own.

CHAPTER FIFTEEN

Lincoln

"HAVE FUN AT YOUR DINNER, BABE," I tell Cassidy as we walk to our cars. "And drive safe."

With a smile, I do a quick scan of the employee parking lot, making sure the coast is clear since we're still keeping our relationship a secret. I press my lips against hers and wrap my arms around her waist, somewhat pushing her against the car. My hips grind into hers while I release a groan. My heart speeds at the taste of her when my tongue slides into her mouth.

I had the day off at the bar, but Cassidy worked the mid-shift, so I stopped for lunch and hung out with her.

She releases harsh breaths when I pull away. "I don't want to be late."

"Nope." I smack a kiss to her forehead.

"I'll be texting and calling," she says, "so make sure you're available at all times."

"Aren't I always available to you at all times?"

"Good point." She stands on her tiptoes to present me with another kiss, wiggles her fingers into a wave, and gets into her car.

Puffing out cold air, I rush to mine, rubbing my hands together to create warmth. Neither one of us remembered to turn our auto-starts on, so our cars are freezing. Sitting in my running car, I wait for Cassidy to reverse out of her spot and leave. It's what I do every time.

Last night, I spilled my truth to her, gave her every component of myself. I told her about my father acquiring the family business after my grandfather's passing and how he'd started committing crimes. It was petty shit at first, but the more he got away with, the more he pushed his limits. Why? I'm still clueless. We had plenty of money, never needed for anything, but for some reason, my dad wanted more. I confessed all the feelings that'd rushed through my body when the feds showed up at my front door and how I'd wanted to jump out of the bathroom window the day I was sentenced to time in a federal penitentiary.

That night, on the drive to Cassidy's, my nerves had been on fire, uncertain of how she'd feel about my admission, about my dark past. She wasn't jumping for joy, but she handled it better than how most people would. She heard me out, was calm and rational, and in the end, she told me to make myself comfortable in her bed.

We didn't have sex, didn't hook up.

We lay in bed, talking about our pasts before falling asleep in each other's arms.

That night, as I lay in her bed, it cemented that I'd done the right thing.

That I was falling for and opening up to the only person who understood me like I needed to be understood. I'm not sure what it is about her, but the scorned parts of our hearts seem to be fitting together perfectly like a puzzle.

A horn blares through the parking lot from her car, causing me to jump out of mine, and I rush over to her. Reaching her car, I find her sitting in the driver's seat with her forehead pressed against the steering wheel. I knock on the window, and she slowly lifts her head as I gawk at her.

Opening the door, I drape my arm along the top of it and lean in toward her. "You honked?"

She smacks her palm against the steering wheel. "My car won't start."

I gesture for her to get out and take her spot. I tinker with the car, trying all the ideas I can come up with to get it to start, but nothing. It doesn't help that she's moving from foot to foot, shivering, while watching me try to fix something I know nothing about.

I'm a numbers guy who doesn't know much about auto shit. A reminder to brush up on those skills because it doesn't impress the girl you're falling for if you don't know shit about how to fix her car.

"If all else fails, you Google it," I say. "Let me grab my phone and try to fix the issue. If we can't, you can get it towed to a shop. There's one right around the corner."

She checks her watch as disappointment clouds her features. "Ugh, I'll call a tow truck and ask Rex or Sierra to come get me."

Tonight is one of her family dinners. If she calls one of her siblings, they'll miss a portion of the dinner, having to drive here and then back.

I scratch my cheek. "If you need a ride, I'm not doing anything."

"It's over thirty minutes away." She shakes her head. "I can't ask you to do that."

"I could use a good drive."

I PEER over at Cassidy after parking in her mother's circular drive. "If you need a ride back, text me."

"I can have someone drive me home." She grips the door handle, slightly opening it, but stops, whipping around to face me. "Unless you want to come in and stay? I told them my car was on crack and a friend was giving me a ride. No one will mind." She fidgets with her bracelet, as if she's nervous I'll say no … or that it'll be weird because everything we are is so up in the air.

A friend.

For reasons unknown, my skin crawls at the term.

No, we're more than friends.

She gave me so much shit all the times I said we were *just friends*, but now that we're on the journey to change that, she's holding back. Things get trickier when I notice Maliki's black Camaro parked in front of us.

Does he know about Cassidy and me?

What he does know is my history, where I was months ago, and plenty of negative stories are circulating about me. Sure, he's been cool with me at parties and the bar, but me possibly dating Cassidy is a different level of simple friendliness.

I have a record.

Automatically, that makes some assume I can't be trusted.

Cassidy pouts her plump lower lip and steeples her hands in a begging motion. "Come on. Be my sidekick tonight, Robin."

I chuckle.

Robin.

That term doesn't make my skin crawl as much.

"Fine," I theatrically groan as if she were asking me to cut a vein or some shit.

Cassidy grins. "You da best, Callahan."

I cut my car's engine and survey the two-story brick home. It's the nicest in the neighborhood, but in my old life, it'd have been considered small.

My old world was full of superficial assholes.

"Is this where you lived, growing up?" I ask her.

She nods. "For as long as I can remember."

We step out of the car and walk stride for stride into the house. A commotion erupts as soon as the door shuts behind us —talking and laughing. We take a quick right, leading us into the dining room with a massively long table lined with people down each side, drinks in front of them. In the middle sits a variety of food bowls and plates.

"Everyone," Cassidy announces, "this is Lincoln. We work together, and since my car decided it was done being my friend, he was kind enough to give me a ride."

We work together.

I gulp.

Is working together worse than saying we're friends?

Hell yes, it is.

An older version of Cassidy and Sierra stands and immediately wraps Cassidy into a tight hug. "I've missed you so much, honey."

"Mom," Cassidy says, squeezing her, moving side to side, "you saw me the other day."

"Yes, but I miss my kids *every day.*"

When they pull away, Cassidy runs her hand along my arm. "Lincoln, this is my mother, Nancy."

From the stories I've been told and her appearance, Nancy is the opposite of my mother—your classic homemaker.

I suck in a startled breath when Nancy hugs me next, slapping my back a few times. "It's so nice to meet you, and I appreciate you giving her a ride. Our family dinners mean so much to us."

"Are you kidding me?" someone says when Nancy pulls away.

All attention shifts to a man at the table, sporting an officer uniform and a cold glare slapped straight in my direction.

Cop.

Criminal.

Bad combo.

"Cass," he says, his voice harsher but his eyes not leaving me, "a word."

"Nope," Cassidy chirps as if the mood in the room hasn't shifted into darker territory. "Whatever it is can wait until later."

A frown of dismay briefly crosses her face before she forces a smile while also shooting daggers at the guy.

She knows what he's pissed about.

Everyone's attention hops between the three of us, watching the show with curiosity.

"Cassidy," he grinds out, slamming his napkin onto the table.

I open my mouth, prepared to tell him if he has an issue with me, to take it up with me, not Cassidy. I'll leave if I'm not welcome. Cassidy shouldn't have to fight that fight for me.

The blonde next to him smacks his arm and shoots him a glare stronger than the one Officer Jackass is giving me, but he pays no attention.

"Kyle," Nancy warns, her tone stern but her voice light and sweet, "we are having dinner. You can talk to your sister later."

Cassidy delivers a smug look at him.

From the conversations I've had with Cassidy, I've learned she's close with her mother. She was the only child living at home when her father's affair came to light. She was the largest shoulder and support system for Nancy. After hearing the stories, I imagined her family to be like a *Jerry Springer* drama, but all I'm getting is *Brady Bunch* vibes.

Except for Officer Pissed Off, of course.

"Everyone, have a seat." Nancy throws her arm out toward the open chairs at the end of the table.

As I survey the table, I halt when my gaze meets Maliki's. My throat constricts at the warning clouding his features. Just as I suspected, he's suspicious of me hanging around with Cassidy. I've gained friendships with most of the guys in my brother's circle, but since Maliki lives in a different town and owns his own bar, he doesn't come around as frequently as the others. Meaning he hasn't had as much time to realize I'm not a bad person.

Next to Maliki is Sierra, Cassidy's older sister. Even though it hasn't been brought up around her when I've been around, I wouldn't doubt her knowing my story. But unlike her fiancé, her lips are curled into an inviting smile.

"Have a seat, guys," Sierra says, pulling out the open chair next to her. "Mom made rib eye, roasted rosemary potatoes, and her famous sweet corn. I'm starving, and I will die if we don't eat soon."

My gaze darts up and down the table as everyone waits for us to take our seats. Cassidy squeezes into the seat next to Sierra. As I take the chair next to her, I quickly glance at the officer —*Kyle*. Chills speed down my spine, the dread of him interrogating me already causing my stomach to curl.

"I'm Rex," the guy across from me says. "Sup, dude?"

Rex is sporting a black leather jacket and a cross necklace. From what Cassidy has said, he's the cool brother.

A mousy, dark-haired girl shyly waves at me. "I'm Carolina, Rex's better half."

Next to Rex is Trey, a guy around the same age as Cassidy. From what Cass has told me, he's the half brother no one knew about until recently. He says hello with a simple chin jerk in my direction.

Chloe, the woman who smacked Kyle, introduces herself before elbowing Kyle to do the same. "I'm Chloe, this guy's— who's actually nice, I promise—girlfriend."

Kyle snorts.

"Quit acting like a little prick," she hisses underneath her breath to him.

"Don't," he says before his dark scowl returns to me. "Kyle."

At least he doesn't introduce himself as *Officer*.

It's annoying when people do that shit.

"Sweetie, do you know what's wrong with your car?" Nancy asks Cassidy as I drape the cloth napkin over my lap. "Did you tell your father, so he can get it looked at?"

Cassidy shakes her head. "I'm for sure not calling him. I'll get it figured out."

"I'll get it looked at for you," Kyle says.

"It's at the bar, but I'm going to have it towed," Cassidy informs.

"Send me the bill for the repairs," Rex adds.

"Now, let's get you some drinks," Chloe comments, her voice overeager, as if she's compensating for her boyfriend. "We have sweet tea, lemonade, water, or I can grab a soda from the kitchen?"

"Lemonade," Cassidy replies before peeking over at me. "My mom's lemonade is to die for."

"Lemonade for me too," I reply with a smile.

Our drinks are poured, and we devour Nancy's rib eye.

"NOT TO SOUND LIKE AN ASSHOLE," Maliki says, sitting next to me on the living room sofa, prepared to most likely sound like an asshole, "but I'm not sure if you two are good or bad for each other."

After dinner, Nancy brought out the dessert. And when I say she brought out the dessert, good ole Nance brought her dessert game. There was a chocolate cake, a cherry pie, and cupcakes. All made from scratch. I'm so full that I could not eat for another week, and I still wouldn't be hungry.

Maliki reminds me of my brother. He is closed off, isn't much of a conversationalist, owns a bar, and is dating a woman the complete opposite of him. Sierra is outgoing, pushes people's buttons, and loud. She and Cassidy share similar personalities.

I bite my tongue, holding back the urge to tell him I couldn't care less what he's sure of. Instead, I cock my head to the side and mutter, "Why do you say that?"

He grips his beer in his fist. "Cassidy tends to have a type … *trouble*, and no offense, dude, but you're trouble."

Here it goes. My past haunting me again.

I want to be trouble and tell Maliki to fuck himself and stay out of our business.

A criminal record shouldn't automatically label me.

"I *was* trouble," I grind out. That's a lie. I didn't break the law. I *knew* someone was breaking the law, and my silence bit me in the ass.

He drains his beer. "Told you, not trying to be an asshole. I get it, man. Your situation was fucked up, and not many people would do what you did for your family. I respect your loyalty. I'm only mentioning it because her cop brother *and* parents, who recently had to deal with her legal troubles with her ex, might not be as understanding."

I slug down my lemonade. I've kept it strictly nonalcoholic tonight.

"Are you going to tell them?" I croak out.

Fear creeps into me like a shady snake at the thought of losing Cassidy because her family doesn't approve of me. Losing her would be a slit to the heart.

"Not my business to tell." Maliki levels his gaze on me. "All I'm saying is, if you haven't told her your past, you should. Not only is one brother a cop but Rex can also hack into anything. Give the guy your first name, and in five minutes, he can provide every digital move you and your family have made your entire lives. Cassidy is a good girl—sarcastic and mouthy as shit, like her sister, but she has a heart of gold. Don't fuck her over."

Our conversation is interrupted by the sound of Cassidy arguing with someone in the other room.

"He's a fucking criminal, Cassidy," Kyle roars from down the hallway.

He managed to keep things casual the rest of dinner but didn't mutter a word in my direction or glance at me again. I had no doubts that he was waiting for the perfect moment to get Cassidy alone to warn her about me.

"Oh shit," Maliki says, shaking his head. "And here we go."

I stand and head in the direction of their voices.

"How do you know that?" Cassidy asks.

"Everyone knows who the Callahans are," Kyle replies. "They were all over the news!"

"You don't know the entire story," Cassidy argues.

"What don't I know?" Kyle's voice rises. "He was in prison. Did he tell you that?"

"He did."

I reach the doorway of the room they're in to find her facing off with Kyle, her arms crossed.

"And in case you forgot, I was also arrested," Cassidy adds.

Kyle shakes his head. "Big difference. You didn't go to goddamn prison."

"White-collar prison," Rex corrects, and my gaze tears across the room to find him sitting in the corner, watching the show in front of him. "Dude, you know that's two different things. He didn't fucking murder someone."

Rex, I fucking like you.

"Prison is prison," Kyle snaps.

"I'm not having this conversation with you," Cassidy says.

Kyle crosses his arms, mirroring her stance. "Do you want me to call Dad, so you can have that conversation with him instead? We can let him know you're hanging out with convicts."

"Oh, don't try to bullshit me." Cassidy snorts. "You wouldn't call Dad if your dick was on fire and he had the last glass of water to put it out."

Rex scoffs, shaking his head. "That was a good one, sis."

Having had enough, I place my knuckles against the door, tapping lightly to make my appearance known. This isn't how I wanted to meet the fam, but I'm not going to sit back and allow Cassidy to take the heat for my actions.

"Don't give her shit," I say, leveling my eyes on Kyle. "Yes, I'm a felon. Yes, I was in prison. My father had committed a crime, and I'd refused to snitch on him. Call me whatever you want for it, but I'd do it again if I had to. My past will not hurt your sister in any way. I'm not trouble. I work at the bar, keep my nose clean, and that's it."

Kyle looks at me, shocked, as if he expected me to sit back and allow Cassidy to fight my battles.

"I can vouch for him," Maliki says behind me, and I'm not sure when the hell he arrived, but I'll take his support. "He's Archer's brother. Dude has kept it real with me since the day he was released. I met him a few times before he was locked up. He's a good guy." He shrugs, sipping on his beer. "We all know our past shouldn't come back to bite us in the ass."

Kyle runs his hands through his hair. "Fine, whatever." He looks at me, and in the same tone he used with Cassidy, he says to me, "A quick word."

I nod. "Sure."

Kyle waves me out of the room and down a hallway, so we're alone.

We land in a bedroom, and he shuts the door behind us.

"I wasn't trying to be a dick," he automatically says.

I chuckle. "You failed at that."

"I'm just … worried about my little sister, you know?" He strokes his jaw. "The last thing she needs is to fall into trouble again. She might've managed to end up with community service last time, but she has a record now, which could result in a harsher punishment."

"I swear to you, I have nothing but your sister's best interests." I silently pray he can see the honesty in my eyes, the deep care I have for Cassidy, and that he'll trust me with her. "I get wanting to protect your sister, but I won't get her in any trouble."

"What are you?" He blinks. "Dating? Friends?"

I feel stupid when I say, "I have no idea actually."

He nods as if he understands that complicated time in figuring out what you are with another person. "Look, I'm giving you the benefit of the doubt because I know your family was good until all that shit went down. I've met Archer, and he seems like a cool-ass dude. Just don't get my sister in trouble."

"That's the last thing I ever want to do."

"Sorry for the interrogation, bro."

"Nah, it's cool. Thanks for hearing me out and giving me a chance, instead of letting my past define who I am."

"If it makes you feel any better, Cassidy has never brought a guy home since high school, so she must really like you. She seems happier than she's been in months. Don't break her heart."

"DID you enjoy meeting your future in-laws?" Cassidy asks when we get back to her place.

I nod and smile, both of them overexaggerated. "Oh, yes, I definitely enjoyed it. I don't think it could've gone any better."

She laughs, shaking her head. "Of course, my brother had to know you've been in trouble with the law."

I slump down on her bed. "It was all over the news. I tend to be more shocked when people don't know or don't recognize my last name."

It's humiliating when I see the recognition cross people's faces when they figure out who I am.

What I am.

It's no secret that Cassidy deserves better than someone with a record, but if she's okay with it, then why would I run away from my own happiness?

I want that life—the life that Archer, Cohen, and Maliki have. A relationship. Another half. Someone to come home to. Someone to be my everything and vice versa. Never have I wanted a relationship before. Never has someone slid into my life, into my head, and—dare I say it—into *my heart*.

Cassidy joins me on the bed, perky and ready for conversation. "Other than that, what'd you think?"

"They're cool. Your mom is a kick-ass cook."

She smiles with pride. "My mom is a kick-ass everything."

I shift to face her, leaning in, and kiss her cheek. "Just like her daughter."

She smiles harder before it slips. "What are we?"

Now, if that question doesn't nearly knock me on the ass. It's not the turn I expected this conversation to take so quickly. It is the turn we need to take though because there's nothing worse than not knowing where you stand with somebody—with someone you want to stand next to, love, and be with.

"What do you mean?" I choke out.

For people who like to talk about everything, we've done a poor job of broaching serious topics. It's almost as if dragging out the complicated questions will change something and ruin us.

Nervousness covers her face as she plays with her hands. "I mean, my sister asked me what we were tonight, and I had no idea what to tell her."

My chest tightens. "I guess we'd better clear that up then, huh?"

She raises her gaze, her eyes searching mine. "We should definitely clear that up."

My heart turns in my chest. "I'm whatever you want me to be."

I want to be her everything.

I want her to want every piece of me for the rest of our lives.

Some might say having feelings so strong with someone you've known for only a few months can't be real. Some might say that there needs to be a longer period to truly fall for someone, but I've spent enough time with Cassidy to know who she is, to know how my day brightens when she's around and how my mind constantly wanders to her when she's not.

"Hmm … anything I want you to be." She scoots in closer, nearly on my lap. "I'd say my husband, my baby daddy, the man obsessed with me."

I chuckle. "Give us some time, and I can be all of those things, baby."

She chews on her lower lip, excitement and nervousness prevalent in her expression. "I'm scared, though."

I raise a brow. "Scared of what?"

"Scared to take the leap with you, to hand myself over to someone and then end up broken. My feelings for you are stronger than what they were with my ex, and what he did tore me apart. If things ended badly between us, it'd kill me, Lincoln."

I stretch out my legs and nod in understanding. "That's why I didn't jump right into having a physical relationship with you." It's something we could've easily done from the beginning, that could've also ended messy. "I wanted to be certain I was comfortable enough for more than sex so that I wouldn't hurt you. And that time wasn't to realize how much I liked you; it was if I'd be good for you, if I'd be able to make you happy … and keep you happy."

"I appreciate that, and I think we both needed that time before jumping into something. My parents' marriage was a complete joke. High school sweethearts. She invested everything into them, only for him to have an affair and completely screw her over. I don't want that to be me."

"I give you my word that I'll never screw you over. Do you hear me? We're alike in so many ways. We both are big on loyalty and honesty. I went to prison for having someone's back. I promise, I'd do the same for you. And I have concerns too."

She blinks at me. "Like what?"

"You recently got out of a bad relationship. Are you sure you're ready for another?" Just as scared as she is that I'll hurt her, I'm scared of putting myself out there too.

"Do you plan on us having a bad relationship?" She furrows her brows.

"Fuck no."

"Then why would I hold my ex's actions against you? Our relationship will be a clean slate."

I shudder. "Other than those few things, which we've now settled, you got anything else?"

She shakes her head before releasing a deep sigh. "I've got nothing."

My confidence beams. "So then, take something."

With that, she grins, crawling into my lap, her weight distributing to my body. Her lips crash into mine, making me come alive, and without hesitation, I dip my tongue into her mouth.

Tasting her and the sweet desserts we devoured after dinner.

Tasting what I keep wanting and wanting and wanting.

My heart thrashes against my chest as I reach around and grip the back of her neck, feeding more of her to me. Kissing Cassidy is a rush I've never experienced. As a man who's had his fair share of women, I've never had these emotions climb through me with just kissing.

The want.

The need.

The urge to give her all of me.

I want to grab Cassidy in my arms and make her mine.

Keep her underneath me while we forget our problems.

I grunt when she grinds into me, her jeans rough against mine, and my cock hardens with every movement. She yelps when I curl my hands around her waist, then turn and ease her onto her back, her hair fanning over the pillow. Luckily, she didn't make her bed this morning, so there's no messing with undoing the bedding to make her comfortable.

I draw back, smacking my palm to the mattress to hold myself up, and stare down at Cassidy. Her chest heaves in and out as she peers at me in expectation, in challenge, as if saying, *What are you going to do with me?*

Slicing my hand up the bed and between her legs, I jerk her thighs open before sliding between them, making enough room for my heavy body. I tip my head down, kissing her, before lowering my mouth to her neck and sucking on the sensitive skin.

"Stop teasing me," she groans. "We've done plenty of foreplay. It's time to get to the main event."

I chuckle. "There's never too much foreplay, baby." My sex game has always been to pleasure the woman first, so that's what I need to make sure I do with Cassidy.

With a strength that surprises me, she hooks her leg around my waist and attempts to flip me over on my back.

Stopping her, I shake my head. "Oh no, baby. Nice try."

She frowns. "I'm going to bite you in the neck and possibly stab you if you don't get me naked soon."

"Oh, I like it kinky, babe." I click my tongue against the roof of my mouth. "And since you were such a good girl today, I'll give you what you need. Let's get you naked."

She glares up at me. "Let's get *us* naked."

"I like the way you think."

Giving her what she wants—what we both need—I hurriedly undress, and she does the same. This isn't how I expected our first time to go, but she's right; we've been waiting for this for what seems like months. Within a few breaths, we're naked, in the same position we were before—her underneath me, me situated between her legs.

Reaching down, I massage my hand between her pussy lips, separating them with my fingers, before slipping down the bed. Her legs tremble when my face reaches her core. I bend my neck and suck on her clit, sliding my tongue between her folds.

I could eat Cassidy for every meal and still be hungry for her.

"More," she moans, writhing underneath me. "I need more."

"I can do that," I reply with a sly smile, moving back up her body.

I take my cock, gripping it, and slide it against her opening.

Back and forth through her soaked slit.

Back and forth before I dive into heaven.

She moans, her back coming off the bed. "Mmm ... I like that ... *more*."

"Jesus, you sure are needy." I slide down and take one long, straight lick against her slit.

"Needy for your cock," she gasps.

"Tell me you want it," I say, flicking her clit before sliding two fingers inside her. "Tell me how bad you want my cock."

"So bad," she moans. "I want your cock so bad, Lincoln. I want to feel your big cock inside me, filling me up in every way."

Her words are my undoing.

"Condom?" I rasp out.

"Nightstand." She points toward it. "Second drawer."

I stretch across the bed, my erection pressing up against her thigh, and she raises her hips, moaning as she grinds against it.

Fuck, she's killing me.

I jerk the drawer open, finding a box of condoms, and pluck one out. Ripping the wrapper open with my teeth, I pull out the condom and slip it down my cock. Cassidy pulls at my ass in the process, dragging me to her, nearly using all of her strength to push my cock inside her.

I laugh, loving how strong her need is for me.

When I slide inside her slick warmth, I suck in a breath. "Jesus, you're tight as fuck," I hiss.

"It's been a while," she says, a shyness overcoming her.

"It's been a while for you?" I work my jaw from side to side. "All I've done since I've been released is yank it in the shower. Baby, I'm about to be born again into sex."

Not going to lie; I've been nervous about having sex with her. It's not that I don't know how to use my dick or that I worry I won't pleasure her, but it's been a minute since my dick dipped into a pussy. And it's been *never* since it's had anything as sweet as her. My fear is, I'll thrust into her and blow my load, becoming a disappointment and embarrassing myself.

Our breathing is harsh as I pump into her. I claim her, rotating my hips from side to side as she writhes underneath me. Her pussy convulses before tightening around my dick, and she says my name when she comes. Her body shakes as her orgasm shatters through her.

"Say it again," I growl. "Say whose cock just got you off."

"Lincoln."

"Yes, baby," I groan, thrusting into her, trying to control my pace, but now that she's gotten off, now that I know her cum is alongside my dick, I can't take it any longer.

Sweat is dripping off my chest, onto her stomach. Raising her legs into the air, I hitch them over my shoulders, wrapping my arms around them, and pound into her.

A few pumps later, I bust inside the condom and collapse on top of her—out of breath, out of energy, out of fucks to give on why it's not a good idea to be with her.

Us together is a damn good idea if you ask me.

CHAPTER SIXTEEN

Cassidy

LINCOLN STARES at me as I'm drying off my hair, fresh from a shared shower. "What are you up to today?"

Last night, we had hot sex.

This morning, we had slow sex—nearly lovemaking.

Then we had slippery, frantic sex in the shower.

"Going shopping with Georgia." Goose bumps cover my arms as I reach for my tee. "She wants to girlie up your place."

I laugh to myself, wondering how Archer will love that. Better yet, he seems to let Georgia do whatever she wants, so he'll probably just shake his head and move on if it makes her happy.

In the same move I pictured Archer doing, Lincoln laughs and shakes his head. "Oh shit."

I nod. "Yep, be scared."

He drops his towel, grabbing for his pants, and my gaze shoots straight to his cock—the one that was inside me while he slammed me against the wet shower wall, our bodies melding into one. Grace was at work, so I moaned while he whispered how good it felt to be inside me.

"I'll see you at work tonight?" He pulls his pants to his waist, buckling them.

"You'll see me at work tonight. Are we having a sleepover at your place or mine?"

"Hmm … wherever you want." He plants a kiss against my lips.

Finally.

Finally, we had sex, and it was perfection.

More than what I'd imagined it would be.

This man was made for me.

He's open, honest, great with his tongue, and he cares about pleasing me in the bedroom. A rare gem in a sea of men with two pumps, who think foreplay is a clit flick before setting off for the finale of sticking their cock inside me.

I'm certain, when he leaves here today, he won't call his buddies and brag about hooking up with me. He won't play mind games, ignore my texts, and call the other girls he's talking to and say, *Sorry, babe, I fell asleep.*

Lincoln is the real deal.

Our relationship is the real deal.

I don't care if he's a felon because that's not what defines him. He's a good man, the man I can see myself spending the rest of my life with, the man I hope whose emotions are just as strong.

"YOU KNOW ABOUT LINCOLN'S … legal problems, right?" I ask Georgia, sitting across from her at the food court in the mall.

We came. We shopped. She bought furry pink pillows, a pink-chandelier canvas print, and rose-gold candleholders. I cannot wait to see them matched with Archer's home. I haven't been there yet, but from what Georgia's told me, its Pinterest board would be labeled *Make My Home As Masculine As Possible with No Character.*

Georgia nods, sipping her açaí smoothie—something I've

never had, but she talked me into trying it, saying Jamie got her obsessed with them. "I do. What do you know?"

"*What do you know?*" She's not giving me details until she finds out what Lincoln has confided in me. I respect that.

She's the first person I've brought Lincoln's record up with. I can't exactly talk to my siblings about it, and I don't have many friends. Plus, with her being Archer's girlfriend and living with Lincoln, there's no doubt she knows about his past.

"He was in prison ..." I bite on my straw.

There's no hesitation before she jumps into her response, and it's with such certainty that you'd think she was telling me a fact about herself. "That pretty much sums it up. Lincoln is a man of a different character—a *good* man. One of the most loyal men you'll ever meet—like Limon to Pablo Escobar loyal. When Archer was acting up, he did everything in his power to set him straight—before and after the bar incident—and has been a great role model as far as helping Archer withdraw from his past mistakes." Her eyes settle on me. "*Prison, felon*—they're scary words, I know, but you can't bundle the terms, bundle the people who've had those titles, as if they were one. Lincoln didn't commit a violent crime. He loved his dad enough to cover for them, to say, *I have your back, no matter what happens*, and because of that, his father received less time. In ways, I respect him for it."

I nod repeatedly. "Me too."

Loyalty is an honorable trait, and yes, some might say that integrity changes when it's for illegal activity, but I don't agree.

"You know," she goes on, "I'm surprised he opened up to you. He's never talked about it with me or even Archer, last I heard. That has to be a hard thing to open up about."

"He told me some secrets. I told him some. He's easy to talk with."

"Are you two ...? *Have you* two ...?"

There's no holding back my smile. "Last night was the first time."

She literally squeals. "How was it?"

I sink in the chair as if all emotions of happiness were weighing me down. "Amazing. Perfection. I've had sex before, but it's different with him. Lincoln is unlike any guy I've ever been with."

"Swear to God, it runs in the Callahan blood. Prewarning: what also runs in the Callahan blood is …" She pauses. "Although I'm not so sure that's Lincoln. The guy isn't as distant as Archer is, and Lincoln seems to have more sense to him. You definitely got the less difficult brother. While Archer is a loner, someone who keeps everything to himself before it eats him up, Lincoln hides his pain behind a smile. I'm not sure which is worse."

"I guess we'll see. He's the only man to have ever opened up to me like that, and coming from a broken home, where my father kept secrets like pets, it means so much to me."

"He's never brought another woman around us. Shoot, I've never even heard of him dating, hooking up, texting. He's not looking for a quick screw. He's looking for a future with someone."

We leave lunch at the food court and return to our shopping adventures. When we're finished, Georgia's car is full, so she calls Archer to come meet us and to fill his car with her purchases.

"We'll drop off the stuff, and you can surprise Lincoln," she says on our drive over.

Too bad I'm in for a surprise from hell when I get there.

CHAPTER SEVENTEEN

Lincoln

SHE'S the last person I expect to see when I answer the door.

The last person I want to see.

If I had a choice to see her or Satan, I'd choose the Devil.

I grind my teeth while asking, "How the fuck do you know where I live?"

She stands in the doorway, a Chanel bag draped over her shoulder—a bag *I* bought her—and her blond hair is cut shorter than before. She winces at my greeting before straightening her stance. "Everyone knows where Archer lives. It's no secret."

With how I've ignored her phone calls and the last words I said to her, she'd be dumb if she expected me to talk to her.

"Better yet," I growl out, "why are you here?"

She pulls on the strap of her bag. "Can we talk?"

Leaning against the doorframe, I release a huff. "What do you want, Isla?" I shoot her a venomous glare. "Can't you put two and two together and realize that me ignoring your calls means I don't want to talk to you?"

She releases a humph before shoving her way into the penthouse. I might be an ass, might tell her to get fucked, but I can't push her back. I don't put my hands on women. At the same time she enters the living room and I'm about to slam the door shut, I hear voices coming down the hall.

Recognizable voices.

Just as I'm gripping Isla's hand to pull her into my bedroom, the door swings open. My heart sinks into my stomach when Georgia, Archer, *and* Cassidy walk in.

You've got to be shitting me.

I have to be the chairman of bad timing.

The three of them halt in their steps, their eyes shooting from Isla to me. Archer, the only one who knows Isla, glares at me without blinking. His hands knot into fists, and I gulp, waiting for him to kick her out of his place. My gaze swings from him to Cassidy. Her hand is pressed against her throat as she anchors her attention on Isla before shifting to stare at me, pain and anger in her eyes.

"Who are you?" Cassidy asks. "His mom?"

Georgia snorts.

The fact that Cassidy can say that with a straight face is impressive, considering she's met my mother and she knows Isla clearly isn't her.

"No, I'm not his mother," Isla snarls.

If there's one way to piss off Isla, it's mentioning her age. She might not be my mother, but she is the same age.

"Oh." Cassidy smirks. "My bad. Who are you then?" Sarcasm seeps through her words, but there's no hiding the hurt in her eyes.

With heat burning along her cheeks, Isla turns to me and ignores Cassidy. "Can we talk in private?"

"Nah, I'm good." I shove my hands into my jean pockets. "I think our time here is over."

Not only am I pissed she's here but I'm also infuriated by her timing. The day after Cassidy and I slept together, she finds another woman at my house. I understand her anger. I'd share the same hurt and irritation.

"We haven't discussed anything during my time here,

Lincoln." A flash of desperation crosses Isla's Botoxed face. "I'm not leaving until you talk to me."

Motherfucker.

With a jerk of my head, I direct her to my bedroom, not having the heart to look at Cassidy. It's a dick move, but I'm not sure what else to do. I'm not sure what Isla would have started saying if we'd stood there any longer. All I can do now is hear what Isla has to say and then kick her ass out.

"Why are you punishing me for the actions of someone else?" Isla snaps as soon as I slam my bedroom door shut behind us.

I scoff, memories of what happened shooting through me like a drug, and it's a struggle to keep my voice low. "You mean, the actions of *your husband*? Surprise, sweetheart, they go hand in hand."

"And what he did was *out of my hands*. If I could've done something—"

"You're right. I should've kept *my hands* to myself. And that's on me, and considering I don't want your husband meddling in my family's life again, you need to leave. And never come back."

She reaches for me, desperate and pleading. "Lincoln, please. I miss you."

I slam my eyes shut. Not because her words hurt or that I miss her. I'm reliving the stupidity of crossing the line with her. It's not that I ever thought I was in love with Isla. We fucked. Plain and simple. Neither of us exchanged love devotions. She'd go home to her husband, and I'd go out and party. Then a few days later, we'd do it again.

It was an unhealthy cycle that lasted a year until all hell broke loose.

Until my stupidity of screwing a married woman blew up in my face.

"You need to go," I snarl, holding back the urge to yell. Stalking to my bedroom door, I jerk it open. "And don't come back. Quit calling. Forget I exist."

"This isn't how it's supposed to be," she whispers, wisping slanted bangs out of her eyes.

"We were never supposed to be." The words come out croaked, and I swing my arm out, begging her to leave.

This time, she listens. Isla struts out of my bedroom, not paying Georgia or Cassidy one glance, and leaves. As soon as the door shuts behind her, I pull at the roots of my hair and groan.

Glancing at Cassidy, I take a deep breath to prevent my voice from shaking. "That wasn't what it looked like."

Georgia kicks her leg out, glaring at me. "Then explain what it was."

"That's none of your business." The response comes out before I can stop it.

Georgia winces at my words. "Okay, rude. Go be a dick somewhere else, please, before I spit in your favorite ice cream."

I've never been an ass to Georgia. She's like a little sister to me, but Isla's visit has fire burning through my veins, and I want to breathe them out, get her out of my system.

Not wanting to have this conversation in front of Georgia—aka the gossip queen—I charge into my bedroom with a load of guilt, hoping Cassidy is behind me.

She is.

"Nice room," she comments, slipping inside before crossing her arms and glaring at my bed in disgust. "Were you just banging her in that bed? I don't think I should sit down on it."

The thought makes my stomach crawl. Isla is nothing but a reminder of my past, of every mistake my father and I made. She's a reminder that I was a stupid guy with no morals who thought his actions had no consequences.

"She means nothing," I grit out.

"Sex must've sucked then, huh?" She rests against the wall as if she truly believes my bed has some sexually transmitted disease.

"If there's anything you won't ever have to worry about, it's me sleeping with her."

"*Have you* slept with her before?"

Do I give her honesty? Do I lie?

Because it's Cassidy, because I always want her to be up-front with me, I nod.

"Interesting." She stretches the word out. "Looks like you had no problem giving older a chance before younger. And from the big-ass rock on her finger, it seems you've also tried them *married.*" A snarl leaves her, disgust on her face—a reminder of how often she's told me she despises cheaters and homewreckers since they're what broke up her family.

I bite my tongue from asking how she's certain Isla was married when we were together. My canines dig into my defense, knowing that she'll most likely ask me to clarify what Isla was when we started sleeping together. And Cassidy is right. From the very first time I met Isla, she's had a ring on her finger. It's fucked up, I'm well aware.

Wanting to change the subject, I clear my throat and say, "Did you figure out what was wrong with your car?"

She nods.

"If you need a ride anywhere, call me Cab Callahan."

She's not agreeing with the convo change being a good idea. "I can call you Homewrecker Callahan or The Man Who Had Another Woman in His Bedroom After Dicking Me Down Callahan. Those might be better for the situation we're currently in."

Right as I hold out my hand to explain myself, her phone dings.

Ignore it. Ignore it.

She doesn't.

Instead, she digs into her pocket, and horror flashes on her face as she reads whatever is on her screen.

"Cassidy …" I drawl out her name as she pales.

"I have to go," she stammers, attempting to shove the phone in her pocket. Her hand trembles, making it difficult, and the phone drops to the floor. "Shit!"

I reach out, prepared to repo her phone to see what suddenly worked her up, but she beats me to it. This time, she grips it in her hand, not bothering to put it away.

"Cassidy," I whisper, "what happened?"

Her eyes are crestfallen as she spares me a quick glance. "Nothing, really, I gotta go."

Without another word and before I can stop her, Cassidy sprints out of my bedroom.

CHAPTER EIGHTEEN

Cassidy

MY HEART IS RACING SO hard that I'm waiting to have a heart attack.

Me moving in with Grace was supposed to prevent this.

What the hell?

Thankful Grace isn't home, I charge into my bedroom, my upper lip snarling, and hold back the urge to punch the man sitting on my bed. "What the fuck do you want, Quinton?"

He chose the wrong day to mess with me. I already walked in on the man I'm falling for with another woman in his bedroom. I'm not in the mood to deal with a crazy-ass ex in mine. I'm mouthy to begin with, and today has pushed all my limits. Chances are, I'll be taking my anger with Lincoln out on Quinton, and it won't be pretty.

Quinton slides his hand over his smooth chin. "You moved in with a judge's daughter, huh?"

I blink at him. "What?"

"Your new roommate's father is a judge." A cruel smirk curls at his lips.

That's why he's here?

To question me about Grace's father?

Dude needs to find a real job because he has too much time on his hands.

I pull in a deep breath to calm myself. "I didn't give her a questionnaire before moving in."

His smirk widens. "Oh, how I miss that mouth of yours."

I hold in the urge to dramatically make a vomiting noise. I don't want him to miss anything about me. I don't want him to even think about me.

I remain in my bedroom doorway, maintaining a safe distance between us. "Look, Quinton, I don't care what you're doing. Keep committing crimes. Don't. I don't give a shit. I got into trouble because you're a coward, but I've moved on."

His back straightens, his smirk dropping faster than his loyalty to me. "Coward?" he huffs. "I'm no goddamn coward."

I imitate his huff. "Who puts drugs in their girlfriend's car, and then when said car gets searched, claims the drugs aren't his? You made me take the fall *for your crime.* I rode off in a cop car, and you drove away in your brother's Mercedes. That, my regrettable ex-boyfriend, is a coward. Be lucky I don't rat you out."

"Why didn't you snitch on me then?"

"I don't want your wrath, *obviously.* I was stupid enough to date you, and now, I want nothing to do with you."

"I'm the one who decides when I'm done with someone. Not the other way around."

I snort. "Think again. I'd never touch a loser like you again, who lives off daddy's money but wants the high of playing drug dealer for a few years."

Wrong words.

I know my mouth has gotten me in trouble again when he jumps up from the bed. His face reddens in fury as he snatches my elbow and jerks me into my bedroom. I gasp as his hand moves to my throat, and I'm slammed against the wall.

"I will end you." Quinton hisses in my face. His grip tightens before he suddenly pulls back, his hands slapping the wall on each side of my head.

I draw in a shaky breath in an attempt to calm myself that does nothing but that. "Don't be stupid, Quinton. It's not smart, breaking into a judge's daughter's house. It might lead to you getting in trouble."

The reality of my words dawns on him.

He drops an arm but doesn't pull away. "You fucking cunt."

I brace myself for another chokeslam or slap or something, but he takes a step back.

"Fuck you, Cassidy."

"Get out of my house."

ME AND MY BIG MOUTH.

That's what I think as I wince and stand in front of the mirror, examining the large bruise around my neck. Arguing with Quinton was stupid, but I couldn't stop myself. Cringing, I carefully pull a sweatshirt over my head, drag the hood up, and tighten it. That way, if Grace comes home, she won't see anything out of the ordinary.

Except that I'm walking around, looking like a damn Eskimo.

If she sees what Quinton did, she'll tell Sierra. Grace might be my roommate, but she's been friends with my sister longer. Grace is also a nice person. She'd reach out to someone out of concern for me. To prevent that from happening, I'll be hiding out until this bruise fades.

As I make myself comfortable in my bed, I look through my phone.

Lincoln has called and texted numerous times, and I've ignored every one of them. Afraid that he'll come over if I don't, I text him back.

Me: Sorry, I have a headache. Can I talk to you later?
Lincoln: Are you sure everything is okay?
Me: It's fine. I'm just going to nap.

Lincoln: Talk when you wake up?
Me: Of course.

So much has happened today.

Lincoln and the random woman who he no doubt has history with. Quinton making a visit and physically assaulting me. The day had started as a fairy tale and ended as a nightmare.

THROUGHOUT THE NIGHT, I sleep like shit.

The next morning, I wake up to find more texts from Lincoln.

I shut my eyes.

The day after we had sex, the day after we discussed our issues with trust, everything falls apart.

My phone rings, and it's Georgia. She's also texted a few times, asking if everything is okay. I've blown her off by replying with smiley face emojis.

"Hey, girl! Taco Tuesday is at our place tonight! Consider it a housewarming-slash-margarita party."

I chuckle. "I'm sure Archer is loving a party at his house."

"Well, it's *our* house now, and if I say we shall party, then we shall party." She laughs. "Plus, he's so happy I finally moved in that he'd let me throw a hundred parties. The fun starts at seven. Come with an empty stomach."

"I wish I could," I say around a groan. "But I have a killer migraine, and I think the move exhausted me. Sorry, but I'm going to sit this one out."

"Okay, but if you change your mind, you know where to come! Let's catch up this weekend, okay?"

"Sounds good."

Opening my nightstand drawer, I grab two ibuprofens and wash them down with water. As I surf through different Netflix options, my phone beeps with a text.

Lincoln: You coming over?

I sigh, debating on my response. He texted a few times earlier, asking me to let him explain himself. I briefly replied, saying I'd talk to him about it later.

Twenty questions had been on my tongue when I walked in and saw some random woman with Lincoln, but then Quinton texted me a picture of him sprawled out on my bed. My throat burning, my stomach churning, I knew I needed to get out of there. Not only because I was worried about being sick, but I also needed to get to my house before Grace did, so I could kick Quinton out.

Yes, my heart had sunk into the pit of my stomach when I saw Lincoln with that woman, especially it being the day after he and I finally had sex. But right now, I'm not in the mood to go back and forth. All I want to do is stay in bed, binge-watch a sappy show, and sleep. We'll discuss his stupid behavior another time.

Me: No, staying in for the night.

Lincoln: Come on. I need my sidekick.

Me: Sorry.

As bad as I want to go and take my mind off everything, I'm in pain, and there's no hiding my bruise yet. If someone bumps into me, if someone touches me in the wrong place, I'll wince.

Quinton wasn't like that when we dated. Yes, after thinking back, I remember the few times he was sketchy, but I didn't think he was dealing drugs.

Not only did I not want them to go to the police, but I also didn't want them to beg me to tell on him, nor did I want them to assume I was involved with his little side business. Knowing my parents, they would've freaked out and tried to stick me in rehab.

Lincoln: Everything okay?

Me: I'm just tired.

Lincoln: See you tomorrow?

Me: See you tomorrow.

I'm not sure if that's true.

CHAPTER NINETEEN

Lincoln

"YOU'RE NOT on the schedule tonight," I say when Johnna, one of the bar's waitresses, walks in.

Johnna shoves a notebook in her apron. "Cassidy asked me to cover for her."

Dread pools through me.

I planned to talk to Cassidy tonight about what had happened. With the anger I'd had when Isla was there, surely, Cassidy had to know there is nothing between us. Not one emotion in my body feels anything but disdain for Isla. I was ready to explain everything to Cassidy, but then her phone rang. The mood in the room hadn't been fucking rainbows, but whatever she'd read on her phone spooked her.

Since she left, I've texted her a few times. When I received no response, I expected to see her at Georgia's party. That didn't work out, just like my plan to talk to her tonight. Cassidy has never opted out of our get-togethers, and now, she's calling off work. My stomach unsettles, and I'm tempted to pour myself a shot to soothe my anxiety.

I fish my phone from my pocket and text her.

Me: You okay?

She replies minutes later.

Cassidy: Yes. I have a migraine and want to rest.

Me: You want me to bring you something when I get off?

The temptation to ask if she needs company hits me. I've picked up countless shifts for people, and someone could return the favor.

Cassidy: Thanks, but I'm fine.

Disappointment shatters through me. I want to be that guy for her, the one she calls when she has a migraine, who she calls when she's bored, whose name she moans when I'm inside her.

That damn guy.

I want to be everything for her.

Even though I shouldn't.

Unease drives through my blood as I text her back.

Me: Let me know if you change your mind.

Another text comes through, and that disappointment from earlier soars because it's not Cassidy.

Isla: Can we talk?

I clench my hand around my phone. Just seeing her name gives me the urge to throw it.

Me: Nope. Go talk to your husband.

Getting wrapped up in Isla was a mistake. Just like all the other women before her. She was crazy, but her husband? Dude was even fucking crazier when he found out we were sleeping together. I was young and dumb. Still, after it ended, I realized that wasn't an excuse for sleeping with a married woman. In my defense, she told me they were separated and in the process of a divorce.

Turned out, that was a lie.

With a curse, I block her number.

The rest of the night, my mind is on Cassidy.

I check my phone periodically, hoping she changed her mind.

Hoping she reached out.

Said something.

But it doesn't happen.

ARCHER GLANCES up when I knock on his open office door. Setting his pen down, he stares at me in expectation as I stand in the doorway.

I rest my shoulder against the doorframe. "Did Cassidy give a reason she called off tonight?"

He shakes his head. "Nah, she talked to Cohen."

Cohen is on baby leave, and I'd feel horrible for waking him. As bad as I'm trying to fight it off, all night, there's been a heaviness in my stomach that something is wrong with Cassidy. When she read whatever was on her phone, that light she carries around like a fucking pet dimmed.

I rub the back of my neck, hoping to relieve the tension. "If you can ask next time you talk to Cohen and let me know, that'd be great."

Archer lifts his chin, anchoring all his attention on me. "What's the deal between you and her?"

"We're"—I hesitate, wondering if I should tell him the truth even though Cassidy asked to wait—"friends."

Tenting his hands together, he levels them on his desk, his voice turning stern. "I know what *faking* being friends is. Georgia and I did it for years."

"Wrong." My voice wavers as I continue, "You and Georgia fake hated each other. I've never disliked Cassidy, and we don't pretend shit."

Okay, the last statement is a lie.

We do pretend that we don't have feelings for each other.

He nods, staying quiet.

His silence pisses me off.

I point at his phone next to him. "Can you ask Georgia if she's heard from her?" I'd text her myself, but like with Cohen, it's late, and I don't want to wake anyone up.

Archer blows out a ragged sigh. "Look, bro, Cassidy might not be the girl for you."

I pull in a breath, trying not to flip my shit on him.

How fucking dare he.

"The hell are you talking about?" I snarl. My stomach twists.

My brother, the number one person in my life, is telling me the only damn woman who's ever made me feel something might not be the one for me.

He's insinuating that the woman I'm falling for isn't for me.

Bull-fucking-shit.

Realizing he's hit a nerve, Archer lowers his voice. "She's on probation for a drug charge."

"And I was recently released from prison. What's your point?"

CHAPTER TWENTY

Cassidy

ONE OF THE most miserable feelings in the world is not being able to sleep.

Two days have passed since Quinton's chokeslam visit, and I've turned into an insomniac. Even with shutting and locking my bedroom door, the panic that he can barge in at any time haunts me, becoming a real-life nightmare since I can't actually manage to sleep to have a nightmare. Attempting to sleep has become as much of a pain in the ass as Quinton.

I dreaded calling off work but had no choice. No way could I wear my Twisted Fox employee shirt without my bruise being on display. Luckily, Johnna took my shift with no questions asked.

It's three in the morning, and I've been bingeing *Shameless* episodes. Just as I hit the remote button that tells Netflix, *Yes, I have no life and am still watching*, my phone vibrates on my nightstand. My back goes straight. Quinton has instilled a fear in me that rises whenever it goes off. I stretch across the bed to retrieve it and see Lincoln's name flashing across the screen.

My body relaxes ... and then my stomach clenches as I ignore the call. When you're a romantic at heart, a guy you're falling for calling in the wee hours of the night is goals. But tonight, there's nothing but anxiety.

Anxiety he'll sense something is wrong.

Shoot, he definitely knows something is off, considering he's calling me in the middle of the night.

A text comes through seconds later.

Lincoln: Just tell me you're okay, Cass. Text me, call me, email me, tell Georgia, whatever. I need to know nothing is wrong.

I bite into my cheek as I read his text, so many raw emotions running through my head. My fingers itch to text him back. My heart yearns to call him and hear his voice—to make me forget about Quinton.

Me: I'm okay.

I owe him a response. He's been there for me. If our situation were reversed, if he'd avoided me this long, I'd blow his phone up *and* show up at his place.

I should tell him what's going on, but I can't. If I tell anyone Quinton is my stalker, they'll want me to go to the police. All that will do is provoke him further. Quinton is stupid and just wasting his time tormenting me. All I want to do is move on from him. It'd be in his best interest to leave me alone, so I can forget he exists.

Too bad all he's done is left reminders.

The texts.

My throbbing neck.

The ugly-ass bruise painting my skin.

He's texted me a few times, apologizing for his manic behavior, to which I replied with middle-finger emojis.

My thoughts are broken by my phone ringing again.

Lincoln.

"Are you ignoring me because of Isla?" he rushes out as soon as I answer, as if he's worried that he'll only get a second to speak.

Yes, I'm pissed about Isla, is what I want to scream.

Ask how dare he.

Mainly, I want to yell to release all the frustration from the past few days.

I exhale a stressed sigh. "I'm sure you'd be upset if you found some rando guy at my house *the day after* we had sex."

"Fair point." He blows out a breath. "I'm sorry, Cassidy. She showed up out of the blue. I want nothing to do with her. I've ignored her for months."

"Who is she?"

The truth test.

Let's see how much honesty Lincoln will give me.

"Can I come over? Explain myself?"

His question blindsides me as chills chase up my back. As I run his question through my mind again, my blood warms. If there's anything that'd make me feel safe, that'd give me a sense of security, it'd be Lincoln.

And fuck you, Quinton, for ruining this moment, when this perfect *man wants to come be with me, to comfort me. You've ruined it by scarring me.*

"Yeah," I breathe out. "You can."

"I'll be there in ten."

NOT WANTING TO WAKE GRACE, Lincoln texts me when he's outside. Tightening the strings around my hoodie, I check myself in the mirror before walking out of the bedroom.

There's no way I can pull this off. Lincoln will know that something is wrong. My heart thuds louder and louder as I tiptoe down the hall, uncertain of how the rest of the night will go. Inviting him here was dangerous. No doubt Lincoln will question me over my wardrobe choice. Before answering, I turn down the thermostat. If I make it the damn Arctic Circle in here, I can use that as my excuse.

Sorry, Grace.

Taking a reassuring breath, I swing the door open to find Lincoln standing before me. It's dark, and I can't see much, but there's no missing his body language.

Lowering his head, he reaches out and rubs the exposed skin of my cheek. "Thank you for letting me come over."

I chew on my lower lip as shivers barrel over my skin. Every part of me wants more of him.

"Come in," I croak, stepping to the side to allow him room.

Shutting the door behind us, he follows me down the hall to my bedroom.

Sitting on the edge of my bed, I wait for Lincoln to speak.

He shuts my bedroom door, and his eyebrows squish together as he studies me. "What's with the sweatshirt?"

Of course that's the first thing he notices.

I play with the strings of my shirt and glance away from him; my goal is to avoid all eye contact. "Grace likes to keep it cold in here."

"Bullshit. Georgia used to complain about how warm she kept it when they were roommates." He eyes me skeptically.

"Maybe she's had a change of thermostat heart." In need of a new subject, I tap the space next to me before slapping my hand against my knee. "You wanted to explain yourself?"

I hope my tone isn't bitchy, but regret rushes through my thoughts. I knew Lincoln would be suspicious of the hoodie. If we don't talk about another subject, that conversation will stray back to what I'm wearing. The problem is, I don't know if I can deter him from it all night.

Lincoln runs his hands through his thick hair before plopping down next to me, his leg brushing against mine. "You not showing up to Georgia's party or to work tonight scared the shit out of me." Shifting, he looks at me, the expression on his face brimming with exhaustion and concern. "I'm not sure if you're avoiding me because of what happened, but I can't …" His voice drifts as he searches for the right words … or the balls to say what is already on his mind. "I can't lose you, Cassidy. I can't lose you over a stupid miscommunication."

My mouth falls open, all thoughts of Quinton temporarily pausing.

"I can't lose you."

As if I wasn't hot enough in this hoodie, his admission sends a shot of warmth through my blood.

How long does it take the air conditioner to freeze this place up?

He squeezes his eyes shut. "That's why I'm here ... to make sure you don't hate me." Slowly opening them, he locks his heavy gaze on mine. "And if you do, then my next mission is to convince you not to."

Just when I thought this damn man couldn't be perfect enough, he has to show up and allow those words to fall out of his mouth. Never in my life have I experienced a man like this— a man who doesn't prioritize hanging with his frat boys over me, a man who's worried I'm upset and stresses about it, a man who has done nothing yet still wants to prove himself.

"I won't lie and say it didn't catch me off guard. It crushed my soul when I walked in to find you with her."

He doesn't break eye contact. "It was fucked up, I know."

"Had I not shown up, I would've never known about her."

"There's nothing to know about her. She means nothing to me."

"But she did once. I saw the hurt on her face when she left." It was the same raw emotion I'd feel if I lost Lincoln.

"Isla and I were *sex*. Nothing more." He signals back and forth between us. "You and me? That's not us. I want so much more than sex with you."

"How did you even get involved with her? It's not like you went to school together."

"She was one of my mother's best friends."

"Oh, wow."

"Back then, I had trouble connecting with women my age—"

"Or younger women, it seems."

He nods. "Fresh outta high school, I started dating one of my mother's friends. It was a short fling, and I guess word got out that I liked"—he clears his throat—"cougars. After graduating college, I got involved with Isla."

"While she was married?"

"She told me she was separated from her husband."

"Did it last long?"

"Almost a year."

"Wow. So, it wasn't just a *fling*. That's a long-ass time."

"On and off for a year, depending on where I was in my life."

"What happened when things broke off?"

"Her husband found out, and then I went to prison. She tried visiting a few times, but I refused. I want nothing to do with her. Her husband is the one who put my family in prison."

"What?"

He nods. "He found out about the affair and became dead set on bringing my family down. I guess there were whispers about fraudulent shit. That, or Isla fed him information after I broke things off with her. I'm not sure."

I like that he's telling me the truth.

"So, she really means nothing to you?"

"Absolutely nothing." His eyes soften. "You're the only woman who means something to me like that. You're the only woman I want to be with, Cass."

We're inches away from each other. Emotions high. My hormones on overdrive. Our eye contact is firm. It's dangerous, given my bruising. I've never connected with anyone like this before.

Unable to stop myself, I scoot closer to him, erasing any distance between us, and stare up at him.

With a slight hesitation, I brush my lips against his. With him, there's no hesitation. As soon as our mouths meet, he slides his tongue into my mouth.

As our lips tangle together, there's a raw emotion that didn't exist during our last kiss. This kiss, we're allowing every emotion toward the other to take the frontline, feeding it to the other.

He brackets his hands around my waist and tugs me onto his lap. There's a slight pain in the movement, but I ignore it. Tilting my hips forward, I rock against him, his cock hardening underneath me, causing me to grind on his lap.

"Cass," he groans, pulling back, resulting in an annoyed huff from me. "We need to talk about us more."

"Kiss first, talk later."

"Cass." This time, he says my name in more of a warning.

"Linc," I mock. "Just a minute. Give me a minute of kissing."

"Fine," he says, feigning annoyance. "We can have some fun before we go into the deep parts."

"Mmm ... deep parts." I grin.

"Jesus, babe. We have to get your mind out of the gutter."

"The gutter is the best place for the mind to be." I go in for another kiss, thankful he's giving in to our desires.

We start slow before it turns frantic, and he's lowering me onto my back.

"We need to get this damn sweatshirt off," he says, hovering over me.

Since his lips are on mine, I don't process his words. I'm so wrapped up in him, forgetting my real life, and I lift my arms to assist him. When I tip my head back, he rains kisses over my cheek while slowly drawing the hoodie over my body. I gasp in pain, knocking me out of my Lincoln haze, and reality smacks into me harder than my need for this man.

"What the fuck?"

I freeze at his tone.

He's staring at my neck in fury as I lie underneath him, wearing only a sports bra. Quinton's damage is on full display.

CHAPTER TWENTY-ONE

Lincoln

ANGER COILS THROUGH ME, tightening around my veins, like a snake as I stare down at her.

Cassidy's eyes are glossy with humiliation and panic. She rubs them, an attempt to blur away the evidence, before looking around the room in panic. She quickly tries to grab the hoodie from the floor, but it's out of her reach. In order to grab it, she'd have to get out of bed.

I glare at her neck as if it were my worst enemy, silently begging for answers while processing what I'm seeing. The skin is bruised, a fusion of black and purple, and swear to God, I see a damn handprint pressed against the dark colors.

"Cassidy," I grit out. "What the hell happened?"

"It's nothing," she rushes out, crossing her arms over her chest in an X motion.

"Bullshit," I snarl. "Someone put their goddamn hands on you. There's a handprint around your throat." I pull back to examine her further, my eyes hardening with every second. "Who did this to you?"

She stays silent.

"Cass, you're scaring me here."

"Just stop, okay." She swats at me, and taking the hint, I

draw back, so I'm no longer above her. Pulling herself up, she wraps the blanket tightly around her, as if a shield to her secrets. "You know what? It's late. You should probably go."

I flinch. "Whoa. How did we go from that to you kicking me out?"

She uses her arm to cover her eyes, to cover her tears. "I can't talk about it."

Reaching out, I gently pull her arm away from her face and use the pad of my thumb to brush away a tear. "Baby, if there's anyone you can talk to, it's me." I fight for my voice to be soft and nurturing, but there's no unclenching my jaw. I'm holding in my anger to comfort her.

She shakes her head, sobbing. "It doesn't matter."

"It does fucking matter," I grind out, and I hate that a hint of my softness disappears to make way for anger. "Give me a name. Who hurt you?"

She stares at the ceiling. "Some guy."

"Give me that guy's information, so I can go rip his fucking head off."

"I can't," she cries out, shutting her eyes as pools of tears resurface. The floodgates finally break, and tears for days fall down her cheeks like a rainstorm. "Please, just drop it. I haven't been sleeping. *Please*. Tonight, I don't want to talk about it. All I want to do is get some rest."

"Okay," I say gently, scooting in closer and staring down at her. "Have you been icing it?"

She slowly nods.

"Are you in pain?"

"No," she chokes out. "I took ibuprofen a few hours ago."

"Do you need more?" I rush out. "Something to drink?"

I have to push back my anger to care for her. It's late, she's exhausted, and right now, what she needs is sleep.

She rubs her forehead with the heel of her hand. "Really, all I want to do is lie down and sleep."

"Do you want me to go or stay?"

"Stay," she whispers, her body going stiff in alarm. "Please …
please stay."

"All right." I slide off the bed, stand, and pull my tee over
my head.

"And please hand me my hoodie." Desperation covers her
tone.

"Cass, you were burning up in here. The secret is out. You're
already in pain. At least don't make yourself sweat to death."

She nods.

I kick off my pants but leave on my boxer briefs. After
carefully climbing into bed, I stare over at her. "Light on or off?"

She hesitates, and from the look in her eyes, I know she's
been sleeping with the light on. She's been in fear of this
happening again. She snuggles into my side, being careful not to
hit the bruise.

"I'd pull you into my arms, but I don't want to hurt you," I
whisper.

She shifts closer. "Please. Being in your arms is what I need."

I drape my arm over her waist, my lips brushing along her
ear. "Get some sleep. I'm right here. Always."

I WANT to wring a motherfucker's neck.

Wring his neck and then his hands, so he can never put
them on a woman again.

I don't give two fucks if it ruins my life.

Someone put his hands on the woman I'm falling in love
with.

He deserves to be ripped to shreds with mine.

With my arm cradled around Cassidy's waist, as if shielding
her from any more harm, I shut my eyes. It's a game I've been
playing for hours now—since her breathing became steady and a
slight snore slipped through her lips.

I came over last night with the intent to lay out everything and explain Isla. As soon as I walked through the door and saw her dressed as if she were about to climb Mount Everest, I knew something was off. The thoughts of her wardrobe dissipated some when her lips hit mine … and then the shitshow started. Nothing mattered anymore—not Isla, not my problems, nothing—when I saw the bruise on her neck.

My blood ran cold.

And then hot with fury.

Somehow, someway, I need to convince Cassidy to open up about what happened. It won't be easy. The more time we spend together, the more I'm learning that Cassidy's been keeping slices of her life from me. I'm falling for this woman whose secrets I need to know.

My attention shoots to the floor when the hallway light flips on, the light shining through the bottom crack of the door meeting the carpet, and there's movement on the other side. Footsteps, quiet and soft. I slip out of bed, careful not to wake Cassidy, and tiptoe out of the bedroom, gently shutting the door behind me.

Grace is in the kitchen, a green turtleneck on, warming up a bagel in the toaster oven. She gasps, her hand pressing into her chest when she notices me. "Jesus, Lincoln. You scared me for a sec."

I smile gently. "Sorry about that."

She tips her head down the hall. "You two *finally* opened your eyes and realized you liked each other, huh?"

I pinch the bridge of my nose. "Something like that."

"I'm happy for you two. I swear, just in the short time she's been here, all she does is talk about you." She turns to open the fridge and grabs the cream cheese before snagging a knife from a drawer.

I pull out a barstool from underneath the island, take a seat, and clasp my hands together. "Have you noticed anything weird going on with her? Anyone coming over? Her being worried at night?"

"No." She shakes her head in hesitation as if checking she hadn't missed anything. "Not that I can think of. We don't see each other much since our schedules are the opposite. Why? Did something happen?"

I rub my temples, debating on how to answer. Blasting Cassidy's information would be an untrustworthy move, but Grace needs to know.

What if the guy comes back?

He could hurt her too.

Grace stares at me in question, a bagel in one hand and knife in the other.

"Nah, she just bailed on Georgia's party and work last night." I shrug. "Just worried me, is all." After I talk to Cassidy, I'll insist she tell Grace.

"I'll let you know if anything catches my attention." She spreads cream cheese over her bagel before holding it up. "Want one?"

"I'm good." I have no appetite.

"There's plenty of food here if you get hungry." She takes in the sight of me. "Although it appears you need sleep more than anything at the moment. Did you keep each other up that late?" A suggestive smile takes over her face. "I do have to say thank you for not being loud. Your brother and Georgia tended to make it known when they were ... *you know.*"

"Trust me, I know."

"Ah, forgot she's your new roomie."

I chuckle. "I plan to get some shut-eye here in a bit. Just wanted to say hi."

"Make yourself at home in the meantime, okay?" She finishes off her bagel and then grabs her bag. "I'm off to teach children."

When Grace is out of sight, I tip my head down and rest my forehead against the granite countertop. The chill pressing against my skin is a relief to my impending headache. The girl I'm falling in love with is going through something. The last thing I want to do is create more stress, but whoever did that to her needs to suffer the consequences for it. She needs to go to the cops, file a report, get a restraining order. If I don't find him and break his neck first.

That should be enough of a consequence for him.

Eh, maybe he needs a little castration too.

I grind my jaw, just thinking about it again.

Convincing Cassidy to turn him in will be one hell of a struggle.

With a stressed sigh, I stand, fill up a glass of water, and chug it down. I refill it and carry it to Cassidy's room for when she wakes.

Sliding back into her bed should be perfect, the best damn moment in the world, but there's that heavy secret looming over us now. I sink into her mattress, my body growing heavy, and finally shut my eyes, giving in to sleep.

THE BRIGHT SUN shining through Cassidy's window wakes me.

That'll be the only damn thing that's bright this morning. I'm preparing for the worst. No way can I sit back and not question Cassidy about who hurt her. No way can I not demand she turn him in.

She was petrified when her bruise was exposed, and it rotted me to the core that she'd been in pain for who knows how long. My guess is, since the day she skipped Georgia's party.

I'm unsure of how late we slept in, but rest was long overdue for us both.

When I peer down, I find her awake and squinting up at me in question.

"Good morning," I whisper, my throat dry.

She offers a sleepy smile. "Morning."

"How'd you sleep?"

"Good." She yawns. "Thanks to our spooning."

How bad has she been sleeping lately?

It appeared to have been days' worth of exhaustion on her face last night.

"Are you ready to talk about it?" I didn't mean for the words to release from my tongue so early. I'd planned to ease my way in and get her to crack without throwing out pressure.

"Nope." There isn't a moment of hesitation in her response.

"Too bad." I lift myself, causing her to do the same along with me. Scooting up the bed, we rest our backs against the headboard and stare ahead. "It needs to be talked about."

"I beg to differ." She pulls the blanket up her body, making sure there's no way for me to catch a glimpse of her bruising. "Subject change."

"Cass—"

"Please." Her voice breaks. "Please don't tell anyone about this."

"I won't tell anyone."

She bows her head. "Thank you."

"Because you will."

Her body tenses, her shoulder stiff against mine. "No, I won't."

My nostrils flare, and like last night, I'm struggling to constrain my anger. "What's your plan then, huh? To just let this guy get away with hurting you?"

Was it random?

Did someone come here?

How did this happen to her?

"It was one time," she mutters with no certainty in her voice.

It's a lie to not only me but also to herself.

"Who did it?" That seems to be the question of the motherfucking year ... that I'll never get the answer to.

"It. Doesn't. Matter," she grits out each word with a huff as if spitting out bad meat.

"You need to go to the cops."

She snorts. "Please, no. This isn't what I want to talk about first thing in the morning."

"If you wait too long, the bruising will fade, and you won't have a case." Shit like this needs to be reported fast. "What if he hurts someone else?"

Cassidy might not care about protecting herself, but she has a big enough heart that she'd be concerned about the guy doing it to another woman.

"I don't want a case," she snaps. "I want it to fade and to forget about it."

My heart squeezes in my chest.

This isn't the Cassidy I know.

"You can ask me a thousand ways to Sunday, and it won't happen," she continues. "This is a part of myself that I'd like to keep private, and I hope you respect that."

I cast a glance in her direction and shift to get a better look at her. The blanket is being used to conceal the damage as if she doesn't want me to be reminded of how bad it is.

As if she doesn't want *either* of us to be reminded of how bad it is.

Is she protecting him or herself?

"Are you shitting me?" I snap. "This isn't me being overbearing or nosy. Someone *assaulted* you, and he needs to face the consequences for his actions."

Her voice turns almost robotic. "It happened. It's over. I'm almost healed. Time to move on."

"Time to move on?" I huff out. "Time for you to get out of bed, and we'll march our asses right into the police station."

"I'm not going to the police. The guy who did this …" She pauses to gesture to her chest, slight sniffles releasing from her, and I know her well enough to know she's holding back her pain, her hurt, her tears. "He's the reason I was arrested … the reason I got kicked out of college, out of my sorority, why I had community service. He's already done enough to fuck up my life. I'm not trying to give him another reason to do more damage."

"He won't fuck anything up. I promise. I'll be here every night. I'll be your personal bodyguard—whatever you need for you to be safe. Whoever that guy is, I swear, you won't have to worry about him any longer."

She's silent.

Another trait I'm learning about Cassidy is her stubbornness.

"Cass—"

Frantically, with shaking arms, she jumps out of bed, as if it were on fire, and her voice cracks. "Discussion over."

I raise my voice. "Discussion not fucking over. I got your back, Cass. Whatever you need, I'm here."

"Just stop!" she screams, stabbing her finger in my direction. "I am done talking about this. You will not tell anyone, do you hear me?" There's a mix of panic, anger, and determination in her tone. "If you do, I swear to God, I'll never speak to you again." Her eyes finally meet mine, her gaze a mirror of her tone, and she claps her hands over her hips.

There is no changing her mind. She's hell-bent on protecting this asshole.

I clear my throat, prepared to say either she goes to the police or I tell her family, but I stop myself.

What do I do?

Keep quiet, so I don't lose her?

Go behind her back and tell someone, only to lose her?

Not to mention, no way in hell am I leaving her alone here.

Throwing one leg and then the other off the bed, I stand. She doesn't say anything, only waits for my next move.

I hold her gaze, praying she's the one who changes her mind.

Nothing.

Heat burns at her cheeks.

My eyes flash to her chest. The bruise is on full display now that the blanket isn't there acting as a protector. My blood boils while endless thoughts of self-doubt and uneasiness flicker through my mind.

"Fine," I finally say, defeated. "I won't say anything." I hate myself as the words climb out of my mouth—with force and pressure.

With regret.

Her body softens, a weight dragged off her shoulders, and for a moment, I'm proud of myself for unwinding that tension. Then I remember what I did, what I said, and how I shouldn't get any recognition for that because I agreed to keep this a secret between us.

"Thank you," she whispers, stepping closer and wrapping her arms around my waist.

I bow my head, kissing her hair, and feel like a fucking coward.

LOYALTY.

It's a hard drug for me.

A problematic drug for me.

I could do what I've done all my life—be loyal and keep my mouth shut.

After helping Cassidy undress and get into the shower, I step out of the bathroom and grab my phone from her bedroom.

I call Archer, and when he answers, I say, "Hey, I need someone to cover for me tonight at the bar."

"Dude," he grunts, "a little late notice. You can't call in this late and expect it to be okay."

"Something came up."

"What's that something?"

"I can't talk about it."

"Yeah, sorry, but I'm not letting you have the night off so you can spend time with a girl."

I clench my hand around the phone.

Now's not the time to mess with me, brother.

"Oh, says the guy who went MIA for nearly a fucking week, and I covered for you," I snap, attempting to keep my voice low in case Cassidy gets out of the shower soon.

"That was different." Agitation spreads along his words. "You can go to Cassidy's after."

"I don't want her alone."

"What?" That agitation alters into concern.

I lower my voice. "I came to her house last night since she was ignoring my calls."

"That probably has something to do with Isla's ass showing up at our place."

Pausing, I look from one side of the living room to the other before deciding to change my mind. With quick steps, I walk outside and shut the patio door behind me. What I'm about to do goes against everything I stand for, but I care about Cassidy too much. I have to tell someone before it eats away at me.

I tighten the phone against my face. "That, and she has a big-ass bruise around her neck after being assaulted."

"What the fuck?" Archer yells into the phone.

"Yeah, tell me about it. Now, do you understand why I'm not leaving her?" I kick at the grass with the same force I'd like to kick her assaulter's ass.

"Is she going to the cops?"

"She refuses to." My answer is a reminder of what I'm hiding for her. It's also a reminder of what I'm not really hiding and how I'm deceiving her by telling Archer this.

"Wait until her family finds out. No way will they let that slide. I'm surprised they haven't shown up on her doorstep yet."

"She hasn't told them, and my guess is, she won't."

"The fuck? I can't keep something like that from Maliki. He's one of my closest friends."

"I know." I blow out a ragged breath. "I know."

"Look"—his tone turns serious—"you need to tell them. Ditch your loyalty for a moment and think about Cassidy's well-being. What if the guy shows up again and does worse than what he did before?"

I scrub a hand over my forehead—an attempt to ease the regret, guilt, and headache pounding through. "I don't know. Taking care of her is my biggest priority at the moment. Just find someone to cover my shift for me."

Subconsciously, I'm not sure if I'm telling my brother this because I need someone to confide in or because I know he'll tell someone he shouldn't.

CHAPTER TWENTY-TWO

Cassidy

FOR THE PAST FEW DAYS, I've been through hell ... and then back after Lincoln showed up.

I'm not sure what I was thinking when I invited him over. In the back of my mind, I knew the bruise would come to light, knew he'd see it, but his comfort was what I needed as a Band-Aid to cover my pain.

Lincoln understands keeping secrets. I trust him, and even though it'll kill him, I know my secret is safe with him.

Will he constantly pester me to turn Quinton in? Absolutely.

Will he go behind my back and do it himself? No.

I've put him in a tough situation, made him go against what he thinks is right, and for him doing this for me, I'll forever be grateful.

Lincoln is in the shower when the doorbell rings. He told me he left the door unlocked and to run in there if there was danger. The poor guy has been scared to leave my side since he arrived last night.

Since I'm not expecting visitors and the last thing I want to do is talk to someone, I ignore the doorbell. If it's important, they'll call or text. If it's for Grace, she's at work, so they'll have to come back later anyway.

I prop my feet up on the coffee table, and the doorbell rings again.

And again.

And again.

Then my phone rings.

The hell?

Lincoln, who apparently has the ears of a moth, walks out of the bathroom, now freshly showered. His hair is dripping wet, and he's wearing black sweats and a tee. "Is that the doorbell?"

It rings again.

"Yes," I groan. "That's the doorbell."

"I got it."

Commotion erupts as soon as he answers the door, a hurricane storming into the living room, a rush of frantic voices taking in the space.

"Let me see it!" Rex, a man who rarely yells, does as soon as he comes into my view. His voice cracks when he continues, "I am going to kill whoever it was!"

"Babe," Carolina says, her tone sharp as she shoots me a despaired look.

"No!" he shouts. "I am going to kill whoever put his hands on her!"

The room falls silent. I stifle back a scream of dread. My leg muscles tighten, begging for me to flee, but I can't move.

I cannot speak or move.

No words are coming to me.

No excuse to justify why I'm hiding this.

I shoot a panicked glance to Lincoln, tears automatically approaching as a whimper leaves me.

That's all I can manage.

A damn whimper as I cover my mouth.

He told them.

He lied to me.

Betrayed me.

Now, my entire family is standing in my living room, staring at me and waiting for answers.

Shock and pain reside in Lincoln's eyes. He stands inches away from me, fists clenched, as we wait for whatever scene is about to unfold.

Rex's hands are shaking. He went through a similar situation with Carolina's ex giving her hell, and he knows the damage that can be done when someone decides they're not finished with you yet. Next to him stands Carolina, a deep concern etched along her forehead.

Kyle stands next to Rex, his face reddened with fury. My mother scurries over to me, nearly tripping over the rug, and collapses on the couch a few inches to my right. Panic fills her voice as he says my name over and over again, tears in her eyes.

"You think I can't hack into your shit and get answers in seconds?" Rex asks. "Who did this to you?" His attention briefly flicks to Kyle. "Wasn't there a guy in her car when she was arrested? Who was it?"

Them not even considering it's Lincoln confirms they heard the news from him.

Kyle shakes his head. "The guy wasn't in the police report." He throws his arm out toward me. "And this one here won't budge on providing a name."

"It doesn't matter," I cry out. "It's over with."

Lincoln curses underneath his breath at my response, but I don't glance over at him.

I can't.

Even though I should, so he could see the hurt and betrayal flowing through me.

I'm thankful that I'm wearing the hoodie. It's been off and on today, depending on my mood. Whenever I get up to use the bathroom, I see myself in the mirror and put it back on. Then as I get warm, I take it off.

Rex steps forward. "It does matter! Someone beat you up!"

"Calm down," Carolina tells him. "You guys can't just barge in here and demand answers."

"Damn straight we can," Kyle inputs.

"I get it, protective brothers and all," Chloe says, coming into view, and I want to die that nearly everyone I'm close with is here to witness my embarrassment. "It's hard for women to open up to their brothers. How about this? You guys chill in the living room and let us girls talk, okay?"

Before anyone answers, Maliki and Sierra walk through the door, their eyes shooting straight to me. Sierra's cheeks are red, and Maliki's fists are clenched.

"Bedroom. Now," Sierra demands.

I nod and hop off the couch, but before I can go to my bedroom, I whip around to face Lincoln.

"You told them," I cry out in despair.

"Did you expect him not to?" Rex asks. "I'd fucking hate the dude if he didn't."

Lincoln shakes his head, torture and guilt clouding his features. "I told Archer, and he must've told them." He gulps, taking a step closer to me. "I'm sorry, Cassidy, but we both know this is what needed to happen."

"Screw you," I hiss, tears approaching. "I trusted you!"

His eyes water. "I know." He bows his head. "I know."

"Archer told Cohen, who told Maliki," Sierra explains. "Archer was unsure what to do about an employee being in possible danger, so he asked Cohen. He told Cohen not to tell Maliki, but Cohen felt he couldn't hide something like that from his best friend."

"I'm going to kill my brother," Lincoln grits out, his eyes not leaving me.

"You should've told us," Maliki says.

"I just found out last night!" Lincoln screams, throwing up his arms. "I've been trying to talk her into going to the police and giving her time to process, not barging in and complicating shit for her. This has already messed with her head enough, and no offense, but she doesn't need people screaming at her while she's recovering. I planned to try to talk it out with her again today. She needs time, like some victims do."

Everyone is shocked into silence at Lincoln's response, no one expecting those words to leave him.

He thought he was going to change my mind.

Wow. Is that why he stayed here with me—to try to talk me into turning Quinton in?

Sierra gently grabs my elbow. "Your bedroom. Now."

I nod, turning my back on the man whose betrayal hurts deeper than Quinton's, and everyone with a vagina follows me into my bedroom.

"Let me see," Sierra demands, taking the lead, her tone as sharp as Rex's. "I'm not going to yell, but I need to see."

While taking a seat on the bed, my mother snivels, her eyes glued to me like her favorite soap opera.

With a heavy breath, I pull my sweatshirt over my head.

"I'm going to kill the bastard myself," Sierra hisses.

"Just …" I shake my head. "It's over."

"Is it, though?" Carolina asks. "How do you know he won't come back and do the same … or worse? From my experience, it's not over until the guy is set straight or is scared enough to leave you alone."

"I think it's time you talk about what happened," my mother says. "Or I'm involving your father."

"Or we have Rex hack into your shit and find out everything," Sierra chimes in.

"Invasion of privacy much?" I huff out.

"I'll take you being safe over you being angry with me," my mother replies.

CHAPTER TWENTY-THREE

Lincoln

THIRTY MINUTES HAVE PASSED since Cassidy went to her bedroom to spill her secrets ... or at least since she left the room with people attempting to get her to spill her secrets.

Thirty minutes of me pacing, of Rex cursing every three seconds, and of Kyle saying he's going to strangle the guy nonstop.

Cassidy is a tough nut to crack.

Doesn't give in easily.

And I've never seen such determination from someone who's breaking inside.

I wouldn't be surprised if they were in there for hours, begging her to talk to them, to give them anything to get the man who hurt her in trouble.

She's a victim.

But Cassidy won't admit that part yet.

We freeze when Sierra comes into view, her attention shooting straight to me. "She wants to talk to you." Her face is unreadable, and she doesn't disclose a word more.

The other women stand behind her.

I nod, shoving my hands into my pockets, and walk around them.

When I enter the bedroom, Cassidy is on the bed, her shoulders curled over her chest. When she raises her head, her face is red and puffy, tearstained, and I rush over to her.

"Baby," I whisper, collapsing to my knees in front of her. I want to console her, hold her, wipe away every single tear, and make sure she never feels pain like this again.

Not only physical pain torments Cassidy.

It's emotional pain.

Tearing her apart.

And I hate it.

She jerks away from me. "How dare you."

She's cold.

Hostile.

Taking out the anger on me that she should be taking out on someone else.

I can take it, though.

I'm strong.

I'll take every emotion she needs to release.

"I …" I stutter for the right words, but there are none that'll bring her comfort, none that'll convince her that I didn't tell Archer about her out of malice. But in reality, I know my brother. In the back of my mind, I knew he couldn't keep that information to himself, not when it came to a woman being in trouble. I had him do my dirty work, hoping I wouldn't have that guilt bearing down on my shoulders. "I didn't know he'd tell."

She sucks in a sob as she glares down at me. "Bullshit. You knew exactly what would happen. You think he'd keep his mouth shut about that? You know how much I trusted you, telling you that, but it turns out, you're just as bad as them."

"You can trust me," I croak out, my hands and voice pleading.

"Please leave."

I slam my eyes shut. "Cass—"

She shakes her head, sniffling back tears. "Get out, Lincoln."

I LEFT.

I left because she needed space, and with her family there, I knew she was safe.

I left because I'm going to get answers.

For years, I've kept my mouth shut for those I love, to protect them.

For my father.

For my grandfather's company.

I've kept so many damn secrets that I could get lost in them.

It was different with Cassidy.

Someone hurt her.

She's not committing crimes.

I went to prison for protecting my father.

I'd go to prison to protect her too.

If she won't tell me what is going on, I'll figure it out myself.

I know just the person to ask for help.

It's also the last person who'd ever want to help me.

LOUIS BERBAN.

Iowa's district attorney.

The main force behind putting my father and me in prison.

Isla's husband.

No one was looking into my father until Louis found out I was sleeping with his wife.

It was bullshit since I thought they were separated. When he found out, all hell broke loose. The first thing he did was tell my mother that I was sleeping with her friend, a woman her age, which broke her heart. He also made it a point to disclose that Isla wasn't the first friend of my mother's I'd *spent time in bed with*.

Him going to my mother caused friction between us. It gave

her more trust issues than she already had. I never went looking for older women. It'd just … happened.

"I thought I'd never see your face again."

I stare at Louis from the doorway of his office. He sits behind his massive cherry-wood desk with built-in bookshelves behind him, shelves filled with law books and family photos.

It was risky, barging into his office and asking his secretary to speak to him. I figured he'd send security out to escort me off the premises, but surprisingly, he told her to send me in.

Pushing his black-rimmed glasses up his nose, he waits for me to speak.

"Trust me," I say, "I never wanted to see yours again."

"Why are you here?" He flicks his Montblanc pen in his hand before sliding it into the pocket of his suit jacket. "To beat me up now that you're free? To keep sleeping with my wife? What?"

Should I tell him his wife is still visiting me?

Considering I need a favor from him, I keep that tidbit of information to myself. I'll make it clear to Isla to leave me the fuck alone or her husband will be hearing from me. For once, I need the law on my side.

I venture deeper into his office, stopping in front of his desk, and stand tall. "I need a favor."

He snorts. "Why would I do *you* any favors?"

"Do me a favor, and I won't fuck your wife again." I step closer, leveling my eyes on him. "How's that sound?"

It's an asshole move, but my attitude needs to match his.

Berban can't lock me up for dicking down his wife. Not that I would, but threats seem to work well. It's what he did to me for months before locking me up.

His dark brows knit together. "You walk into my office, talk about fucking my wife, and want a favor from me? Did they beat the sense out of you in prison or something?"

"You scratch my back, and I'll scratch yours. Or rather, I'll leave your wife alone."

Not that I'd touch Isla with a ten-foot pole, but she's Louis's weakness. Dude loves her more than he loves anything.

He leans back in his leather chair, crossing his arms. "What can I help you with, Callahan?"

"I have a friend who's in trouble."

He keeps staring, not muttering a word.

"And I need help figuring out how to get her out of trouble."

"What do you want me to do?"

I gesture to his computer. "Look up her record. There's a guy who's messing with her."

His back straightens. "Define *messing with her*."

"She's bruised up." I make a circling motion around my chest. "My guess is, from a guy she was arrested with. His name isn't in the police report, but I'm hoping your report has additional information you can give me."

"What's her name?" He pounds a finger onto the keyboard.

"Cassidy Lane."

He freezes. "Lane ... as in the daughter of the mayor of Blue Beech?"

"I think so."

I knew Cassidy's father was the mayor of their town, but she doesn't talk about him much.

Surprisingly, Louis types on his computer, moving his mouse as he reads the screen. "Hmm ... she only has one charge. A drug misdemeanor. It appears she was pulled over, and there were drugs in the car. Not enough to consider distribution, but it was pretty damn close."

"What else?" That information is shit I could've easily googled or had Rex hack to find.

"That's about it. Police report said she was pulled over with her boyfriend. She denied the drugs being hers, but the boyfriend said they didn't belong to him either. It was her car, so it became her charge. When they asked where she got them, she wouldn't answer any questions. She was bailed out six hours later, put on probation since it was a first-time offense, and sentenced to community service." He shrugs. "Not much there for you."

"The boyfriend." I hastily point at the computer. "Does it give a name?"

He squints at the screen. "A man by the name of Quinton ..." He pauses, recognition dawning on him. "Landing. Quinton Landing."

"Well, fuck me," I mutter.

He nods. "That might be a problem for you, huh?"

"Could be, but at this point, I don't care."

In the Iowa investment industry, Landing Holdings was the biggest competitor to Callahan Holdings. As Callahan Holdings began to spiral, Landing rushed in to poach our clients, giving them the notion they could get in trouble by allowing *criminals* to work with their money. They painted us as people who couldn't be trusted. That we stole money from our clients and would be spending the rest of our lives in jail. The Landing family is as conniving as they come.

Now, I need to figure out if Quinton is the one who hurt Cassidy.

Time to hunt him down.

I attended private school with his older brother, so I can always start there.

"Can you pull up his address for me?" I ask Louis.

He looks at me as if I grew a horn out of my head. "No."

"Come on."

He shakes his head.

"You put me in prison ... give a man a little favor now."

"I've told you all I can." Even after everything that's happened, there's a hint of remorse on his face.

CHAPTER TWENTY-FOUR

Cassidy

IT TOOK me forever to convince my family to leave.

Correction: *most* of my family to leave.

Sierra and Maliki have stayed, wanting to *hang out* for a while.

Code word for: babysit me.

While in my bedroom with my mom and the girls, I revealed my bruise but held my ground. I'm not telling them who did it or providing any details.

It's my story to tell.

And I'll tell it when I'm ready.

If I'm ever ready.

They tried and finally gave up—at least on getting a name. When I asked them to have Lincoln come into my bedroom and talk, I wasn't sure what I was going to say.

Betrayal had sunk its claws into my thoughts. None of this would have happened—my entire family wouldn't have shown up like a circus—had he not told someone. A light of hope had begun to surface that day, positive thoughts of forgetting about Quinton approaching, and my future with Lincoln was all I was looking toward. And then Rex had barged through the door like a madman, dissipating all that confidence.

Because of Lincoln, they know.

Because of Lincoln, my family sees me as dishonest, as weak, as someone who needs to be watched.

Johnna is covering my shift at Twisted Fox again tonight. Cohen was understanding when I texted and told him. It's time for me to come up with a plan. As much as I love working at the bar and living in Anchor Ridge, what happens now?

Now that people know what happened to me.

I don't want to be known as Cassidy Lane, the girl who was abused, needs saving, and couldn't hold her own against some jerk.

I'm in the living room, staring at the TV yet not processing anything happening on the show. Maliki and Sierra are in the kitchen, whispering and warming up frozen pizzas. My head rises, my gaze shooting toward the entry, when the front door opens.

Grace appears, strutting into the house, wearing a wool jacket, pencil skirt, and kitten heels. She smiles at me, dimples popping out along her fair cheeks, and drops her computer bag to the floor before relaxing in the chair next to the couch.

"Hey, babe," she says. "You have the night off again?"

I stare at her, blinking, struggling to get a read on her. "Do you know?"

"Know what?" She genuinely looks confused, which confuses me because I was under the impression that the group told each other everything.

Gripping the hem of my sweatshirt with my hands nearly trembling, I drag it up to reveal my bruise. It happens without thought, as if my brain told my body I could trust Grace.

Or maybe I'm sick of hiding it.

She gasps, her mouth falling open, her eyes wide. "Oh my God! Who did that to you?"

"An ex." My voice is fainter than a whisper as the truth releases from my lips for the first time, and I shove the sweatshirt back down.

And just like that, Grace is the first person I've muttered those words to. I'm not going into specifics and telling her it was Quinton, but it's more than what I've given anyone else. I'm not sure if it's because there's an ease, a comfortableness, with Grace or because I finally want to talk about it so I can stop thinking about it incessantly.

All her attention is on me, her forehead creasing in concern. "Did you call the cops?" She jumps up from her seat. "Do you need anything? Ice? A drink?"

I was worried about telling Grace this for two reasons: one being that she might think it's unsafe to be my roommate and the other being that her father is a judge and she might ask him to step in.

"I thought I could trust Lincoln, but he ran his mouth. So, my family knows." I blow out a breath. "I'm surprised the news hasn't hit you because I'm pretty sure Georgia knows."

Her face softens, and a genuine smile that's meant to be helpful and comforting spreads along her lips. "It's a personal matter. Yes, we're a tight-knit group, but if one of us confides in another, that secret stays with that person. Georgia wouldn't tell your story, wouldn't disclose your secrets, unless she knew it was okay with you for her to do so. Just like I won't mention this to anyone unless you're comfortable with it."

"If only Lincoln had followed that same structure."

"I'm sure it sucked for him to break your trust." She sighs. "But what happened to you is serious. Someone physically assaulted you ... and it's scary. Trust me, I know. But are you protected now? Will they come back and continue messing with you? Violence tends to lead to more violence."

"I know; I know."

"I'm sure Lincoln was trying to protect you because he cares about you."

WE'RE in the living room, munching on cauliflower pizza, when the front door opens again, and Lincoln stalks into the living room.

He's called and texted a few times, but I've ignored them. Uncertainty of where we're at has stopped me every time. I trusted him, and he proved I'd been stupid in doing that. Maybe he didn't plan on Archer telling my family, but he still went behind my back and told Archer. What I had shown Lincoln, told him, was supposed to stay between him and me.

Not Lincoln, me, and my entire family.

If the tables were turned, I'm not sure what I'd do either. *If one of my friends or family were hurt, would I keep that secret or reach out to someone in concern?*

Everyone goes quiet, Sierra even pausing the show we're watching, when Lincoln comes to a halt in front of me.

"Is it Quinton?" he asks, staring down at me, not sparing a glance in anyone else's direction. "Is he the one who hurt you?"

A sudden coldness hits my core.

How does he know Quinton?

All attention plasters to me.

"That's none of your business," I grit out, clenching my fists, my nails digging into the sensitive skin of my palms.

"Quinton?" Sierra asks. "Quinton who?"

"No one!" I shout. "Just some stupid guy I hung out with at school."

"Quinton Landing," Lincoln says, his voice firm. "The guy you were with the night you were arrested. The guy who went free while you didn't. Is *he* the one who put his hands on you?"

Why would he do that?

Say his name in front of everyone.

In seconds, my sister and Grace will be looking up Quinton Landing. Sierra will examine every social profile of his before sending the information to my brothers.

Lincoln won't sit back and allow me to remain silent.

I slap my hand onto the couch before standing. "Can we talk in private?"

He nods.

I walk around the coffee table, all eyes on me, and Lincoln follows me to my bedroom.

Whipping around, I face him, a deep scowl on my face. "Why would you do that?"

"Do what?" He raises a brow, and my outrage heightens that he'd ask *do what*, as if he didn't just barge in here.

"Go and say his name in front of everyone." I shake my head, grimacing. "How'd you even find out about Quinton?"

When I dated Quinton, I didn't talk about him with my family. Sure, I briefly mentioned I went on a few dates with a guy, but I tended to be more private, knowing how they like to get involved. I was in college, living the life, and wanted to keep that life to myself for as long as I could.

"Why wouldn't I say his name?" Lincoln asks. "Is he the guy who did that to you?"

I bite into my lower lip.

"It was him, wasn't it?"

I'm not much of a liar.

There's a difference between lying and hiding information from someone.

As Lincoln stares at me, his eyes filled with concern, I can't lie to his face.

I bow my head and nod, a flight of embarrassment soaring through me, though relief also treads behind it.

"Please, Cass, please turn him in," he begs, his voice nearly breaking.

"Just …" I blow out an uneasy breath. "Give me a day to digest everything, okay? I hadn't planned for this to happen today. I'm bruised up." I move my gaze to him, narrowing my eyes. "I'm very upset with you, and I need to let my mind rest for a minute before I do anything."

His stare is pained in my direction. "I don't want you staying here alone."

"Grace—"

He keeps talking. "Grace won't be able to do anything if Quinton comes back to mess with you."

I nod in agreement. Nor would I want to put Grace in that situation. I feel bad enough that Quinton came here, and all night, I've waited for her to ask if it's safe to stay here. Grace doesn't like being alone; she checks that the alarm is set numerous times before going to bed at night. There's a history there that I haven't felt comfortable enough to ask about yet.

"Trust me, no one in my family will leave me alone right now. Even though I wish they would for a moment." My shoulders slump. "Quinton hasn't returned in days. He came over, we fought, and it happened. He freaked out as soon as he realized what he'd done."

"If no one can stay with you, you call me, okay?"

As much as I want to tell him I'd prefer it was him staying at my side, I don't.

I don't because I'm still so angry with him.

"Okay," I whisper.

"Promise not to ignore me."

"I'm not making that promise," I say. "I'm angry with you, Lincoln. Pissed off beyond belief that you went behind my back."

"Hate me if you want, but at least I'll know you're safe." He takes my hand in his, careful at first, waiting to see if I'll pull away, and when I don't, he uses it to pull me into his hold. "If it takes you hating me to keep you safe, then I guess the heartache and pain I'm experiencing is worth it because your safety is the most important thing to me. Not my heart, not my feelings. *You.*"

I shake in his arms and choke back a sob.

What do I do?

I can't forgive him. I trusted him, and he broke my heart.

CHAPTER TWENTY-FIVE

Lincoln

"WHAT DID you do to make Georgia not hate you anymore?" I ask Archer, sipping on my coffee and narrowing my eyes at him. "I still can't believe you said something to Cohen."

Sleep was like a blocked-off street to me last night. All I thought about was Cassidy.

Is she safe?

Will Quinton hurt her again?

Will she ever forgive me?

With our talk after I returned to her house, mentioning Quinton, I don't think she hates me. I'm scared that she won't trust me any longer, and if you can't trust someone fully, can you be with them? I don't want to have a half-assed relationship with someone who is on the fence on whether they can share their deepest secrets with me.

I'd been tested, and I failed.

I failed and told my brother what I'd said I wouldn't.

Somehow, someway, I need to earn her trust back while also fighting for her to go against Quinton.

In the end, do I regret telling my brother? No.

Because it might convince Cassidy to turn Quinton in.

There's a stronger pulling force alongside me now.

Archer gapes at me. "Dude, don't try it. You knew I'd tell him."

I scrub a hand over my face, not admitting that he's right.

"And as far as the Georgia hating me question, I'm not sure how she doesn't hate me." He chuckles. "My advice is to do everything in your power to make things right and earn her trust back."

"It's hard to earn back her trust when all I can think about is that motherfucker hurting her."

"Don't get yourself in trouble, brother. You've already gone to prison once."

I shift in my seat. "What would you do if someone did that to Georgia?"

He delivers a dark look at the thought. "Rip their head off and feed it to them through a straw."

That's how my brother understands feelings. You ask how he'd feel if it happened to someone he loved. Otherwise, the dude is cold as the Arctic.

"Exactly," I deadpan. "You can't expect me to sit back and forget about it. I want to rip his head off and feed it to him through a spoon ... it'd be more hands-on."

Archer holds up a finger. "A. I don't have a criminal record." He holds up another. "B. I'm in love with Georgia. Are you in love with Cassidy?"

I stay quiet.

Am I in love with Cassidy?

It's an internal battle.

I've never been *in love* with anyone. Or so I thought.

But what is love? Is there a specific destination, a specific rhythm your heart follows until a light dings inside your head that says, *Hey dumbass, you love this person?*

How do you know you love someone when love is an invisible thing?

"Think about it," he says, interrupting my thoughts. "Think

about the risk and your feelings for her. And then do whatever you need to do to protect her."

WHAT I'M ABOUT to do will create the opposite of convincing Cassidy not to hate me.

But hey, if I already started off by disappointing her in this situation, might as well keep adding to the list that'll only lead me deeper into the hole of her possibly never speaking to me again.

"I have some information," I tell Maliki and Rex.

Not only did sleep evade me last night, but I also spent most of the time looking up Quinton. From what it appears on his Instagram, dude is a prick who regularly uses hashtags like #richkids, #getlikeme, #bejealous. His feed is full of photos of him and his frat brothers in their loafers and button-ups, lined up with beers in their hands, and sporting Gucci belts. I had to pour myself a drink out of embarrassment for him.

Hopefully, it'll change to #iscurrentlyincarcerated next.

Before leaving Cassidy's, I put Rex's and Kyle's numbers into my phone. We've shared a few texts here and there, but I asked to get together, so I could give them everything I know about Quinton. Kyle is a police officer, and from what I've heard, Rex is our generation's Kevin Mitnick—only without the criminal charges.

That's what led me to Rex's kick-ass house, and I'm not that easily impressed when it comes to real estate. The guy has everything teched out. I could spend all day asking him questions.

"Whatcha got, bro?" Rex asks.

"The guy who hit her is Quinton Landing. He's also the guy who was in her car the night she was arrested. He got to walk free. She obviously didn't." I suck in a deep breath. "A while back, she told me her ex was the biggest drug dealer on campus, to which she didn't know, and he borrowed her car. That's why there were drugs in it. If you put two and two together, Quinton's face lights up in guilt every damn time."

"Landing." Rex snaps his fingers, searching for words. "Name sounds familiar."

"From Landing Holdings?" Kyle asks.

I nod. "I'm going to pay him a visit. Is Cassidy still at Sierra's?"

Maliki texted me last night, letting me know that Cassidy was crashing with them.

"She is, but last I heard, she plans to stay at her place tonight," Rex replies with a hint of disapproval. "We're going to make sure one of us is there with her at all times."

Oh boy, Cass will love that.

"Let's rewind back to your previous statement," Kyle says. "It's not smart for you to *pay him a visit*. You're fresh out of prison, and the last thing you need is to go back."

It's a struggle not to smile at his comment. His concern over me returning to prison means he doesn't see me as a threat to his sister. If he did, he wouldn't give two shits about me being locked up again because it'd mean I'd be away from Cassidy.

"And here we thought you didn't like him," Rex says to his brother with a smirk.

Kyle shoots me an apologetic smile. "Sorry, dude. I was worried about my sister."

"Nah, it's cool," I reply. "I'd probably do the same if I had a sister."

"Do you know this Quinton guy?" Rex asks.

"Not personally," I reply. "I looked at his social media, know his brother and family, but that's it. I wanted to make sure I gave you guys his name, so you're as updated as I am." I turn my attention to Kyle. "You have connections to look into him, to possibly get him arrested even if Cass doesn't go to the cops. That's your job." I direct my gaze to Rex. "Your job is to try to find whatever shit you can on him ... and to get me an address."

REX SCORED me the address I was looking for in ten minutes. They weren't lying. Dude has skills. Without waiting for them, I got in my car, plugged the address into my GPS, and was on my way.

Thirty minutes later, I'm pulling into a neighborhood I've frequented enough that I know the gate code. Apparently, they don't change that shit for years. I drive past million-dollar house after million-dollar house and cut a right before parking across the street from a two-story red-brick home.

It seems too expensive for a college student, so it might be his family's home, or he could live off-campus. I'm sure the guy would rather be in a home like this than some stinky frat house. Not sure if this is where he's at, and wanting more information, I snatch my phone from the cupholder to call Rex and confirm this is Quinton's current address. I stop after unlocking my screen when a silver Benz pulls into the drive.

The driver's door opens, and a man in a fitted black suit steps out.

A man I recognize.

I do the same, slamming my door shut behind me, and unlike him, I'm in a black jacket and jeans when I move toward him.

The guy, as if sensing my presence, turns around, squinting in my direction. "Lincoln Callahan?" He cocks his head to the side, attempting to appear casual, but there's no missing the way his shoulders straighten. "What's up, man?"

That's right.

Be nervous because your family shit-talked mine to death.

Without bothering with small talk, I say, "Where's Quinton, Christopher?"

He sniffs, his face overconfident. "What do you want with my brother?"

I clench my hands. "I want him to stop putting his hands on women."

The air goes quiet, leaves blowing across the drive and over our feet.

"The fuck are you talking about?" Christopher asks, that overconfidence slipping away like the clients he poached from us.

"He hurt a woman, choked her, and she has the evidence." A tone of certainty and warning is clear with my response.

"What?" he hisses. "Is she going to the cops?"

"She's considering it."

"What's her name?" he stutters, his Ivy League education not strong enough to have trained him for this conversation.

"You'll find out when she files the police report against him."

I stop myself from disclosing Quinton's drug dealing. It'd be stupid to talk to Christopher because he'll call his brother to give him a heads-up as soon as I leave here.

Before I turn around to leave, Christopher, with a voice brimming with snark, says, "Might want to be careful. You wouldn't want to go back to prison, would you?"

This smug motherfucker.

"I've already been there once," I sneer at him, my lips curling into a cold smile. "What's another sentence? Especially if it's punishment for beating the shit out of the guy who put his hands on my girlfriend."

That smugness falls to the ground along with the leaves. "I'll talk to my brother."

Without a word, I turn around and return to my car. He stands in his drive, watching me, before hastily shoving his hand into his pocket and dragging out his phone.

I do the same and dial Rex's number as soon as I return to my car. "That's his brother's address. I need Quinton's campus addy."

"On it."

Just in case Christopher gets slick and calls the police for my trespassing, I drive off, and Rex has a new address for me as I'm pulling out of the neighborhood.

"Text it to me," I demand.

"You're not doing this alone," Rex argues. "We don't want you to get in any more trouble."

"I got this. You just go to Cassidy in case Quinton tries to get to her."

CHAPTER TWENTY-SIX

Cassidy

"HEY, SIS," Rex says over the phone. "I need to come over. My Wi-Fi is down, and I have some work to do."

Even though he can't see me, I roll my eyes. "You're going to make a thirty-minute drive to my house to use Wi-Fi when you can go to any coffee shop or to another sibling's—who all live much closer to you, by the way? Seems legit and not at all suspicious."

He chuckles. "Someone needs to be there with you. Maliki has to go into work, so I'm clocking in."

Clocking in.

I hate that I'm like a job to them.

"Look, I'm fine here on my own," I say, chugging the rest of my water. "Plus, Grace is here, so I won't be alone when Maliki and Sierra leave. Problem solved. Go fake need Wi-Fi somewhere else."

"The Wi-Fi is down everywhere else."

He hangs up, and ten minutes later, there's a knock on the door. I answer it to find Carolina and Rex standing in the doorway. Since he lives a good half hour away, no way was he sitting at home, struggling to connect to Wi-Fi.

"Oh, look," Sierra says, gasping dramatically. "What a surprise."

"Shush," I grumble, shooting her a dirty look. "You knew the *surprise* was coming."

Carolina gives me a hug hello, and then Sierra gives me a hug good-bye. She tells me to call or text if I need anything.

"If you're going to play babysitter, at least order some pizza," I tell Rex as we make our way into the living room.

He chuckles. "I can do that in exchange for the Wi-Fi."

"Oh, yes, the Wi-Fi."

"CAN I say something without you being pissed at me?" Rex asks.

Grace, Carolina, and he are all in the living room with me as we watch TV and devouring slices of greasy, cheesy pizza.

"Depends on what it is you say." I pop a pepperoni into my mouth.

"You shouldn't be mad at Lincoln," he says matter-of-factly. "You know that, right?"

I point at him with my slice of pizza. "Yep, that definitely pisses me off."

It's a topic I've battled with myself over. Since I kicked Lincoln out, I've done nothing but think about our argument, think about how I asked him to leave with such sorrow filling my heart. I've thought about what I'd do in a situation like that, whether it be the person I'm falling in love with, a close friend, or a sibling.

How hard would it be to keep something like that from others?

To know they could be in trouble but wouldn't do anything about it?

To know that something worse could happen?

"Come on," he says with a chuckle. "Hear me out first."

My brother is brilliant, one of the smartest men I know, and his problem-solving skills are out of this world. He also has a heart of gold. At the beginning, his and Carolina's relationship had some bumps in the road because she was keeping secrets from him—the same way I did with Lincoln.

"Fine," I mutter. "Let me hear it."

"Our situation was similar but not similar."

I scoff, "Uh, that's not a great way to start because it doesn't make any sense."

He sets his plate to the side, scoots to the edge of the couch, and rests his elbows on his knees, pinning his attention on me. "I was worried about Carolina and looked through her phone … and hacked into her ex's shit … all to protect her." A glimpse of frustration flashes along his face at the memory, and Carolina scoots in closer to him, squeezing his knee. "When you care about someone that much, you care about their safety more than them possibly being mad at you. Had Lincoln not gone to someone, had he not wanted you to go to the cops, I'd be questioning his feelings for you. At least talk to him, and please, for the love of God, go to the cops."

His words are another punch in the reality face for me.

Would I have questioned Lincoln's actions later if Quinton were to come back and do more damage or if he decided he wanted me to permanently go away, so he wouldn't worry about me tattling on him?

And had I forced Lincoln to keep that secret, how bad would it have torn him up inside if Quinton were to take things more serious?

I sigh. "I know … I'm just coming to terms with everything."

"Have you thought any more about going to the cops?" Rex asks, an expectant look on his face.

I stay quiet and slowly shake my head.

"When my ex threatened me with a sex tape, I was terrified to go to the cops," Carolina starts but then hesitates when all eyes fall on her. "I was scared of retribution from him, but I knew it was what I had to do. I had to do it for me, so I'd no longer live in fear and also to protect other women he might hurt in the future." Her eyes are wide as she focuses on me. "It's scary, I know, but you'll feel better. I had a longer timeframe to do it since most of my proof was digital, but it's not that easy with you. When your bruises fade, the chances of him getting the punishment he deserves will also fade. I'll go with you. I'll be by your side if you want someone who's experienced it."

Carolina, my brother's sweet best friend turned girlfriend. They're opposites of each other—her quiet and reserved, him loud and outgoing.

"Me too," Grace says. "Whatever you need from me, I'm there."

Their support means everything to me.

It's a comfort to know I have women at my side who understand what I'm going through and are offering to help. And Carolina and Lincoln are right about Quinton having the power to hurt another woman if he gets away with what he did to me. Or what if he sells drugs to someone and they OD?

I play with my hands in my lap. "I'll think about it." Standing, I force a smile. "I need to use the bathroom."

Moving toward my bedroom, I dig my phone from my pocket and call Lincoln.

He doesn't answer.

CHAPTER TWENTY-SEVEN

Lincoln

"YOU TOUCH HER AGAIN, and I'll kill you."

Growing up, I got along with most people, so I wasn't involved in many fights. That changed when I went to prison. There, you have to prove yourself, prove you can't be messed with. Prison is where I established my fight experience.

Tonight's fight isn't to prove myself.

It's to prove that Cassidy can't be messed with. Quinton needs to know that if he pays Cass another visit, there will be hell to pay.

On the drive to Quinton's campus apartment, my mind raced with reminders of Rex and Kyle telling me to wait for them and Archer warning me to stay out of trouble. Going back to prison isn't something I want, but if it's for Cassidy, I'll do it.

The new address Rex provided was correct. No one spared me a look as I took the stairs to the fifth floor, knocked on the apartment door, and asked if he was Quinton. The moment he said yes, I gripped him around his scrawny throat, dragged him through the entryway, and threw him against the wall—similar to what it appeared he'd done with Cassidy.

He yelled, "What the hell?" at the same time I kicked the door shut with my shoe, blocking out as much noise as I could.

He cries out when I draw back my fist and punch him. My fist stings when it connects with his jawbone, a throb shooting up my veins. He slides down the wall and slumps to the tiled floor like a crumpled pile of laundry.

I kneel down to his level, inches from him, spit flying from my lips as I snarl, "Go near her again, and I'll kill you."

It's not an empty threat.

Cassidy's bruise will haunt me until the day I die. I'd do anything in my power to prevent any harm or hurt to Cassidy.

"Fine, whatever," he groans, his head falling against the floor, small sprinkles of blood next to him. "She isn't worth this shit." He nearly rolls into the fetal position, in fear of another strike from me. Sweat lines his forehead. Blood, alongside slobber, drips from his mouth.

I bend my knee back, gearing to give him a swift kick to the ribs, but he cowers, staring up at me in alarm.

"Hurt me any worse, and I'll make sure you go back to prison." His eyes are panicked, his words sputtered. "Don't think I don't know who you are, Lincoln Callahan."

I scoff, my hand sore and shaking. "Go to the cops? How about we go now, huh? We can explain why I beat the shit out of you." I deliver a mocking smile. "It'll be fun."

He spits at my feet.

"Stay away from her." I bend at the knee, my face in his. "Her brother is a cop. I have connections from being *locked up*, and we've hacked into your shit. Mess with her again, and you'll regret it. Your daddy won't be able to get you out of that mess with your drug-dealing ways."

I shoot him a cold smile full of warning before nudging his knee with the toe of my shoe. I spent less than ten minutes with the asshole, but hopefully, I've knocked some sense into him. As I'm walking out, I rub my hand down the outside of my pants, wiping away Quinton's blood.

I'm practically bouncing on my toes from the adrenaline while returning to my car. Quinton didn't put up much of a fight and backed down in seconds. If he's scared of me, then he'll stay away from Cass.

As I slide into the driver's seat and pluck my phone from my pocket, I find a missed call from Cassidy. My palms sweat as I stare at her name, my heart pounding harder than it did when I was punching Quinton, and I don't waste a second before calling her back.

"Hey," I breathe out into the speaker when she answers.

"Hi," she replies, her tone timid and shy.

There's a brief silence as I wait for her to speak, unsure of where to go with this conversation.

"I've decided to go to the cops," she finally says. "I'm going to turn Quinton in."

For her to tell me that, I feel a relief stronger at this moment than I did the day I was released from prison. I want Cass to get her justice more than I wanted mine.

Quinton will look real pretty when they bring him in beat up.

"Will you go with me?" she asks.

Her asking me this means so much. It hands a piece of the trust she lost from me back, giving me another chance to prove to her that I'll be by her side, that I'm always here for her.

"Of course," I reply.

She shouldn't even have to wonder if I'd go with her.

"Will you …" She hesitates, and I hear her heavy breathing. "Will you stay with me tonight?"

"I'll be there in twenty." I need to run home, shower, and then be back at my girl's side.

CHAPTER TWENTY-EIGHT

Cassidy

I'M DOING the right thing.

Those are the five words I've been singing to myself like a lullaby song on repeat in a newborn's room.

"I'm scared," I tell Lincoln as I change into my pajamas.

I called and asked him to come over.

He did.

If I dig deep inside myself, if I claw into my heart, I have no doubt I can trust Lincoln. Am I still upset over him telling Archer? Yes. But I'd much rather have a man more worried about my safety than pacifying me.

His arrival shocked everyone in the living room. I hadn't told them that I invited him over, nor had I told them that I'd decided to go to the police. I needed to know that Lincoln had my back, would be by my side, before I made any declarations. Lincoln made small talk with everyone as we all yawned like we'd been on no-sleep binges.

Ten minutes ago, Grace went to bed, and after confirming Lincoln was staying with me fifteen times, Rex and Carolina went home. It's nice, knowing I have so many people who care about my well-being. I should've known I wasn't so alone earlier.

"Scared of Quinton?" Lincoln asks, stopping to stare at me from across the room.

I nod. "After my arrest, he threatened me, my family, to do things to us. I'm terrified he'll retaliate."

Lincoln peels off his shirt, revealing his six-pack. "He seems more bark than bite."

"How do you know?" I raise a brow, eyeing him up and down—not only in curiosity, but also because, damn, he's hot. Even in situations like this, I'm still attracted to him in every sense.

He blows out a breath. "Honesty is the best policy, right?"

"Honesty is the best policy."

"Your brothers and I ..." He rubs at his forehead. "We tracked Quinton down."

"Why am I not surprised?" I mutter.

"Quinton's family owns a competing business to my family's. After my father's and my arrests, his family went and poached all of our clients, forcing us to shut the company down. As soon as I found out the name, I knew who it was."

"So, you'd met him before?"

"Before tonight? No. But I know his brother. We went to school together."

"Whoa, what do you mean, before tonight?"

"I paid him a visit ... told him to leave you alone."

That's when my eyes travel to his hands. I noticed a few scratches on one but didn't pay it too much mind because there's already enough stuff on *my mind*. Now, it makes sense. "Is that what the messed-up fists are from?"

There isn't one inch of shame on his features. "Possibly."

"Lincoln"—I release a heavy sigh and sink down on my bed—"I don't want you getting in trouble over me."

"Cass," he says, his voice soft-spoken. "I'll never stop standing up for the woman I'm falling in love with."

Good thing I'm sitting because this is the moment I'd fall on my face.

Our conversation comes to a halt.

My brain, though?

It spirals, spinning with countless emotions and questions.

I'm not sure how I'm looking at him, but as he peers at me, panic sets over his features.

He blows out a deep breath, a labored breath, and falls to his knees in front of me. "Cass, I know we've been on the fence, but when I saw what happened to you, it killed my soul."

I stare at him, bewildered.

He continues speaking, continues warming my heart, confirming that this won't be the end of us and that I can still be happy. "Your pain caused me pain. Is there a possibility I can get in trouble for kicking his ass? Maybe. But I'll take those consequences if that means he'll stay away from you." He abruptly stops, his face nervous and frenzied as he eyeballs me. He grabs my hand in his, massaging the top of it, and softens his voice. "When it comes down to it, yes, I'm falling in love with you. I didn't go into this thinking that, and it's only been a couple of months since we started hanging out, so it might be considered early, but you feel what you feel, you know? I've never felt this way with anyone, and from what I guess, it's love because it's surreal to me."

Oh.

My.

Freaking.

God.

Did he say that?

I wish I could rewind that moment and listen to it over and over again. All my awareness is on us, on our connection, on our emotions toward each other. I squeeze his hand, my heart jumping in my chest, thankful for *finally* some happiness and some damn good news. Lincoln has been my savior, and I'm so happy I found a man who knows how to handle me, how to care for me, how to love me. And in part, I'm going to do the same for him.

Dropping his hand, I reach down, and with shaking hands, I cup his chin. Tears fall down my cheeks, my feelings for him finally being thrown out in their truth.

I taste the salt of my tears as I say, "I'm falling in love with you too. I'm sorry for being angry with you ... for keeping the Quinton thing ... the bruise from you." My words are all flowing into nearly one, as I'm frantic and scared that I won't be able to express all my feelings before this moment is over. "I was just in shock, but I love you."

His hand blankets mine over his face, shaking over my shaking ones, as we pour out our truths like the drinks we serve.

Straight up.

No bullshit.

All honesty.

Me and him.

I sniffle back the tears. Unlike what they've been lately, these ones are from relief, from happiness, from the excitement of being loved. He nuzzles his face in my palm, his rough scruff rubbing against the sensitive skin. We relax against each other. It's as if a tension bubble had been popped.

When he pulls away, our eyes meet, and he reaches out, his thumb abrasive as he wipes away my tears. "I love you, Cassidy."

I gulp, nodding, and blurt out, "I love you, Lincoln."

IT'S the ass crack of dawn when my doorbell rings.

And rings.

And rings.

Oh God, here we go again.

Last night started in hell and ended in heaven. After Lincoln and I finally broke down and explored our emotions before throwing them out to the other, the night relaxed. When he asked to see my neck, to see how it was healing, there was no hesitation this time. He stared at it, anguish in his eyes as if he wished he could heal it with them.

We lay in bed that night, his finger running along the bare skin of my thigh, and talked for hours—about anything and everything.

Lincoln slips on a pair of sweats, throws on a hoodie, and says, "I got it," before leaving the bedroom.

"Oh, man, do I have some fucking news for you," I hear Rex say from the other room.

I hurriedly dress and join them in the living room, where Rex is standing with a stack of papers tucked underneath his armpit. Grace is on the couch, staring at him in curiosity, while we all await his early morning pop-in information.

"Quinton, your little ex," Rex starts, his gaze darting to me. "The guy has quite the drug setup going on. Not only is it him and a few friends, but there are dirty cops on his team as well." He snatches the stapled papers from his arm and throws them down onto the coffee table. "You gotta read this shit."

So much dawns on me.

Quinton being comfortable with one officer and then uneasy when the other showed up.

Him doing the bro hug with the officer.

He'd been working with the first one who approached my car.

"We need to do something about this," Rex says.

"I know a way." Lincoln grabs the stack of papers. "I'll be back."

He smacks a kiss to my cheek and leaves without providing any additional information.

CHAPTER TWENTY-NINE

Lincoln

THIS TIME, I don't bother going to his office.

I go straight to the source and pray he doesn't call the cops on me.

Isla answers the door, wearing a pink silk robe. "Lincoln?"

"Where's Louis?" I rush out. "I need to speak to him."

"What?" she stutters, a string of disappointment crossing her features that I'm not there for her.

"I need to speak to your husband."

She stares at me, speechless.

It's a plus for me that their doorway is massive enough to fit a semi, and I duck around her before rushing inside their home, marble flooring underneath my squeaky sneakers. Louis is sitting in the kitchen, a full breakfast plate in front of him and the paper in his hands, all old-school style.

He frowns when I come into his view. "Jesus, why do I keep seeing you?"

I'm sure the man your wife had an affair with isn't what you want to see before starting your day.

I hold up Rex's papers. "I have a case for you."

He puts the paper down and picks up his coffee. "If it's

about the assault, you need to take that up with the police. We don't deal with small crimes like that."

"Is a massive drug operation on a college campus a big enough crime for you?"

He pauses mid-sip of his coffee. "Go on."

I slam the folder down on the table in front of him, causing his coffee cup to rattle. "It's all right here. Texts, voicemails, the guys involved. My guy managed to speak to a man who used to work for them. When he told them he wanted out, they beat the shit out of him. If you can grant him immunity, he'll tell you everything you need to know from the dirty cops they're paying off, to their connections, to where they're buying and making the drugs." I blow out a breath before going on. "Cassidy, the woman he assaulted, is filing a police report against him today. Her brother is a police officer with Blue Beech PD. His thoughts are, as soon as they talk to Cassidy, they'll go pick Quinton up for questioning. That means, he'll basically be delivered to you."

He gawks at me. "How do I know this is factual evidence?"

"I know I'm not the guy you want to trust, but this is worth looking into." I gesture to the documents, the ones I read during stoplights on my drive here. "You think I had time to forge these? That I'd make this shit up?"

He pays the evidence a quick glance, a *this is a joke* glance. "I'll look through it."

"That's all I'm asking. And there are some dirty cops in there you might want to look into as well."

That piques his interest, and he starts thumbing through the papers.

"Do with it what you please. I have to get back to my girl."

Isla gasps as I walk by her, and I don't glance back once.

CHAPTER THIRTY

Cassidy

"YOU'RE the bravest person I know," Lincoln tells me on our way into the police station.

It's scary.

More terrifying than the one I was actually taken to when I was arrested.

The drive here was filled with me battling with myself. Me coming here would be a clear *fuck you* to Quinton, and that scared the shit out of me. I remembered his intimidation, all the threats he'd put against my family and me, and I silently prayed that they were all empty.

Surely, he wouldn't be that dumb.

Not to mention, Quinton isn't a hardened criminal who likes to get his hands dirty. We went for couples pedicures on the regular.

I'm brave because I have a great support system. Brave because I have my family and friends with me. Some of them have stayed outside, not wanting to overwhelm me—Grace, Georgia, Lola, Carolina, Chloe, and Rex.

We take small steps into the station. Kyle, my mother, Sierra, and Lincoln all at my side, forming a line of protection with me. All eyes turn to us at the sound of the door shutting, and the first officer I see is him—the one who was chummy with Quinton and arrested me instead. Fear spirals up my spine, and if my hands weren't clasped with Lincoln's and my mother's, I'd be out the door, running and changing my mind.

Kyle shakes his head, muttering a curse underneath his breath, knowing he's the dirty one since I described him to a T on the drive here. It's one thing my brother hates—dirty cops. He plays by the rule book as best as he can, treats everyone with respect, and doesn't use having a badge to his advantage.

When I make it to the front counter, I clear my throat before saying, "I'd like to report an assault."

The woman nods and asks me to follow her before calling for a man to come with us. A heavier-set officer steps up and waddles his way toward us, gulping down a coffee on his way.

This is it.

There's no going back.

We cram into a small, chilly room. I take the chair across from the officers, my mom occupying the one next to me and Lincoln collapsing into the one on my other side. Everyone else stands behind me, and a sense of comfort settles through my body at the feel of Sierra's hands clasping my shoulders, a gentle squeeze of assurance that she's here for me.

The officers are kind as I speak and don't seem frustrated as I slowly ease into the story of what happened the night Quinton came to my house and put his hands on me. My mother cries, short sobs coming from her, but I stay strong. Not one tear drips down my face. A few times, my voice nearly breaks, but I suck in deep breaths to stop it.

I am strong.

I got this.

He will go down for touching me.

Goose bumps rush up my arms when I ease the sweater off my shoulders, revealing a cotton cami and the bruise. The woman officer snaps photos from dozens of angles and has me sign my statement before sliding a restraining order across the table. After I fill it out, they tell me they'll be in contact.

As I walk out of the station, a heavy weight the size of an elephant drops off my shoulders.

CHAPTER THIRTY-ONE

Lincoln

"I DON'T KNOW how welcome you are here."

My attention shoots to Archer's line of vision at his aggressive tone. He's gripping a towel in his hand and shooting daggers at Louis, who's walking in our direction, wearing determination and an expensive suit, sticking out like a sore thumb in the bar.

"Not here to see you," Louis deadpans.

"It's cool," I tell Archer, stalking over to them.

Archer stares at me like I've lost my mind before understanding dawns on him. I filled him in on Cassidy and Quinton's situation—not giving him all the details because I know Cassidy wants some specifics kept between us.

I jerk my head toward the end of the bar. Louis nods, his strides long as he meets me.

"What's up?"

This has to be good news, right?

He wouldn't pay me a visit for the fuck of it.

"You handed me some useful information," he says with a nod of certainty and appreciation.

"I know," I reply, wanting to get to the point. "Now, are you going to do something about it?"

He has to.

Quinton needs to go down for his crimes.

He was arrested shortly after Cassidy made her statement, but it didn't take long for his attorney to show up, and he was bailed out in an hour. The power of having money and people in high places. Quinton's issue now is that he has Louis against him, and this motherfucker likes to bring criminals down. He's a fighter, and he has been featured in documentaries about how many cases he's won and how well he convinces jurors that criminals need to go down for their crimes. He doesn't fuck around, and that's exactly who we need on our side to take Quinton down.

"Already started," Louis replies. "We've tracked him, and we know he's been bailed out. We've kept it hush-hush, not going to his attorney, until we find out what cops he's working with." He taps his hand against the bar. "Just wanted to keep you updated."

With Kyle's connections, he's informed us on everything Quinton related the best he can. Cassidy's restraining order is active, and we make sure she's not alone. She calls us overbearing, but we're not giving Quinton any chance to retaliate.

"I appreciate that." I tilt my head in his direction. "How about a drink on the house?"

Louis shakes his head. "Not interested in having a drink poured by the man who was sleeping with my wife."

Louis is the most straight-to-the-point, no-bullshit man I've met in my life.

With that, he turns and walks out of the bar.

IT'S Cassidy's first night back at work.

It seems like it's been forever since she's been here, and I've missed her. I've been waiting in anticipation to see her walk through those doors.

I've missed all the jokes she added to her drink orders, missed our closing times together, missed walking her out. Most of all, I've missed just spending time with her, hearing her laugh, seeing her smile.

I'm so damn pussy-whipped.

So damn Cassidy-whipped.

She's been hanging out with Georgia, Lola, and Grace today. Even though there isn't one of us guys with them, I have no doubt that with the four of them, they'd kick Quinton's ass if he tried to pull anything.

She wanted her bruise to completely heal before returning. Our close friends know what happened, but she doesn't want other employees or customers to see any signs of the bruise.

I've stayed at her house, in her bed, every night since the evening before she reported Quinton. We've ordered takeout, binge-watched TV shows, and talked.

You know what we've also done?

We've exchanged *I love you*s as if they were simple hellos since the night we tore out our hearts and gifted them to the other. That night, sitting on her bed, is really the first time the words fell from my mouth. The Callahan household wasn't one to express themselves. We didn't share hugs and *I love you*s. With the exception of my mother a few times, Cassidy is the only other person I've said those words to. Hell, she's probably the only other person who will have my heart enough for me to do so. She owns every piece of me in so many ways.

All eyes are on her when she struts into the bar as if nothing has changed, and she didn't spend days in her own personal Quinton hell.

That's right.

My girl is strong as hell.

A fighter.

"Welcome back, Cassidy," Cohen calls out. "We're glad you're here."

Archer nods and echoes Cohen. "Welcome back."

I grin, a smile I can't contain creasing my face, and a pleasant hum warms my blood. She wastes no time in circling the bar, heading straight in my direction, and kissing me on the lips. There are no gasps of shock. It's no surprise to our friends. Even though we haven't come out and told people we were dating, from the way we've been around each other, from my sleepovers and protectiveness of her, they'd be stupid if they didn't know.

"Back to reality," I say against her lips before pressing mine against them again.

"Back to reality," Cassidy says. "Only now, it's better."

I raise a brow. "Oh yeah?"

"Yeah, because now, people can know we're in love with each other ..." She stops and winks. "And that someday, you're going to be my baby daddy."

CHAPTER THIRTY-TWO

Cassidy

TACO TUESDAY IS EXACTLY what I need for my first night out.

My bruise is healed, but sometimes, as I'm getting dressed or in the shower, I peek down at my neck, expecting the reminder of Quinton's abuse. At times, I feel like the journey I've taken on since my arrest has been the one intended to make me a stronger woman. Even with my father's infidelities, my parents did everything they could to create a perfect *unicorns and rainbows* life for me.

Quinton prepared me for the real world and taught me how it's not always perfect, not always safe, and not always the way you want it to be.

It also led me to the man who stole my heart and protected it through that journey.

Tonight's dinner is being thrown at the Callahan-slash-Georgia penthouse. The last and only time I've been here was the day I walked in on Lincoln and Isla whispering like two kids on the playground, and as everyone knows, I hate whispering.

I expected my stomach to turn, for nausea to swarm my body, but when I walk in and see my friends, I smile.

Smile because, like Lincoln, I've found something real—

authentic friendships I know will last over time. No matter what happens, no matter if I get in trouble, no matter if I try to run and hide, they'll have my back.

I rode with Grace. She hasn't stayed at the house much and doesn't mention where she's been sleeping. I'm worried her absence has something to do with me. Maybe she's worried Quinton could come back to finish me off and hurt her in the process.

The aroma of fresh-baked tortillas, quesadillas, and tacos smacks into my nostrils as I take a look around. There's no stopping me from laughing when I see the décor Georgia bought the day we went shopping. That day seems like an eternity ago after all the events that took place.

"Hey, girl, hey!" Georgia says, wrapping me up in a hug and leading me into the kitchen, where Silas and Archer are.

Silas is cooking while Archer is standing next to him, talking with a beer in his hand.

"Cassidy," Archer says as Georgia grips his shoulder, leaning into his side. "How have you been?"

I smile, happy that he asked. "Good … better."

"I'm glad you're okay. I'm happy for you and my brother." He blows out a breath, and his face softens into an expression I've never seen him wear before. "I'm sorry for going behind your guys' backs and telling Cohen. I was in shock, unsure of what to do. As an employer, I know shit that happens out of work might not be my business, but also as an employer, I care about my employees—even with as standoffish as I am. I also know how much you mean to my brother, and if someone was hurting you, I wasn't sure how much further they'd go. So, I called Cohen to ask for advice, knowing that he'd call Maliki because that's the kind of guy he is."

"It's okay," I reply with all honesty. "You did the right thing."

Silas whips around, a spatula in his hand. "Does this mean you and baby Callahan are together?"

"It sure damn does," Lincoln says loud and clear as he enters the kitchen. With swift steps, he comes up behind me, wraps his strong arms around my waist, and places a gentle kiss on my ear. "Hi, baby."

"I'm swooning," Georgia says. "Seriously swooning."

Same, Georgia. Same.

A blush caresses my cheeks as everyone stares at us.

This is what I originally wanted from Lincoln.

This is what I wanted all those times I joked around with Lincoln but never thought I'd get.

His hands on me.

His mouth on me.

Him claiming me in front of everyone, making me feel wanted, making me feel like I could get a man who wouldn't turn his back on me.

Silas grins. "I like it. Another couple breaking through our *only friends* rule." He shakes his head. "Now, we're waiting on Grace and Finn."

"And then you and Lola," Georgia adds.

"Nah, Lola and I will be the only two who stick to the *just friends* pact."

"I wasn't aware we'd made a pact," Georgia replies.

"No, we did. In the beginning, Cohen said things were to stay strictly platonic between us and you and your friends." He shrugs. "Cohen made the rules, and we were supposed to follow them."

"Yeah, well, too bad Cohen doesn't make our rules," Georgia says with a frown. "And I'm going to kick his ass for telling you that."

"And speak of the devil," Silas calls out when Cohen, Jamie, and baby Isabella walk into the room.

Cohen has his tiny daughter wrapped in his arms, her head resting on his shoulder as he holds her tight.

My mind wanders to when Lincoln will be a father—how he'll hold our baby, how he'll love it, how we'll be as parents.

Whoa, getting way ahead of yourself there, Cass.

I can't help it. I want everything with him.

"What devil are we speaking of here?" Jamie asks, running her hand along Isabella's back as she sleeps.

"Your other half telling his friends that my friends and I are off-limits," Georgia says, resting her hand on her hip. "The audacity."

"I think he's learned his lesson on saying relationships are *off-limits*," Jamie says with a twinkle in her eyes as she stares up at her fiancé. "We broke the ultimate *off-limits* rule."

"True that," Silas says. "The baby mama's sister. That's on a whole different level."

Cohen narrows his eyes at Silas. "A particular situation, thank you very much."

He seems to be protective of Jamie and their relationship, but from what I've heard, it was hard in the beginning, so I don't blame him.

"Are the tacos ready?" Finn asks, walking in with Noah hanging off his back.

"Just about," Silas calls over.

I help Georgia along with Lola and Grace, who join us from the living room, set all the toppings for the tacos and quesadillas out on the massive kitchen island.

We eat. We drink. We play games.

Everyone, at least once, comments with how happy they are for Lincoln and me.

It's a great night to start my new life.

"MY FIRST TIME IN YOUR BED," I say to Lincoln, lounging against his headboard, moving my legs up and down his smooth sheets.

He was having a conversation with Archer, and out of exhaustion, I ventured to his room, undressed, and slipped into bed.

"About damn time," he says, shutting the door behind him. "I've been waiting for this day for what seems like forever."

"Oh, really?" I smile before giggling—the giggling is a result of too many margaritas since in sober life, I am not a giggler. "What were you waiting for?" Another damn giggle.

Ugh, I'm going to hate my giggling self in the morning.

He nods toward the bed. "To fuck you on those sheets. To screw you from behind and have you mask your moans with my pillow." He licks his lips, and I can imagine they taste like margarita salt since I convinced him to drink one with me. "To hold you when we're finished making love, and then in the morning, I'll make *your* favorite breakfast—Belgian waffles and scrambled eggs."

"What are you waiting for then?" My eyes flutter in his direction—another side effect of the damn liquor—and I slowly crawl across the bed on my hands and knees to where he's standing at the foot.

He hisses when my face comes into line with his waist, and I tug at his belt buckle.

I waste no time unzipping his pants and taking his cock out. Draping it along my palm, I rub a finger up and down the skin as it jerks in my hand.

"Oh," I say, wrapping my hand tightly around his cock and slowly stroking him. "This cock brings me so much pleasure."

His legs go straight, his body stiffening as I increase my pace. "And you bring it more pleasure."

Being with Lincoln is sex I've never experienced.

His touch is a different breed of intimacy.

When I glance up at him, his eyes are glued to my hand, to our connection, and I want to provide a better view. His knees buckle when I slip my fingers down his cock to make room for my mouth.

I stare up at him, watching his face and the changes it makes.

The way it forms an O when I suck on the head.

The way his mouth drops open as a gasp escapes it when I swirl my tongue around his balls.

The way he rasps, "Jesus Christ, Cass," from his throat.

"I'm close," he hisses. "Turn around, get on your hands and knees, and stick your ass in the air."

Anticipation showers through me as I do what he said. He climbs onto the bed behind me and places his palm to the base of my back, pushing me down to my stomach, and lifts up my legs. I gasp when he tears my pajama shorts and panties down my legs, and he tosses them over his shoulder as I peer back at him.

Bending over me, he grips my hips, tight and firm, and hauls me back up to my knees. Holding me in place as he stretches across the bed, he opens a drawer in the nightstand and plucks out a condom. I bite back the urge to ask why he has condoms in his drawer because he didn't ask me about the condoms I had in my nightstand.

Did he wonder the same thing when he got one from my nightstand?

Shoving his pants down his waist, not even bothering to take them off, he slips two fingers inside me.

"You're already soaked for me, baby," he practically growls.

"Always," I whisper, nearly panting for him.

Without warning, he thrusts inside me.

I hiss before releasing a long moan, taking in his large size, and hope Georgia and Archer are no longer in the living room. He lifts my shirt with one hand, holding it away from my waist, while lowering the other around my body to play with my clit.

He pounds into me.

I fuck him right back.

It's been too long since he's been inside me, and for once, I couldn't give two fucks about foreplay. The only playing I want is him inside me for as long as he can last.

Our harsh breathing occupies the room, the only sounds coming from us as we get each other off. My body swells with pressure, with intimacy, with love, and just as I'm about to scream out my release, his large palm grips the back of my head, shoving my face into the pillow.

Just like he wanted to.

My orgasm rips through me, just as strong as the first night we had sex, and he holds me tight as he finishes himself off, our flesh smacking together and making its own rhythm.

He groans out my name and slaps my ass as he comes inside the condom.

CHAPTER THIRTY-THREE

Lincoln

"DOES this mean we'll be new roomies?" Georgia asks the next morning.

Somehow, I got suckered into making *everybody* breakfast. Well, *buying* everybody breakfast because the first Belgian waffle I tried was an absolute fail. So, I told everyone to get dressed, and we're sitting at a table at Yellow Peep to get our waffles.

As soon as we sat down, I was reminded of Cassidy and me coming here after her community service—the day she thought she didn't look *dressed* to come into a restaurant like this when she didn't even realize how damn beautiful she was.

She is.

Inside and out.

"Oh my God." I hear from Cassidy, and at the same time, she covers her face.

I glance up to find the same waitress, Taylor, who helped us before, standing at the front of our table, a bright smile on her face.

Her smile broadens when she notices Cassidy and me, and she gestures to us with her pencil. "From the looks of it, I'm hoping this means you no longer see her as your little sister?"

Cassidy adds her other hand to cover her face as she groans.

Georgia snorts, her attention bobbing between Taylor and us. "What?"

"Nothing," Cassidy and I answer at the same time as she uncovers her face.

"Nope," Georgia says, shaking her head. "As soon as we give our drink orders, we're going to need that story."

"They came in a while back," Taylor chirps, apparently ready to answer for us. "And they were going back and forth about him seeing her as a little sister, and she was upset because she didn't want to say she was attracted to someone who saw her as a sibling ... something along those lines."

"I can't believe she told them that," Cassidy hisses so only I can hear.

Appeased with the answer, Georgia orders a mimosa with Cassidy doing the same. Archer and I opt for coffee and water, and Taylor scurries her tattletale self off to get our beverages.

Georgia straightens her napkin in her lap and leans into us. "Now, back to the conversation we were having prior to finding out you used to think of her as a little sister." Her gaze whips to me.

Archer grunts before mocking his girlfriend's voice. "Yes, totally. We don't need to discuss new roommates as a couple at all."

She turns to pat his chest with her palm. "That's right, baby."

Archer shakes his head and laughs, pinning his attention on Cassidy and me. "I'm just fucking with you. It's only fair to let my brother's girlfriend move in since I already moved Georgia in. Cassidy, you're welcome whenever."

Cassidy smiles at the invite before it collapses into a frown. "I don't think I can do that to Grace, though."

Georgia nods, wisping strands of hair out of her face that fell from the pigtail buns on the top of her head. "Yeah, I felt horrible too. I almost didn't do it, and that's why I waited until you agreed to move in because I didn't want to leave her alone."

Cassidy rubs the back of her neck, and I do the same, feeling a wire of tension up my neck. "If I do, will she have to move in with her parents?"

Georgia nods. "Probably."

"What's the deal with that?" I cut in. "What if we tell her we'll spring for rent until she finds another roommate? Problem solved."

I love the thought of Cassidy moving in with me, the thought of us calling the same place home and going to bed together every night.

Taylor delivers our drinks, all her attention on Cassidy and me, like she's waiting for me to drop to one knee and propose or some shit. It's as if we're the new couple she's fangirling over. It could be a compliment, but I hate attention on me, and from the way Cassidy tenses every time it happens, it's the same for her.

Georgia shakes her head, and with certainty, she says, "Grace won't stay somewhere overnight without another person there."

I cock my head to the side. "Why?"

"Not my story to tell," Georgia replies, not making eye contact with anyone and instead focusing on her mimosa. "But there's a reason I didn't agree to move until she had another roommate."

"I get that."

Cass and I have spent a lot of time with Grace since we've been hanging out at their house so much. Lately, she's been acting strange. Cassidy has noticed it too.

Is she worried that Cassidy will move out?

Hell, does Cass even want to move in with me?

I shake my head, remembering the smile she had when Archer invited her before the dread of leaving Grace clutched at her thoughts.

"It's cool," I say. "We're good where we're at, and Grace doesn't seem to mind me hanging out there." I reach under the table and squeeze Cassidy's thigh. "We have plenty of time to move in together."

"And who knows? The penthouse might be completely open for you two," Georgia says.

That catches my attention, and I focus on the couple across the table from us. "What?"

"We *maybe* found a second home—"

"A second home?" I blurt out. "A second home for what?"

"For us to hang out in ..." Georgia says before trailing off, as if she lost her train of thought.

"How did we go from you saying *let's be roommates* to you saying you're moving out?"

"Technically, we don't close on the house for another month," Georgia says. "Plus, Archer isn't selling the penthouse. He wants to keep both, and it's good news for you. When we move out, you guys will have the place to yourselves."

I stare at them, blinking, while processing the news that I wish Archer had given me. We're supposed to tell each other everything, especially something as big as this.

"The penthouse is yours to stay in for as long as you'd like," Archer says. "Georgia just keeps on girlie-ing up shit, so I figured we needed our own place for that."

The discussion has changed from Cassidy moving in with us to Georgia and Archer moving out. It'll be weird, not having them there with me, but I understand their reasoning. If I had the option to have a place with Cassidy solo or with roommates, I'd for sure take a place for just the two of us.

Now, I just need to figure out when we can make that leap in our relationship.

CHAPTER THIRTY-FOUR

Cassidy

I WALK into the kitchen to find Grace grading papers, notebooks spread out along the table and her laptop to the side. "Hey, girl."

She grins up at me, shutting her computer. "How did last night go? The first night at the boyfriend's?"

"It was …" I'm no doubt beaming like those love-drunk yuppies in movies. "Amazing."

"Aw, yay! I'm so happy for you, Cass. You really deserve it. I think you're a great match." Her voice is genuine and soft, and if I were ever to cast an angel in a movie, it'd be her with that tone, her strawberry-blond hair, and her fair skin.

She stayed with her parents last night because I'd given her a heads-up that I was staying the night with Lincoln. He'd asked me to since it was something we'd never done before, and he said he wanted his sheets and bedroom to smell like me.

Hell, I wanted his sheets and his bedroom to smell like me to ward off any middle-aged women who might try to become his cougar.

Although I was unsure of how deep her not wanting to stay home alone was until breakfast this morning, I'd known she wasn't a fan, known she was always nervous at night, but I'd thought it was similar to me—a girl who had always been surrounded by company and wasn't used to being alone. After seeing the uneasiness on Georgia's face when Lincoln asked why, I know it's something deeper than that.

The nervousness on her face matches the nervousness on mine after Quinton's visit. Something similar happened with her, I'm sure of it, but what I'm not sure of is how to start a conversation about it.

Or if I even should.

I pull out the chair across from her, and my voice becomes hesitant as I take a seat. "Is there something wrong?" I lean back against the seat and take her in, wanting to make sure I don't miss her reaction to my question. "Are you unhappy about Lincoln spending so much time here?"

She stares at me with intent, her hand resting against her chest. "Oh, absolutely not. Why would you think that?"

"You've just seemed ... off lately."

She flicks at the corner of a paper. "Is it that noticeable?"

So, there is something.

"Kind of." I stare at her, determined to help with whatever she's struggling with, to be a friend like she was with me during my Quinton issues. "I don't want to overstep any boundaries, but does it have anything to do with me? If so, I want to be able to fix whatever it is. I want you to be happy and comfortable."

She shrinks in her chair before nodding. "I have been nervous about you moving out now that you and Lincoln are together." Her words become more rushed. "Not that I'd blame you. I'd probably want to do the same with the man I love, so I wouldn't take any offense to it. That doesn't mean it hasn't crossed my mind more often than it probably should."

I'm happy she's not upset about Lincoln crashing with us, but my heart breaks that the thought has been haunting her.

"You don't need to worry about me moving out," I say, reaching forward and squeezing her hand. From the fear on her face, that won't be happening unless she finds someone or says she's okay with living alone.

She sits up straighter in her chair, as if my words were connected to a chain that lifted her back up. "You know, I don't care if Lincoln moves in here. It'd actually—and no offense because I love you being here and want to keep you forever—be nice, also having a guy with us, you know? Two girls living alone can be scary at times."

I love the sound of that.

Although I'm not sure how much Lincoln will love it.

I know he likes the penthouse, but after Georgia and Archer's news at breakfast, he might feel a little differently.

Grace turns quiet, her breathing hitching, and as she plays with her hands, I know there's more than what she's telling me.

"Grace," I say softly, "we're roommates. You can talk to me, you know that? Just like you kept my trust, I'll always do the same with you."

She blows out a breath and glances around the room as if she's worried someone is hiding in the shadows. "I haven't told anyone this, but I was dating the principal at our school."

"Oh." I'd tell her that's great, but from the expression on her face, it's not.

"He's married." She bows her head in shame.

"Oh."

"I didn't know that, though," she blurts. "He's new. It's his first year, and I guess his wife was still packing up their belongings and everything before moving out here after he got the job. He didn't tell me that he was married. He said he'd *been* married, but that he and his wife had recently divorced." She holds in a sob that becomes a sniffle. "I didn't think much of it, and then, the other day, his wife showed up at the school to surprise him … after we messed around in his office." She covers her face. "It's humiliating and heartbreaking."

"Oh my God, why didn't you tell me?" I feel bad because she

was at my side during this Quinton mess when she was going through her own issues.

"You were dealing with something way more serious."

"I'll talk to Lincoln, see what he thinks, but no matter what, you don't have to worry about losing me as a roommate." I switch to the seat next to her. "Now, come on. Let's make some roomie hot chocolate and Netflix it up."

"I TALKED TO GRACE."

Lincoln peers over at me, and I'm almost positive my sentence came out in somewhat of a slur. We might've had one too many hot chocolates, but they were putting Grace's mind at ease. What the guy had done was messed up, and from the few details she gave me throughout the night, she was really falling for him.

Which is weird because I thought Finn held the key to her heart. As bad as I wanted to ask what happened with that, I didn't want to bring it up, in fear there were bad memories there as well. Maybe Finn turned her down, or maybe they just flirted, but that was it. Although I would have put my money on the two of them being the next to date.

Heck, I would've put my money on them dating before Lincoln and me when I first started working at the bar.

"You did, did you, drunkie?" Lincoln asks with a laugh.

I nod, swaying as I walk toward him. "And I can't move out. You and I are staying here." My words come out in short blasts as if I were slamming my foot on and off the gas pedal of my mouth.

Lincoln nods. "I figured that'd be the case, and it's cool. We can keep doing what we've been doing. It works for us."

"She offered for you to move in ... said it'd make her feel safer, *and* I definitely feel the same."

He stares at me from my bed, scratching his jaw. "I mean, I'm cool with that. As long as I get to be with you, I'm happy."

"Yes, but our apartment is definitely no Archer penthouse."

"I don't give a shit about that. All I care about is having you and a bed. Nothing else matters."

IT'S the day before Lincoln's birthday.

And good thing I questioned him dozens of times because he didn't give me a birthday reminder. Tomorrow, we're going to celebrate with our friends, but today, I have something special for him.

At least, I hope he sees it as special.

I told him we were taking a trip to Blue Beech, and he was excited even though the last dinner was a hot mess.

My mother is throwing him a birthday dinner. After the initial shitshow of when Kyle questioned me about him being a convict, everyone seems to be getting along now. In fact, Lincoln now texts my brothers on the regular, like they're friends, which makes me happy. I love my brothers, and for them to like the guy I'm dating is a big deal.

My mother is also a Lincoln fan, which is why, when we walk in, there's a birthday feast laid out on the table—all of Lincoln's favorite foods. It's what she does for our birthdays along with fixing two birthday cakes—one for everyone else and then a personal one for the birthday person.

Everyone yells, "Happy Birthday!"

My mother scurries around the table and gives him a tight hug, singing the "Happy Birthday" song to him. Lincoln laughs, shaking his head, and hugs her back.

"Wow, looks like you've sure won her over," I say with a laugh.

Lincoln winks at me when they pull apart. "Like mother, like daughter."

Just as we're about to sit down, Lincoln's phone rings in his pocket. Dragging it out, he looks at the screen before holding it up.

"Let me take this real quick," he says, walking out of the room.

I'm taking a seat and pulling my chair in when Lincoln returns with a bright smile on his face. As he holds the phone in the air, he's practically dancing.

"I have good news," he says as if it's an announcement.

"What's up?" Rex asks.

Lincoln points at me with his phone. "And, babe, you should be receiving a call soon, but I can't keep this from you. Louis wasn't supposed to tell me, but he thinks you should know."

I frown at *Louis* even though I shouldn't. I appreciate all the help he's given with Quinton, but I hate that he's connected to Isla. It makes me uneasy because all I remember is the look of heartbreak she gave when Lincoln told her to leave.

She loves my boyfriend.

Therefore, I don't like her.

Lincoln sets his phone down before sliding his hands together. "First, they have Quinton in custody."

"Hell yes," Kyle says while Chloe squeals, shimmying in her chair.

Quinton hasn't sent a text or made an unwanted visit since his arrest.

"With the evidence they have, he should be facing some time," Lincoln continues. "I don't know all the details yet, but we did it." He walks around the table and stops to high-five Rex. "And secondly …" He pauses, going quiet while taking the seat next to me. Wrapping his arm around my shoulders, he beams down in my direction. "Cass, Louis plans to expunge your record."

"What?" I gasp.

He nods, and Kyle jumps out of his chair, knocking his fists in the air.

"Holy shit!" Rex shouts. "That's fucking awesome."

My heart batters against my chest, and I repeat, "What?" because I have no other words.

For so long, I've accepted being a criminal. Having that misdemeanor was a part of me, forever who I would be. That might change now.

Lincoln nods. "Yep, say good-bye to your record."

Tears are in my mother's eyes. "That means … that means you can go back to school, get a degree, go back to do whatever you want."

"Best damn birthday present ever," Lincoln says, smashing a kiss to my forehead.

WE'RE STILL RIDING the high of Quinton going down and me losing my record when we get back to the townhome. We talked on the way home, and Lincoln decided he wanted to move in with us.

Best day ever, seriously.

I'm ecstatic for us to take the next step in our relationship.

All the lights, except for the hallway bathroom, are off when we walk in, which is strange because Grace's car is parked in the drive. She rarely leaves the lights off. The girl sleeps with a night-light and has one in every room.

Lincoln glances at me, his brow raised in concern. "You think everything is okay?"

No.

Dread soars through me. "I hope so." I take small steps to the bathroom and knock on the door. "Grace?"

Sniffles come from the other side of the door, but no response from her.

My hand is trembling when I knock again. "Are you okay?"

Again, silence and sniffles.

"Just go in," Lincoln whispers, motioning toward the door.

I nod, hoping she doesn't see this as an invasion of privacy. Lincoln stands to the side, out of view of the bathroom, so they can't see each other. I play with the door handle, tinkering it from side to side to see if she'll tell me to stop, but nothing. Slowly, I open it, sliding between the crack, and shut it, my back pressing against the door.

Grace is crouched down on the floor, back to the tub, tears in her eyes, and … a pregnancy test in her hand.

"I'm pregnant," she croaks out, her hands shaking.

Oh my God.

CHAPTER THIRTY-FIVE

Lincoln

Three Weeks Later

"I'M GOING to miss working with you," I tell Cassidy.

"Oh, stop." She swats at my arm. "I'll still be there on the weekends, and don't think I won't be sitting at the end of the bar, studying it up while you're working."

"You promise?"

"I absolutely promise."

I chuckle. "Nothing like studying for law school in a bar."

"Studying for the bar while in a bar," she singsongs. "If I ever write an autobiography when I'm some famous attorney, I shall make that the title."

Cass is going back to school. It's online for now until she figures out where she wants to go or even if she wants to attend somewhere where she'd have to live on campus. She's made it clear to her mother that she's not going back to her old college because there are too many Quinton memories.

"I don't want the old typical college life," she told her mom.

I was worried she didn't want to go because of me, because we now lived together, because she thought we couldn't make it if she was gone. I didn't want her to give up on her future. She swore up and down that wasn't the case.

She's even changed the route of what kind of law she wants to practice. Before everything with Quinton went down, her plan was to go into law and become a defense attorney because that was where the money was.

Now? She wants to become a prosecutor to take down people like Quinton.

I'm so damn proud of her.

Before she was expelled, she was a few years back from earning her bachelor's degree, so law school is still far down the road, but she can do it. She's a fighter, and when she has her mind set on something, it gets done.

She climbs across the bed and into my lap, wrapping her arms around my neck. "I'm so happy I found you. So happy and thankful for our love."

I brush my thumb over her cheek. "Me too, baby. Me too." I shut my eyes. "I'd probably be living in a ball of sorrow had you not skipped your way into my life and told me we'd be sleeping together eventually."

She saved me.

Showed me what love was.

Hell, she showed me that love actually existed.

I'd be a skeptic, someone who called it a joke, had Cassidy Lane not come into my life.

She throws her head back and laughs. "All those times I said we'd sleep together sure caught your attention, huh?"

"It sure did." I open my eyes, meeting hers, and smile. "And what else was it you always said? That we'd sleep together and have all the babies?"

"Oh, yes, that was definitely another subject that was regularly brought up."

Another subject that I can't wait to happen.

She bows her head to kiss me.

I kiss her back. "I love you." *More than you'll ever know.*

"And I love you," she says, raining kisses along my cheek. "I can't wait to be your wifey and have little Lincolns running around." Lacing our fingers together, she squeezes my hand. "What's your favorite love song?"

That's one we haven't touched on for me, surprisingly.

"Hmm …" I tap the side of my chin as if contemplating the question strongly. Not that I listen to *love songs* on the regular. I go with the first thought. "Umm … '*Next To Me*' by Imagine Dragons. Why?"

"Just preplanning what song we dance to first at our wedding."

I chuckle before kissing her hard.

I love this woman.

She loves me.

Straight up.

No bullshit.

We got this.

KEEP UP WITH THE TWISTED FOX SERIES

Stirred
(Cohen & Jamie's story)
Shaken
(Archer & Georgia's story)
Straight Up
(Lincoln & Cassidy's story)
Chaser
(Finn & Grace's story)
Last Round
(Silas and Lola's story)

ALSO BY CHARITY FERRELL

TWISTED FOX SERIES

(each book can be read as a standalone)

Stirred

Shaken

Straight Up

Chaser

Last Round

BLUE BEECH SERIES

(each book can be read as a standalone)

Just A Fling

Just One Night

Just Exes

Just Neighbors

Just Roommates

Just Friends

STANDALONES

Bad For You

Beneath Our Faults

Pop Rock

Pretty and Reckless

Revive Me

Wild Thoughts

RISKY DUET

Risky

Worth The Risk

ABOUT THE AUTHOR

Charity Ferrell resides in Indianapolis, Indiana with her future hubby and two fur babies. She loves writing about broken people finding love with a dash of humor and heartbreak, and angst is her happy place.

When she's not writing, she's making a Starbucks run, shopping online, or spending time with her family.

www.charityferrell.com
Find me on:

Made in the USA
Monee, IL
05 July 2021

72948653R00152